MOON

of the

TURNING
LEAVES

ALSO BY WAUBGESHIG RICE

Moon of the Crusted Snow
Legacy
Midnight Sweatlodge

MOON

of the

TURNING

LEAVES

A Novel

WAUBGESHIG RICE

wm

WILLIAM MORROW
An Imprint of HarperCollins*Publishers*

MOON OF THE TURNING LEAVES. Copyright © 2024 by Waubgeshig Rice. All rights reserved. Printed in the United States of America. No part of this book may be used or reproduced in any manner whatsoever without written permission except in the case of brief quotations embodied in critical articles and reviews. For information, address HarperCollins Publishers, 195 Broadway, New York, NY 10007.

HarperCollins books may be purchased for educational, business, or sales promotional use. For information, please email the Special Markets Department at SPsales@harpercollins.com.

Originally published as *Moon of the Turning Leaves* in Canada in 2023 by Penguin Random House Canada.

FIRST US EDITION

Illustration on page i and flower illustration throughout by Joshua Mangeshig Pawis-Steckley

Library of Congress Cataloging-in-Publication Data has been applied for.

ISBN 978-0-358-67325-5

23 24 25 26 27 LBC 5 4 3 2 1

To my son Ayaabe,
who guided us out of the darkness when the world changed.

MOON

of the

TURNING
LEAVES

PROLOGUE

A GUTTURAL HOWL TORE through the lodge and breached the birchbark walls. The younger women caught their breath. The air inside the small domed structure grew thicker with each measured exhalation flowing from the young woman sitting upright against a pile of blankets draped with soft rabbit fur, her protruding belly commanding the attention of the midwives, her cousins, and her aunts. The fire burning in the middle of the birthing lodge painted her young, crumpled face a flickering orange. Her partner, the only man inside, nervously swayed on the soles of his feet while his mother and grandmother watched under concerned brows.

A large pot of water and cedar boughs boiled on the blackened grill in the centre of the lodge, steam and embers and the medicinal aroma of the tincture floating up and through the hole in the bark ceiling above. The birthing woman's long, thick black braids hung down the front of the tattered light-blue button-up shirt covering everything but her belly, rising and falling with her breath as she recovered from the push. The young man knelt low beside her, rubbing her back and holding her hand while whispering assurances into her ear.

Two midwives—an elder and a younger apprentice—knelt before her, watching for the black hair of the child's crown to emerge. The older woman squinted to peer through scratched glasses, while the other one softly commanded the delivering woman—her younger cousin—to prepare to push. She drew a long, energizing breath through her nostrils, and her cheeks ballooned as she exhaled through pursed lips. Her breathing quickened, tightening the space around the ten people huddling closer to fulfill this birthing rite.

The young man's mother stepped forward from her perch beside the fire to deliver him a hand drum. She only nodded at him, to avoid betraying the anxiety that was peaking deep within her long into this night of labour. She'd delivered her son nearly two decades earlier in a loud, bright, white room in a city hospital hundreds of kilometres to the south. The moment replayed in her mind as they entered this birthing lodge to receive her grandchild, and she wondered if that hospital still stood.

The expectant father stood, taller than all the women gathered, and struck the drum four times. His voice cracked as he attempted the opening notes of the welcoming song, and he cleared his throat loudly to sync his melody with the beat. The shadow of his head bobbed against the tied boughs and birchbark that made up the interior wall of the birthing lodge, built high enough for the young man to stand comfortably. The skeletal saplings that ran up each wall were buried deep into the ground and woven together tightly to stand year-round. The beating rhythm of the drum invoked a count of the babies born in this ceremonial space in the decade since they tied it together: eight in total, but only five who survived beyond birth and infancy.

The younger midwife spoke softly to the expectant mother, low enough for only them and the elder midwife to hear. The young woman tightened her lips, her nostrils flaring with each heavy breath. Two of her cousins brought two plastic tubs of water closer. The elder midwife grabbed a pinch of cedar from a wooden bowl near the firepit and threw it onto the flames. The tiny green leaves popped and crackled, pumping a sharp evergreen aroma into the air.

The young woman pressed her chin to her chest to push again. Sweat rolled from her creased brow and down her ruddy cheeks. She cried out in another burst of pain and her partner sped up his drumming, outpacing the tempo of his own voice. His mother and grandmother bounced to the beat in front of the fire, while the shadows on the wooden walls around them danced.

The midwife asked her cousin for another big push. Her shriek stilled the shadows and caused her partner's song to falter for a moment. The baby's head emerged, its black hair glistening in the orange light of the fire. Face down, the child made no noise. The mother shouted and pushed again, but the baby remained in place, silent. The pause, although infinitesimal, was enough to panic them all. The elder midwife stepped forward swiftly to kneel beside the other.

"Wiikbinaa-daa," urged the elder, repeating again, "Let's pull!" She wrapped her thin fingers around the infant's slippery head, cradling the chin and the back of its skull. The apprentice placed her hands atop the midwife's. The drumbeat stopped in the sudden severity of the moment.

They remained silent while they pulled. The young mother threw her head back in one last immense inhalation, followed by a searing wail. In that instant, the baby's shoulder came free, and in the midwives' careful grip, the arms, torso, and legs slid out behind it. The elder midwife fluently pulled the glistening blood-streaked body into her elbow and scooped mucus from the baby girl's mouth as she cradled her. A small but piercing first cry echoed through the lodge.

The new parents, exhausted, cried together in a relieved half embrace. By the fire, the new grandmother and great-grandmother beamed through tear-streaked cheeks. The younger midwife wiped down her cousin's baby with a soft, white rabbit pelt, which turned pink with each pass across her blotchy skin. Still in the elder's arms, the baby cried louder as her young lungs quickly expanded.

The girl was washed first in the tub of lukewarm sterilized water. Cedar water was poured in from the pot that simmered on the grill into the second tub, creating a translucent medicinal blend. The elder midwife dipped her hand into the warm essence and scooped it onto the newborn's skin. The faint-green liquid streaked across her torso and beaded in the chubby creases of her arms and legs, the baby's skin gaining colour with each beat of her young heart. The baby's mother watched the ceremonial cleansing while sipping from a copper cup of water.

After the baby's skin and scalp were dried with a faded and tattered blue towel, the young midwife carried her over to the eager and anxious new parents. She lowered the child onto her mother's bare chest. As the baby nestled, the lodge roused in whoops of joy and celebration. The parents thanked their daughter for coming to them, and giggled together as they gazed in awe upon the new life they'd created, delicate yet full of wonder.

The young father looked from his daughter up to his mother by the fire. Her long dark hair hung loosely, framing her slender face. She smiled and nodded to let him know it was time. The new mother kissed the top of the baby's head one more time, cupped her little frame into both hands, and raised the child in the direction of her grandmother. She took her granddaughter into her bare arms and carefully caressed the girl's torso with her callused fingertips before resting her weathered palm upon it, trying to feel the first beats of her heart outside of her mother. She looked to her daughter-in-law and smiled again before clearing her throat to commence the naming ceremony.

"Boozhoo." Her voice punctuated the convivial ambience hanging in the lodge. "Niimkiikwe ndizhnikaaz, mkwa ndodem. Bjiinak ngii-ooshenh'," she said, introducing herself as a new grandmother in Anishinaabemowin, the traditional language of their people. The rest acknowledged her with a celebratory holler, and she switched to English to tell the story of the girl's name so everyone could understand.

She told a story of a dream of a beam of light coming down from the sky—but it was only a glimpse. She told how the same dream came twice more in the following weeks, longer each time. In the vision, it appeared to be early fall, when the leaves have just begun to change. But the land she was seeing didn't look like their current home.

As she walked through the bush, the trees were tall around her, she told them. Large pines were on her right. Maples and oaks stood scattered throughout. But mostly she remembered the white birch trees, leaves just starting to turn. She felt a warm breeze coming from behind her, and she heard waves but couldn't see any water.

Then the light came again, the beam from above, descending slowly and touching down in the bush ahead. She couldn't tell how far away she was from where the light met the ground, but she felt like it wanted her to follow it. She didn't hear voices in her dream, she told the onlookers, but the light in the bush seemed to be calling to her.

Then, she told them, she stepped over a small hill into the middle of a clearing, where the gleam shone down, and she saw a tiny flower alone in the grass. "It had wrinkled purple petals with yellow and white in the middle," she described. "I don't think I've ever seen a flower like it. Not around here, anyway. I tried to look up again to where the light was coming from, but that's when I woke up."

The new mother's face swelled with emotion as she stifled a quick sob and smiled, teary eyes sparkling in the glow of the fire.

"I didn't have to think about that dream anymore," the grandmother said, concluding her story. "That flower I saw is this baby's name. Like that flower, this child is special. She's beautiful. She is a light that will help lead the way out of this darkness. Her name is Waawaaskone. A flower, in the language of our people."

"Waawaaskone," repeated the new parents. Sharp pops rang out as more cedar and tobacco were tossed on the fire.

In the sacred safety of the birth space, all stood but the new mother. The grandmother extended the baby's small, plump body outwards. She turned to face the opening to the lodge, which pointed east. The baby slept soundly now, still wrapped in the faded blue towel. Her grandmother's strong bare arms elevated her to eye level, presenting her proudly to the direction where the day begins.

"Waawaaskone," she proclaimed again.

"Waawaaskone," the rest repeated.

The grandmother pivoted to the remaining three directions, declaring the girl's name. The crowd followed her movements and voice, repeating the name for all of creation to hear. The chorus faded into the bark walls and the ground below, and she lifted the baby skyward to speak her name one last time, followed by the echo of the helpers. The ceremony was complete.

ONE

WATER LAPPED AGAINST THE low hull of the boat, its
rhythm synchronized with the pulls on the float line as the
small white plastic pods that kept the net afloat knocked
against the shiny metal of the vessel. Hand over hand, fifteen-
year-old Nangohns yanked the white nylon net over the gunwale trim, pulling in the green and grey fish that flopped onto
the curved deck. The rippling water around the small boat
bounced jewels of light back up towards the sky. Nangohns
hunched her long torso over to survey the morning's haul.
Three smallmouth bass so far, another three pike, and a couple of smaller pickerel. She looked from her deeply tanned
hands to the bin on the floor of the boat and estimated she
had pulled in about half of the net already. She'd hoped for
a few more fish.

Two days had passed since Waawaaskone was born, and
Nangohns had proudly taken on the responsibility of harvesting the food for the feast to celebrate her niece's arrival. On
short notice, she had decided that netting fish in the lake was
the best option for a quick return. But it had only been a couple
of weeks since the last netting, and she worried the lake's stock
was running low. A lot of the fish caught so far this season had

seemed undergrown, and she'd heard similar complaints from other fishers.

The tin thirteen-footer she'd rowed out in rocked as she hauled in the net, but she kept her hips loose to prevent it from tipping. Since the age of five, Nangohns had practically lived on this lake, splashing along the shore with her brother, Maiingan, and other kids, rowing out to other inlets to explore, and walking along the ice and cutting holes to fish in the winter. The lake lay just steps from their settlement, which they called Shki-dnakiiwin, or new village. It was wide and deep, and teeming with fish when they first arrived, and her people called it simply Zaag'igan, the word for "lake" in their language. From the middle, rocky and sandy shores were visible in every direction, illuminated by the sun, which had cleared the treeline in the east.

Nangohns looked north, back at the settlement. When she and her family had made this land their new home, a half-day's walk from the crumbling homes and buildings of the old reserve, they had laid out their new community in a loose circle. The open space in the middle was kept clear for ceremonies, celebrations, and the play of children. Over the water, Nangohns could hear the chatter of little ones in the distance as the community awoke just beyond the shore. The lodges lining that central space were inhabited by the five extended families who first came to Shki-dnakiiwin, led by Nangohns's father, Evan Whitesky. She could see her own family's pair of domed dwellings, made of a frame of tied saplings and covered in canvas and plastic tarps, lying closest to the shore, on the outskirts of a permanent camp of ten more wooden lodges ranged around the central gathering hub.

The ceremonial lodge was the largest structure, standing about a metre taller than the other buildings, and easily within

Nangohns's line of sight from her vantage out on the lake. Like most other buildings in this community, it was shaped into a dome, stretched out on the ground like an elongated oval. Walter, the eldest survivor, had instructed Evan and the other younger adults to build it this way, in the manner of the old medicine lodges of the Anishinaabek.

To Nangohns, Shki-dnakiiwin was physical evidence that separated the time before—what they called Jibwaa—from the world she knew now and that made up most of her memories. When her parents and their people were building this village, they erected an extra two dwellings on the periphery, in case any holdouts hoping for the lights to come back on at the old reserve—named Gaawaandagoong for the abundant white spruce trees there—would eventually turn up, needing shelter. Like her uncle Chuck, her mother's cousin, who at first refused to live in the bush. And Dave, the elder Walter's nephew, who remained in the community garage at the old site for as long as he could, half believing the machinery there, the power transformers and trucks, would one day work again. Nangohns remembered those two, among a handful of others, trudging through the snow, cheeks gaunt, eyes bloodshot, to join them after most of the holdouts had died off.

The final few floats that buoyed the net thudded against the gunwale as Nangohns brought in the last of it. Five more fish, all notably smaller than usual at this point in the season. There were thirteen altogether in the heavy green bin. A few twitched in their final nervous throes of life, but most had died shortly after being caught in the white weaves of the net, unable to move and push water through their gills.

Nangohns sighed and looked back to the shore. Adults were beginning to bustle in the central glade and along the shore, some collecting firewood, others hauling water in buckets. Most

9

of the plastic tarps and canvas coverings of the dwellings were being readjusted or removed, in preparation for the coming summer heat. Seeing people out now for daily tasks turned her attention back to the head count for tonight's feast. After everyone ate, the rest of the morning's catch would likely last her family a week at most.

A loon flapped its wings low to the water as it passed through her line of sight. She grabbed the handles of the long, light aluminum oars, the oarlocks creaking and rattling as she settled into place to row homeward. As she pumped her right hand to slice the oar's blade through the water and point the bow to the shore, the outlines of the muscles in her arms stretched and constricted in a steady tempo as she paddled herself smoothly to land.

The bow came to a stop on the muddy shore, scraping loudly as the hull dug into the rocks below. With the boat firmly planted among the lush green reeds of the shoreline, Nangohns stood, turned, and climbed up onto the seat in front of her and made her way to the front. The metal benches had captured the heat of the morning sun and warmed the bare soles of her feet. She leapt over the side and splashed into the shallow cold water, which came up to her calves. The summer solstice was approaching, but the lake would remain fairly chilly until the peak of the summer heat. Nangohns walked around to the bow and began to tug the boat out of the water and up onto the shore.

"Need help?" a familiar voice murmured from behind. She turned to see her father walking down the grassy slope to the shore. Evan Whitesky's hair was freshly tied into a braid, and the sun reflected off the sheen of his black crown. He raised his hand to shield his eyes from the glare coming off the water.

"Kaawiin," replied Nangohns. "It's not that heavy this morning, sorry to say."

She pulled the boat up onto the grass and let it sit. Evan came to her side and they peered down into the bin of fish, shoulder to shoulder.

"If I caught those with a hook I woulda thrown 'em back," said Nangohns. "But they got caught in the net, so most were already dead."

"We'll make use of 'em," Evan said, reassuringly.

"Might be time to find better fishing spots," she suggested after a short pause.

"Let's just clean these for now," her father replied, pulling the bin of fish out of the tin boat and turning to walk back up the slope. Nangohns followed, carrying the other, empty bin and the tattered nylon net.

They ambled up from the shore and onto a plateau where their family's two domed lodges stood, each entrance facing a large central firepit. The larger structure to the west was draped in green canvas tarps, faded by sunlight but mostly intact. A slightly smaller lodge was covered in a shiny, crinkled blue plastic tarp that rustled with any movement. The green house stood tall enough for full-grown adults to walk around upright inside with sufficient headspace. The blue dwelling stood lower, primarily a sleeping space, and a separate home for Nangohns's brother, Maiingan, and his partner, Pichi, and now their newborn, Waawaaskone.

Evan carefully placed the haul of fish on the grass in front of the firepit. Nangohns tossed the big plastic bin and white net aside as they each took a seat on one of the stools arranged around the pit. The morning sun climbed higher and the soft humidity from the lake began to bead on their sun-darkened foreheads and bare shoulders.

"Aapiish Ngashi?" Nangohns asked, not seeing her mother around.

"She went out to the garden earlier to get some stuff to cook with these giigoonyik. Then I think she was gonna go see your aunties for a little visit," Evan said. "I think a bunch of them are gonna come by. They all wanna see your little shimis."

"Where's the rest of them, then?" asked Nangohns.

"Inside sleeping still. Still pretty tired from it all."

She wanted to see the baby girl again, but didn't want to disturb the new parents.

They sat in the comfortable late-spring stillness. The sun climbed higher, accentuating their arid surroundings after several days without rain. The flies would descend upon them soon, to feast on bare arms and legs, and they could only cover them up with long sleeves and pants or swat them away until the woodsmoke from the evening fires provided a shield.

Evan set to cleaning the fish, and Nangohns to mending the net, which they both agreed could use some work. She grabbed a handful of the fine mesh from the bin and pulled it up to eye level. The nylon threads keeping the net together were still strong enough to trap with, but, scanning it up and down, she noticed some dire holes. It was their last net of this kind.

"Hide ties won't work for a net," Evan reminded her. "They'll just soak and get loose and fall off. Maybe some spruce roots would work."

Within her short lifetime, they would have been able to buy new nets hewn from thin but sturdy nylon strands from the people in the towns and cities to the south. Food and tools would come to them by air. In the winter, provisions came up on trucks that rolled along the ice.

But her father rarely indulged her questions about things like airplanes, trucks, and satellites, and Nangohns had mostly given up asking. The words and markings on their older tools and clothing—the things they hadn't made themselves—had become increasingly intangible to her. Now it seemed that almost everything that had come from Zhaawnong—from the south, that other world, down there—was fading away and falling apart.

She had been three when the power went out, and only five when her father had led their people off the old rez and into the bush. But Nangohns held on to fading memories of bright lights and soft furniture and rumbling cars and trucks that once took them from place to place.

"Maybe I can take down some of the net on the side and use that to patch some of these holes," she suggested.

Evan grunted in the affirmative, arranging buckets and preparing to clean the fish. He picked up one of the wooden logs that served as a stool next to the firepit and placed it beside another smaller one. On top of that log sat his long, curved fixed-blade cleaning knife in its original leather holster. Like the net, it was a manufactured tool that could no longer be traded for, and thus was wielded with great care, meticulously cleaned and sharpened, and never overused.

Nangohns waited for something from her father beyond the gruff acknowledgement.

"I bet there's more nets lying around somewhere," she said evenly, hoping she sounded pragmatic. "We just gotta go out and look. Spend a few days down Zhaawnong, checking out some lakes down there."

Evan paused mid-reach into the fish bin and looked up at her, the cleaning knife in his other hand. "We went around, a few times over the years," he said, turning back to the buckets below him. "We brought back just about everything we could find. You and your brother were just kids back then."

"I remember," Nangohns shot back. And she did remember, relatives who had gone and not come back. She remembered hearing murmurs about failed expeditions. Her sharp retort hung in the short distance between them until the baby cried from within her brother's lodge. Nangohns shrugged and turned her focus back to the white threads in her hands.

Evan looked back down to the fish and wiped strands of his long dark hair out of his face and tucked them behind his ear. The cuts of white fish piled higher, and the zigzag lines of their muscles made mesmerizing patterns in the bucket. About three-quarters of the catch would be cooked to eat tonight. The rest would be smoked and preserved. Evan had been counting on more hauls of fish from the big lake over the summer. They'd need more for winter rations.

They had managed to feed themselves effectively and efficiently in recent years, hunting moose and deer in the fall and geese and ducks in the spring, mostly with bows and arrows, but occasionally with the dwindling supply of rifle bullets and shotgun shells. They snared rabbits and squirrels in winter, and fished through the ice when the lake froze over. Ahead of winter, meat was smoked and dried in old bottomless refrigerators placed over firepits. They gardened and grew squash and beans, and harvested berries from the bush. And there was manoomin—wild rice—that grew naturally in the shallower parts of the big lake. Some of the elders who were still around when they arrived—like Evan's parents and Walter—remembered how to grow and harvest it. Keeping everyone fed was a constant effort, but lately these efforts allowed for the occasional celebration, like the one scheduled for the coming evening.

As dusk fell, the great fire in the centre of the settlement grew in size and heat. Sitting on a log on the outskirts of the gathering space, Evan watched a small but bustling crowd grow around the blaze, first a couple dozen people, mostly kids, and then double that—nearly the entire population of Shki-dnakiiwin. The elevated murmur of adults conversing was punctuated by the occasional crackle and collapse of burning wood in the large firepit. Children ran in circles around the oval lodges, playing tag and laughing. A large black pot full of manoomin simmered on the grill over the fire.

Maiingan was busily frying fish in bubbling duck fat in a massive cast-iron frying pan over the grill. A little beyond the fire, Evan's granddaughter slept in Pichi's arms, surrounded by a crowd of well-wishers. The baby was wrapped in a brown and white blanket of rabbit fur that the older women and men periodically tugged down softly for a better look at her sleeping face. Behind Pichi stood the baby's grandmother, Nicole, resting her hand on the young mother's shoulder and beaming every time someone gleefully uttered the girl's name, which she'd bestowed upon her two nights before. She looked up and caught Evan looking her way, once again sparking their shared elation as new grandparents.

Evan also saw his friend Tyler in the group, squatting low with his wiry limbs jutting out of his faded black T-shirt and cut-off jeans, looking at the girl and beaming. He noticed Evan gazing his way and, with some parting words to the young mother and the others, he stood up and walked over to where Evan picked the last few bones from the prepared fish cutlets.

Greeting Evan as "mishoomis," grandfather, Tyler took the stool beside him. As he took in the happy scene in front of them, he pulled the hide tie out of his black hair, allowing it to fall freely on his shoulders and down his back. "See that?" he asked

Evan, subtly tossing his head. "Still as black as the night I was born. Good thing you're a grandpa now. You got an excuse for them smoky streaks in yours!"

"Pfffft," Evan replied, friendly but clearly envious, instinctively tucking the grey streaks from his temples behind his ears.

"Ho-ly, she's beautiful, bud. You should be proud."

"Miigwech, niijii. But geez, when I was them kids' age," he said, nodding towards some of the older boys roughhousing by the fire. "I wasn't even sure I'd live this long. Now here I am a mishoomis."

Evan looked from his granddaughter to the rest of the crowd. The outlying clusters of people gathered around the fire comprised members of the five main families that had survived the collapse and now lived here, who in the time before used the surnames Whitesky, McCloud, Meegis, North, and Birch.

The fish sizzled in the frying pan. Maiingan flipped the pieces with a metal spatula fastened with pine gum to a thick twig that replaced a long-ago broken plastic handle. Evan asked Tyler if he'd noticed how many fish were in the bucket.

Tyler raised his eyes at his friend in concern.

"Not much," Evan replied for him, meeting Tyler's gaze. "Nang set the net last night and pulled it in this morning. Only got about half of what usually comes in this time of year. All small. I'm scared to set it even one more time."

"Maybe we're gonna have to start going to some of them other little lakes. Maybe start using them old rods a bit more too," said Tyler.

"If we had any line for 'em, you mean?" replied Evan, sounding harsher than he had intended.

Tyler paused, waiting for his old friend's face to tell him more.

Evan softened. "You sound like my daughter," he said, noticing Nangohns settled in on the far side of the fire and back towards the communal structures with a couple of the younger adults, including Amber, the midwife who'd helped deliver baby Waawaaskone, and her partner, Cal. "But I'll remind you what I told her. Our nets are barely hanging on. You want to talk about fishing rods . . ."

"Yeah and you probably lost all your fancy lures to snags years ago, eh?" Tyler patted Evan playfully on his chest.

Evan grumbled amicably.

"Look," said Tyler. "We've got work to do before winter. For sure. But we still got lots of moose jerky left over from the spring. And we'll get more moose in the meantime. That daughter of yours is a real deadeye with that bow."

"She is," agreed Evan. "Doesn't seem that interested in much else other than being in the bush. She's a good friend to Pichi and them other ones their age, but she hangs out more with the older ones like Cal and Amber. Is that normal for a teenager?"

Tyler raised his eyebrows and shrugged. "There was never no normal when it comes to teenagers."

"Speaking of them hooved ones," said Evan, returning to the subject of food, "they don't come around this way much anymore. They know we're here. We gotta go out farther and farther every time to track 'em down. The rabbits don't seem to snare as easily anymore, either. And who knows how long that wire's gonna last."

"You're a grandpa now, man," Tyler said after a pause. "You can see the new generation. Look. Right in front of you. You're worrying too much. We've always found a way. We will now. They will too."

A ripple of laughter erupted from the group gathered around Pichi and the baby. Gloria, the elder midwife who had guided the baby's birth, was giving Nicole a playful nudge, and the crowd was gradually moving from the baby to the food as

Maiingan finished up the first batch of fish. Evan took in everything at once, in the orange glow of the fire. A bit beyond them, he saw the silhouette of one small child tackling another.

"We should go see Walter tomorrow to talk about it," Evan said, but lightly, to show his friend that he had heard him and appreciated the counsel.

"I'll run it by him tonight," replied Tyler. "Forget all that for now, though. We got food to eat. It's a party!" He raised his hands in a victorious gesture before clasping one down hard but affectionately on Evan's bare shoulder. The slap was loud enough to make Maiingan turn in their direction.

"Ow, goddamn it!" Evan yelped, half in pain, half in laughter, as he gave Tyler a hard shove and knocked him off his seat. Tyler hooted out a laugh on his way to the ground. They both stood and made their way over to the feasting area on the other side of the fire, where Waawaaskone's celebration was getting underway.

From the other side of the fire, Nangohns watched her father and his friend walk towards the gathering. Her companions, Amber and Cal, had stolen off by themselves for a quiet moment together after a long day of work, she suspected. The two had been inseparable as young teens when the community settled here, and in the last couple years they'd blossomed into a full-fledged item. In their mid-twenties now, they were among the younger couples. Nangohns figured it wouldn't be long until they had kids of their own, but she had always felt too shy to ask them about it. Next to herself, Cal was one of Shki-dnakiiwin's best hunters, and although her aim and stealth were unsurpassed, she envied his speed and strength. Amber was rapidly becoming their most experienced midwife, following in Gloria's footsteps. And Nangohns's mother, Nicole, discovering that her own daughter would rather be hunting, had taken Amber under her wing, teaching her about the medicines.

Nangohns looked at Pichi, her round cheeks pushed outward by her wide smile as she peered down at Waawaaskone. The baby slept soundly despite the commotion around her. Nangohns listened to the playful squeals of the other kids nearby, and wondered what life would be like when Cal and Amber finally did have a child, leaving her to spend time with the younger children. Maybe she'd take to the bush even more. That's where she felt the most comfortable, after all, and where she could do their people the most good.

Her joy about the small baby was overshadowed by concern over the meagre fish, and her mind clouded with thoughts of the future. She imagined what her father and Tyler had said to each other, and what might become of it.

TWO

THICK RAINDROPS FELL ONTO the tarp roof of the lodge
in a steady hum. First just a few modest taps, and then, in
moments, a downpour, cascading so quickly that the sound of
each bead of water became indiscernible from the others. The
roar of the deluge was welcome after ten days without rain.

In the middle of the central lodge a fire burned, the reflection of the flames dancing in the eyes of the twelve figures
loosely assembled in the long, oval space. Walter and Gloria,
the eldest of the community, had shown Evan and the others
how to build the lodge in the old style, with the eastern doorway the primary entrance and exit. The western opening was
only used to close major ceremonies, like funerals. Movement
within the lodge was always contingent on the fire: one could
only walk around it clockwise, upon entrance, exit, or to
move places. That is the way of the old medicine lodge of the
Anishinaabek, Walter had told them then.

Aside from Evan, Nicole, and Tyler—in his usual place
over the fire—gathered there that evening were Evan's parents,
Dan and Patricia, standing in their moccasins with long strips
of hide looped into the waists of their old, loose pants to hold
them up. Dan wore a threadbare sleeveless white T-shirt, and

Patricia was in an oversized faded purple athletic tank top. They were just a little younger than Walter, elders now in their own right. J.C., Walter's nephew, and his partner, Amanda, one of the last of the old band councillors, stood nearby, perched in the doorway chatting with Tyler's partner, Nick. They were a little older than Evan. Along with Nicole, they were the ones who had led the survivors from the old town into the bush ten years before.

The leaders of that migration had also included Candace, another of the former councillors, seated by the fire with her son, Cal, and his partner, Amber—both now considered young trailblazers themselves. Behind them, talking with Nicole, stood the only relative newcomer, Meghan, a white woman who had come up from the south the first winter after the blackout but was by now one of their own. She regaled Nicole as they waited with a story about her son, Makwa, the child she'd borne seven years earlier with Jeff, Evan's cousin. To Nicole, she'd gone from mysterious foreigner to family in the twelve years since she arrived.

Dan spoke up over the pounding rain, his forehead creasing into rivers of wrinkles as he looked up at the ceiling. "Gchi-gmiwan nongo naagshig," he said, acknowledging the heavy evening downpour.

"Hopefully them strawberry bushes will start to catch up now," Evan replied.

At the peak of the dry spell a few days earlier, Nicole and Maiingan had returned from a meagre medicine walk with Amber and Cal, reporting that the berries were late, and that the bushes lacked their usual colour for this time of year. As he listened to the rainfall, Evan hoped the water would help draw the red of the strawberries and white yarrow from the land around them.

They had all agreed to convene at sundown, when the smaller children would be in bed and the older ones would be able to occupy themselves with old scratched checkerboards marked by stone play pieces and tattered books read by candle-light made from moose and deer tallow.

Tyler quietly rearranged the logs of the fire with a rusty steel poker. He had lifted the canvas and nylon tarps from the bottom of the structure to let in the cooler outside air. The others caught up in quiet conversation, waiting for the meeting to formally convene.

The chatter stopped when the figure of a tall man in a rough moose-hide vest and loose blue basketball shorts appeared in the doorway. His bare paunch protruded slightly from the vest's tan lapels. In his left arm he cradled and carried his medicine bundle: a pipe, tobacco, sage, an eagle feather, and other ceremonial items and medicines wrapped in another long cut of hide, stained and smooth from years of handling. His long grey hair was tied back in a tight braid, accentuating his squinting eyes as he entered the dim fire-lit space. His pace was slow but smooth and deliberate.

"Holy shit, why's everyone so quiet?" said Walter. "Is this my funeral or something? Did I get struck by lightning out there?"

Affectionate laughter rippled through the group. "Who's that keeping the fire? Tyler? I can't tell from here." He squeezed his eyes tighter, almost closing them entirely. "Jesus Christ, all you long-haired Indians look the same in the dark. Get a hair-cut and get a real job!"

He raised and shook a loose fist in jest, and set his bundle down on one of the woven blankets laid out in front of the fire. Evan could remember when the blanket was brought up as a gift for the former chief and council from a deputy minister in the old government's Indigenous Affairs department.

Walter moved through the assembly, hugging and greeting each person individually. Now somewhere in his seventies, he still towered over most of them. He walked clockwise around the fire—the way they had been taught—to finish his round of greetings, then leaned down to take a pinch of dried tobacco out of the bowl beside Tyler near the fire. He closed his eyes and whispered a prayer, elevating his fist close to his heart to hold the semaa, his tobacco offering, tight. He opened his eyes and tenderly lowered his hand to offer his prayer medicine to the fire. Tyler followed by throwing a small dash of cedar leaves onto the burning logs. Walter stepped around the rocks of the circle that contained the blaze, and eased himself down with a pronounced groan onto the blanket on the western side of the lodge, across from Tyler. "Nmadabik," he kindly commanded the others, and they lowered themselves onto the blankets on the ground surrounding the firepit, gathering close enough to see each other's faces in the light of the flames.

Walter's eyes no longer strained as he looked into the fire before him. He rested his forearms on his bare knees, his moccasins folded under his crossed legs. The patter above slowed to a quieter pace; the heaviest of the downpour had passed.

"Mii zhgo wii-niibing," he proclaimed. "Summer's almost here."

Several hummed an acknowledgement and nodded.

"The rain is nice, though, eh? It's been pretty dry the last little bit. It was probably almost a month, if we were counting the days, since we had a good rain like this one. So the berries are behind. The gardens aren't coming up good. I even heard some of the medicines around here aren't as easy to find like usual." He glanced towards Nicole.

Nicole straightened her back and told the group about her medicine walk with Maiingan and Cal and Amber three days ago. With the birth of Waawaaskone, she had hoped to harvest a flower her Auntie Aileen used to tell them was good for babies. She remembered Aileen showing her how to harvest and then boil the root, which could then be rubbed on a baby's gums to help soothe the pain of teething. Her granddaughter, still only days old, wouldn't need it for a while yet, but Nicole had hoped to gather some to have on hand for the sleepless nights to come. But the bushes weren't even budding. They were able to bring back some yarrow and cedar, but not much else. The land was dry.

"We had dry summers before," Walter piped up. "Everything usually catches up. But if the rest of this summer stays dry, and then the next one too, it's gonna be hard to keep up."

He paused to peer back into the fire.

"Weather's been changing since before we came out here," said Walter. "But I think there's a bigger problem facing us right now that I worry we're responsible for."

Evan turned to Tyler, who tightened his lips.

"Whenever we have to go out and get a moose or a deer," Walter continued, "we have to go farther and farther to track one down. Sometimes we even gotta stay the night out there in the bush. Even the four-leggeds know enough not to hang around here no more. We've been in this place for some ten winters. We haven't moved nowhere. There's a reason our ancestors always picked up and left whenever the seasons told them to. Anishinaabek were meant to move."

Walter's voice went suddenly hoarse, and a rumble came from deep in his throat as he tried to clear it.

"Nbi," he said, holding out his hand. J.C. handed him a brown metal water bottle. Walter unscrewed the shiny top, took a generous swig, and handed it back to his nephew. "Chi-miigwech," he said.

Tyler tossed another dash of cedar onto the fire.

For all of Evan's life before the blackout, his community had been consigned to one place. Generations had been unable to move and live in the old way, and by Evan's childhood, the majority of their food and supplies came to them. It wasn't a lot, but they survived. Even then, they still went out into the bush to get whatever else they needed. But for the last ten years, hunting and harvesting were how they'd been getting all their food.

"The other big problem is with the giigoonyik," Walter continued. "We've been using the net too much, and that big lake, it just can't keep up. We're not the only ones who need the fish. The birds do too. And they need the manoomin. If we take too much, everything else could suffer. There needs to be a balance with all the life in the waters around us. Right now, we're upsetting that balance."

Evan sensed several bodies around him readjusting nervously. Tyler's eyes were cast to the ground.

"We're all too young to have experienced this, but this has happened before," Walter went on. "It's what happened to our ancestors when they used to live on those big waters down south, before they were pushed up here. The zhaagnaashak brought in big boats with big nets and they took almost all of the fish out of the lakes. Then they cut all the trees down. It was in a different lifetime, and in a different world, really, but it wasn't that long ago. That was Jibwaa, back before. And when the lights went out and we lost everything we had from the world of the zhaagnaashak, we were given a chance to live another way. We left where we were and we came out here. As hard as that was, and as many as we lost, it's part of our history."

A log crumbled into embers in the fire, sending up a crackle of sparking ash.

"I tell you all this tonight," Walter said, "because I think we're gonna have to make a decision soon. Another matter of life or death for our people."

A soft, expectant clamour moved over the group. Walter paused to allow the brief confusion to calm.

"We need to go back home," he said.

Evan felt his chest pound. He looked to Tyler, who gazed back stoically this time. He turned to his parents, and saw their hands clasped on his mother's knee. Meghan and the younger ones kept their eyes locked on Walter, awaiting an explanation.

"We've been up here for so long that some of us forget where we originally came from," he continued. "And I don't think the young ones hear enough about our real homelands, where the birch trees grow by the big water. That land is who we are. It's time to undo what's been done to us. It's time to go back home."

Nicole and Evan locked eyes, not sure how to respond. Finally, from the northern side of the circle, Cal, the youngest in the group, spoke up.

"So we gotta pack up and go south, then," he affirmed.

"Not yet," the elder responded immediately. The creases at the corners of his eyes and around his cheeks mapped out a lifetime of grief and healing. "After all that happened that first winter, when evil came to us on the old rez and threatened everything we had, everything we were, we haven't had any contact with the world below."

Meghan, whose gaze had been fixed on Walter, bowed her head. Of everyone present, she'd had the most recent glimpse of the world before: a city in turmoil, violently unravelling. She had told everyone here all she saw. Infrastructure and communications failing in a matter of weeks after the power went down, followed by burglary, violence, and elevating chaos.

Nick had witnessed it too, as a student in the same city at the time, but he escaped weeks before she did. Neither of them told those stories anymore, though, and no one had returned to the city, once called Gibson, since.

"We need to know what's happening down there first," Walter declared. "We need to know before we decide if a big move is something we can do. We have new babies here. We can't put them, or anyone else, in danger."

"We gotta go scout it out," acknowledged Evan, thinking of his new granddaughter, Waawaaskone, just days old.

"Haven't we tried that already?" Candace's voice cracked from the other side of the circle. "We never find anything."

Amanda wrapped an arm around her friend's shoulders.

"We lose people," Candace concluded, choking back emotion.

It was true. There were two missing from their circle that night. Isaiah, another of Candace's sons, Cal's older brother; and Kevin, Tyler's younger brother. They had left on a similar expedition deep into Zhaawnong four years earlier, seeking supplies and answers about the blackout. They never returned. Their departure had only widened the void for those they left behind.

Evan remembered helping Isaiah pack the night before he headed south. Their plan was for the two men to pack light and move fast. They didn't have a fixed destination in mind, but had prepared for a month-long trip: two weeks down, or until they found something, and two weeks back. They would resupply as needed in the bush. Both knew their way around.

Evan worried that Isaiah hadn't packed enough quick-dry clothing and had brought him some of his. He had teased his friend for insisting on bringing his long-dead cellular phone, which since the first night of the blackout had been as good as

27

a brick without power and a functioning network to connect to. When Evan asked why he was bringing it, Isaiah had joked about finding service and ordering a pizza, before throwing the device, wrapped in a blue rubber case adorned with the logo of the Toronto Maple Leafs, into his pack.

Back in the lodge, Cal's voice rang out, startling Evan from his memory.

"I'll go," the young man proclaimed, straightening his long back and lifting his square jaw.

Amber let out a choked cry. "What?" She was shocked.

Cal took her gently by the shoulders. "We've been saying this for years now," he said, looking deep into her eyes. "You know Walter is right. And I wanna know what's down there."

Amber said nothing and kept her eyes trained on his. His mother, Candace, exhaled a shaky breath and slouched forward, looking down into her clasped hands.

Cal spoke to the group. "I wanna do what's right for our people. This is a chance to go back home." He turned back to Amber. "I wanna honour our ancestors. And my brother. And you should come too."

Walter interjected that they wouldn't be taking volunteers just yet, but that he did think they should go sooner rather than later. "If a team goes right at the start of summer, they could be back by the fall, just as the leaves turn."

"Walking all the way?" asked Cal.

"Unless you figured out how to flap them arms of yours," J.C. responded dryly. "Yeah, walking all the way."

Nervous laughter joined the ambient noise of the ongoing rainfall. Cal shrank a little into the ground.

A trek by foot all the way down to the north shore of the Great Lakes could take a month, thought Evan. Depending on what remained of the roads, and in the towns and cities along the way. For all this while, Zhaawnong, the world to the south, had been a vast void, and they could only speculate who or what still lived there.

"We'll have to be ready for anything," Walter continued, as if reading Evan's thoughts. "I wanna have another meeting in two nights with more of you. I'll talk to the others who I want there. The rest of you, just show up. Nahaaw, baamaapii."

With that, Walter dismissed the group and urged them home to sleep, asking that nobody speak of this for the next couple of days. The circle broke, and the assembly got to their feet without saying much to each other, shuffling slowly clockwise around the fire towards the exit. "Evan, Nicole," Walter called out. "Stay back, would you. I wanna talk to you both. Tyler, you too."

Evan and Nicole whispered a few quick goodbyes as the space emptied. Tyler stayed in place by the fire, his eyes fixed on the coals, only glancing up briefly to loft a quick smile at Nick, who was leaving with the rest.

When they were alone, Walter, still sitting cross-legged on the ground, gestured to them to take their seats again. He made a fanning motion in Tyler's direction. Tyler's long fingers tenderly broke stems of sage that lay in a neat pile on the blanket in front of him. He placed them into the cracked ceramic bowl, then stuck a long strip of birchbark into the fire to catch a flame. He guided the light under the small pile of sage in the bowl. He brought the burning medicine around to the other three, and they all took turns waving the thick grey smoke over their bodies and heads.

"Some heavy shit, eh?" said Walter.

Evan's shoulders relaxed with a sigh, and Nicole leaned forward, almost leisurely.

"Big time," said Evan.

"I think it's our only choice," Walter declared.

Nicole's lips flapped in an exaggerated exhale. "I think so too," she agreed.

"Is it so bad," asked Tyler, "that we have to go?"

"It will be," said Walter. "We've lost so many people already. We can't lose any more. We've been working so hard just to survive that we're not growing. Even with that little nooshenh of yours that was just born, our numbers are going down. It's time we went out to have a look. We have to try."

"With a bigger group." Evan predicted his next line.

"Yeah, with a bigger group. Maybe five or six of you."

Nicole bit her bottom lip. Tyler's eyes widened.

"It sounds like you've already decided who you want to go," Evan said.

"It's not my decision," Walter replied. "That's not how we do things around here. But yes, that's what I think is best. I think you two should help figure out who should go. And Evan, I think you should help lead the way."

Nicole's face betrayed worry, but she nodded silently in agreement. "I think so too," she said.

THREE

THE TENSION IN NANGOHNS'S bow released in a sharp snap, and the arrow hissed through the air in the blink of an eye before landing in the deer's side with a quick thud. Its hind legs kicked back, its front legs scrambling forward towards the shelter of the bush beyond the edge of the clearing. In a few frantic pounces, it was out of sight, veiled by the darkness of the thick spring canopy. The beast's heavy gasps faded into the insulated scrub. Nangohns looped the bow around her shoulder as she listened to the sound of its flailing hooves on the forest floor grow dim. Confident in her shot, she was in no rush to chase after the animal. She sauntered over to the treeline and entered the shade.

Glistening drops of blood speckled the leaves and branches on the ground. Nangohns crouched for a closer look at the red trail. Blood streaked across a birch leaf and dripped off a blade of grass. Scattering this essence about the land was the final act of the deer's dying heart. Nangohns followed the trail of blood up through the trees and over a low hill. She had seen the arrow go right into its lung. If it had punctured the other as well, it couldn't have gotten very far.

The rain two nights earlier had left a comforting dampness on the earth and in the trees. It restored the grass in the small meadow, its green hue returning, and with it the deer came back to graze. When she awoke that morning, Nangohns knew she had to hunt. The recent, much-needed downpour was sure to bring a few deer out to the clearing. By the time she planted herself behind a shrub on the other side of the glade, it wasn't long until a target appeared.

The red track became wider as she approached her kill. Here, the animal had slowed, unable to breathe, blood filling its lungs. Nangohns stepped over a fallen tree and proceeded towards the peak of the incline. At the top she paused, and saw the inert buck resting in finality down the other side. The arrow's shaft and fletching protruded straight up from the fatal wound, and a last trickle of blood oozed from the puncture site. It was one of only about a dozen synthetic arrows she had left, and she was pleased to see it still largely intact. She would clean and use this one again.

Walking up to the animal slowly, Nangohns dug in her pocket for her tobacco pouch. She stopped just a step from the deer and gazed across its hefty frame. Its eyes bulged into nothingness and its tongue lay on the dirt it could no longer taste. It was a fully grown adult and would feed them for weeks. Feeling proud and thankful, she opened her small deer-hide satchel to take some semaa into her left palm. She squeezed her fingers firmly over the dried brown leaves, harvested from their own community garden the fall before. They crumbled into the creases of her palm, and she closed her eyes to whisper a prayer of gratitude.

Evan, who had been standing on the ridge Nangohns had traversed moments ago, waited until his daughter had raised her head and exhaled before he moved to join her.

"Double lung shot, eh?" he noted as he appeared a few strides behind her. "Nice job."

"Miigwech," she replied. "He's a pretty big target."

"You're one of the only ones around here who can make that kinda shot, no matter how big they are."

Nangohns shrugged. She'd been working on it, practising every day.

The two of them surveyed the felled deer.

"Might have to clean him back here, eh?" said Nangohns. "I dunno if we can get him on that roller."

One of the two-wheeled trailers they'd salvaged from the old site was still useful enough to cart large animals back to the settlement, as long as the distance wasn't too great. The limp rubber on the metal rims could gain enough traction on flat stretches, but it took multiple people to pull and push it at the same time, especially with fully grown deer in the cart. Any adult moose was too big and heavy and almost always had to be quartered and dressed on site, leaving the internal organs behind for scavengers.

Evan expected his son, Maiingan, to arrive any moment, so they both sat on the ground as the blackflies descended into the small hollow and began to swarm the dead buck. Evan and Nangohns swatted them from their bare shoulders and faces. The mosquitoes had returned in full force as well, thanks to the heavy rain, and they buzzed endlessly in their ears. The morning was otherwise calm.

"Noos," Nangohns spoke up.

"Yes, my girl?" Evan replied.

She cleared her throat, and her eyes darted to the buck before looking back at her father's face. "I wanted to say . . . to tell you that I know what's going on."

Evan's back straightened at the question. "What do you mean?" he asked evenly.

"I know—everyone knows—about that meeting you guys had the other night."

Evan swallowed and tried not to look sheepish. "There's not even fifty of us here," he said. "Sometimes I wonder why Walter thinks anyone could keep a secret."

Nangohns offered a smile and a reassuring chuckle. They both looked again at the dead beast, speckled now with black insects throughout its beige and white coat. The swarm around it grew bigger.

Nangohns took a deep breath. "I want to go," she proclaimed, looking deep into her father's eyes.

A panic rose up in Evan's chest, which he tried to suppress. "Go?" he was finally able to vocalize.

"On that trip. When you go south, I want to come with you."

"Nang . . . no," he said flatly, after making some effort to compose himself. "Zhaawnong . . . it's too dangerous."

"How do you know that?"

"Because Izzy and Kevin didn't come back."

She looked at her father. "It was only a few years ago. Maybe they just kept going. They could still be out there. All the more reason to—"

Evan sharply raised a hand to silence her. "No," he said. "They promised they'd come back and get us."

Nangohns's face flushed. "Something could have happened. We can't know for sure."

"I guess not." Evan lowered his hand, but his body remained planted, resolved. "Don't forget, Nang, they're not the only ones who left and didn't come back."

Nangohns remembered the search parties. She had still been a little girl. The summer after the blackout, a pair of young men set out to seek answers in another reserve about

34

one hundred kilometres to the west. Winter returned before they did, and they were never heard from again. The next summer a team of four loaded up canoes to paddle south on the big river, but only two returned. One of the boats had capsized in the swollen waters shortly after their departure, and two of them drowned. The other two came home, starving. They were never the same. They refused to leave the old reserve and eventually died, like the rest who stayed behind.

Evan and Nangohns were silent for a moment as the dead buck lay there, presiding. Finally Nangohns turned to her father. "Noos, you know I'm one of the best hunters here. I know this land around us just as well as you older ones. You raised me this way, remember?"

Evan kept his mouth closed, staring at the insects landing on the deer's smooth flank.

"I'm fast. I'm strong. I can run through the bush with my eyes closed. I can walk through the night and make it wherever I need to go. I can disappear anytime, and no one would see or hear me."

It was true. Nangohns knew no other life as intimately as life in the bush. She settled in here—almost seamlessly—at the age of five. Two winters later she was on solo excursions through the woods, sometimes leaving on her own in the morning and not returning until dusk. Evan and Nicole never worried, because she always found her way back. Three winters after that, she killed her first deer with the compound bow Evan had never really mastered. By then she spent most of the daylight hours firing arrows at targets made of dull-blue Styrofoam chunks ripped from under the docks at the old reserve site. She rarely missed, so few of the shafts ever broke.

"I don't need no bullets. I just need one arrow. I take good care of them, so they last."

As Nangohns pleaded her case, Evan was taken by her assured eyes, which reminded him of her mother's.

"I'm good with the knife. I can get the meat ready quick. I hunt with respect. Just like you raised me."

She wanted to go on. Her reasons were coming fast, but her words weren't sounding the way she had planned. She paused, giving Evan time to consider what she had to say. He kept a straight face.

"This life is all I know, Noos," she began again. "Every spring I help plant. Every summer I fish and gather. Every fall I hunt and save the food for winter. And in the winter I go around and make sure everyone has wood. Just like you did when we were little kids at our old house. You believed in our future, like I do now. You raised me this way."

Evan remembered his rounds through the community with Isaiah and Tyler back then. Before the collapse—the time they called Jibwaa—all three were employed by the community's public works department, ploughing roads, cutting grass, clearing brush, and more. Then, when everything fell apart, the community's survival became their responsibility. They delivered food and firewood to dark, cold houses. During that first winter, they towed bodies on sleds to a makeshift morgue in the garage at the band office. He was then only a decade older than his daughter was now.

He remembered her childhood and adolescence too, when she was eager to go out into the bush while the other children were content to stay back in the settlement, playing by the shore and learning the basics of handcrafting moccasins and other small tasks. She went out at night to catch smelts in streams when many of her peers were home in their beds.

"Hmmmm," Evan murmured, if only to assure her he had heard everything she said. "I know what you can do, my girl. You know these ways better than all the other kids your age. Better than plenty adults. We still don't know what's there, Zhaawnong. I don't want to put you in danger. You're my kid."

"Not knowing and just staying put is dangerous too," she pushed back. "I don't want to let us, let everything we've built, just waste away. That could happen. You know it. And I'm not really a kid anymore."

Evan cleared his throat and peered into the lines of his stained palms. "We'll talk to your mother about it," he relented.

The Whitesky family, now a unit of six, milled about as the late-afternoon sun began its slow descent into evening. Shortly after Evan and Nangohns had reached their temporary truce, Maiingan had arrived and they'd determined that they could wheel the massive deer out on the trailer and break it down back home. Once the arduous trek was done, the deer had been cleaned and butchered with old knives honed and sharpened on rods and whetstones. The processing of the buck began late in the morning with the help of Tyler and Nick, and most of the meat had already been distributed amongst the other families in the compound. Evan held back two large chunks of the hind. He sat on a stump in front of the firepit, cutting the slabs of purple meat into strips to be smoked and dried for jerky.

Maiingan moved logs from the pile beside the lodge to the fire. He stepped into the structure briefly to grab small strips of birchbark and a flint stone. Pichi nursed Waawaaskone on the long bench across from Evan, and Nicole sat beside her, awaiting the end of the baby's feeding to take her and give the young mother a break. Nangohns sat with her back resting against the lodge, enjoying the calm of the late afternoon before the nightly arrival of mosquitoes.

The sleeping baby came off her latch, and Pichi handed her over to Nicole. "Nbaan nooshenh," the grandmother said softly, encouraging the child to sleep. The first weeks of motherhood were going smoothly. The midwives still visited almost daily, and they assured Pichi and Nicole that the baby was developing well. The routine of taking care of this fresh existence was a balm.

Nangohns arose and walked towards the small gathering before her. She eased onto another of the upright logs they used for seats near the fire.

"How you feeling?" Nicole asked as her daughter joined the circle.

"I think we're gonna be sore tomorrow after driving that trailer through the bush," she replied.

Evan glanced at her from under his downturned brow as he continued to cut.

"Well, you guys did pretty good," said Nicole. "Miigwech."

"Nahaaw," said Nangohns. She looked down at her dark moccasins and cleared her throat. She raised her head to look at Evan. He felt her gaze and knew what she was about to say. Maiingan stopped striking the flint for a moment and looked up in his sister's direction.

"What?" asked Nicole, looking up from the baby in her arms, sensing the tension.

"I know what's going on," Nangohns replied, not missing a beat. "I know what everyone's planning. I wanna go."

"Go where?" Nicole asked, but it was clear what her daughter meant.

"On that long walk Zhaawnong. I know I could help. I'm a good hunter, and I know how to be in the bush."

Nicole, Maiingan, and Pichi sat in stunned silence. Evan

set his blade down in the bucket on top of the strips of deer meat and placed his hands on his lap.

"I already told Noos all about this," Nangohns continued. "I wanna come to that meeting tonight. I know it's happening. I'm gonna tell them why I should go."

Her parents could not deny that Nangohns was one of the best-suited for this undertaking. But Nicole wasn't ready to admit it. After a few minutes of heated debate, Nicole looked towards the sky and tried to breathe. She looked at her daughter, her eyes wet.

"My girl," Nicole sighed. "Put yourself in my place. You are my daughter, on the edge of adulthood. If you go now, I'm worried any hint of the little girl that made me smile during those darkest days will be gone for good. Even if you return, that child will be lost to me forever."

Nangohns's eyes went to the infant in her mother's arms. She wanted to soften, but knew this was her only chance to prove her case. "I will return. I will bring everyone back safely. And when I do, I'll be who I've always been."

Nicole shot back, "Nang, you don't realize the danger— how dangerous it was, how it used to be out there."

"How could I know that?" Nangohns could no longer hold back. "You guys never tell us anything about Jibwaa, about what used to be."

Nicole erupted. "We tell you the good things!" Her voice echoed down the slope and over the water below them. "We don't need to talk about the evil, because it's not here anymore."

Nicole looked down at the baby in her arms and tried to compose herself. Evan moved to her side.

Nangohns softened her voice but remained still, addressing all of them. "If we wait around here too long, we'll die. That baby will die. We need to go down so we can survive. So we can grow. And if we lose hold of everything we've gained here, if we weaken, the evil will find us."

Nicole had no rebuttal. Waawaaskone let out a faint whimper as her tiny limbs stretched out in her grandmother's arms. Nangohns accepted her mother's silence as permission to attend the meeting. She looked at her father a final time and nodded. He nodded back and returned to his work on the deer.

Maiingan returned to striking the flint onto the small bundle of bark and shavings, and soon he was blowing on a tiny ember. They went on in silence as Nicole held her granddaughter tight to her chest and peered into the western horizon, awaiting the sunset.

FOUR

THAT NIGHT, NANGOHNS JOINED her brother and parents for the larger community meeting. Nearly all of Shkidnakiiwin's adults were there. She listened as Walter shared his vision of starting over where the birch trees grow by the big lake, their people's original homeland. Stories of the old days on the Great Lakes were told long into the night.

In the days that followed, the precarity of their food supply also came into clear focus. Hunters and harvesters corroborated more distinctly what most people had only muttered in passing up to that point: returns were dwindling. But many still resisted the proposed migration.

Evan warned Walter and the council that there would be holdouts, as there had been a decade earlier. Nangohns joined him as he canvassed the settlement about the proposed expedition. Some with young children were worried about uprooting their families and taking them on a long, dangerous exodus. A few wanted nothing to do with it, refusing to join or send their loved ones on another doomed adventure Zhaawnong in hopes of finding a home they had, in their lifetimes, never known or in many cases even seen.

But as Nangohns saw on those visits, most of the families that made up Shki-dnakiiwin trusted her father. They also trusted Nicole. They remembered what a hungry winter felt like. After several days of discussion and debate—in homes, around fires, and in the ceremonial lodge—a community decision was made to equip and send a small group south, towards their ancestral home, and to bring back by summer's end news of the world below.

Ten days after Walter had first convened the group on a rainy night to hand the task of leading the mission to Evan, the community gathered at dawn to give thanks and announce who would be making the trip Zhaawnong.

The sky was a luminous purple in the east. The horizon bloomed into pink, then orange, then an odd burst of white before the sun peeked above. The still morning carried a slight chill, even this close to the onset of summer.

A sacred fire burned steps from the shore of the big lake. The absence of wind left the water's surface perfectly undisturbed, like a mirror, except for the occasional splash of fish jumping in the coves. The lake reflected the brightening sky above, doubling the sunrise for those gathered on the shore.

The assemblage of more than forty people stood on the beach and a few steps inland in a loose crowd, long black hair hanging loose or in braids, faces tanned a deep bronze from the prolonged sunshine of the spring season. Most wore patched wool sweaters, hooded sweatshirts, and long-sleeved canvas work shirts against the morning chill.

Standing in front of the small fire, the elder and medicine keeper Gloria beat her hand drum four times to signal the beginning of the ceremony. Tyler assumed his usual position as firekeeper on a flat rock beside her. In the immediate circle around the ceremonial centre stood the elders and near-elders:

Walter, Amanda, Candace, Dan, Patricia, and a few others. None remained in the community that were older than this core group.

Four other hand drums, held by Patricia, Nicole, Amber, and Nangohns, joined in a mid-tempo rhythm. Gloria began singing a welcoming song, and after her lead, the others joined in. The beats echoed across the lake.

Evan gently nodded his head to the beat and mouthed the words of the song. Families in the crowd huddled together on the shoreline in the morning coolness, awaiting the warmth of the higher sun on the cusp of the summer solstice. The beat of the drums carried the ancient melody across the water.

After the final notes of the last verse resonated through the crowd, the drummers struck their tight skins four final times in unison, and the song was complete.

"Hoo-ah!" shouted a few in the crowd, followed by smatterings of "Nahaaw miigwech."

Patricia lowered her drum and stick to the ground, resting them on the hide carrying case. She reached forward to gather a trace of semaa from the birchbark bowl next to the fire. She picked up an eagle feather that lay on a separate blanket, beside other medicines and ceremonial items like a pipe. Holding it between her wrinkled thumb and index finger, she began to softly stroke the grey vane with her other hand, lining up the thin barbs neatly. Her mouth made a sharp smack as she opened it to speak.

"Boozhoo ndanwendaagnak," she began, greeting her relatives, and then formally introduced herself with her name and clan before delivering an opening prayer. She turned to each of the four directions to give thanks, speaking in nearly fluent Anishinaabemowin, proudly enunciating the long syllables. She rotated again to face the fire and completed the thanksgiving prayer.

43

When she was finished, she sprinkled the grains of dried tobacco onto the fire before stepping back to take her place alongside the other singers. One by one, community members stepped up to the fire to give their own brief, silent prayers, although Nangohns noticed a few older adults hanging back.

Tyler threw a flash of cedar onto the fire after each tobacco offering, and once all the offerings had been made, Walter stepped forward from beside Dan and Patricia to speak.

"Boozhoo, good morning, everyone," he said. "Chi-miigwech. We give thanks for a new day and a new beginning. Every dawn is a new opportunity in this life the Creator has given us. Mother Earth shows us her beauty with every sunrise. Even on the cloudy days we give thanks for what she is bringing us. We're here today to talk about starting over. We're thinking about the days ahead, even beyond the next winter."

Over the last few days, people had talked of little else beyond the proposed expedition to explore the vast terrain to the south in hopes of blazing a trail to the rocky shores of their ancestral waters, said to be so big that no shore was visible on the other side.

"We want to go back home," proclaimed Walter. "Back to the place near that big lake where all the birch trees are. Wiigwaaswaatigoong, our ancestors called it. But we can't all just pick up and go yet. It's gonna take us a while to get ready. And the journey is far."

They had looked at one of the tattered old maps and determined that the trip would take thirty days. Too long for them all to go at once. Evan's team was to make the journey and then come back to guide the rest.

"We have to acknowledge, though," continued Walter, pointing his long nose and bushy eyebrows to the ground, "the young men who went that way and didn't come back. We honour them today."

In the crowd, Evan could make out Joanne, Kevin's mother, weeping quietly. Her grey hair hung to her shoulders, still shorter than everyone else's; she had cut it to grieve the loss of her son when she'd finally accepted that he might not return.

"Izzy and Kevin respected the land," said Walter. "Our next steps will follow the path they set for us, into a world we haven't seen in more than twelve winters. We need to be prepared for what we might find."

Walter explained that there were six volunteers, and called on Evan, who with Nicole had been in charge of preparations, to speak.

Checking the tightness of his thick black braid at the back of his neck, Evan cleared his throat and stepped forward. The smooth hide of his moccasins sank into the grey sand of the shore. The familiar sensation made him want to remove his footwear and stand barefoot, despite the cold air low to the ground.

"Nahaaw, miigwech, Walter," Evan began. He looked out to the faces in front of him. "You all know me, I'm gonna keep this short, just like me," he said, with his usual hint of self-deprecation drawing chuckles from the crowd. "Me and Nicole have talked to you all at some point over the past few days, so you know what we've been asked to do. I don't gotta go over all the history and all that. We know that picking up and moving again is gonna be hard, just like last time. Some of you aren't on board yet, and we respect that. But some of us gotta go. Right now."

He looked out into the crowd. He could feel their worry, and detected a few stony faces, frowning above folded arms. But it was clear the dissenters were content to let him speak, and announce who would be joining him on the walk south.

The first name called was Cal's. As he walked up to the fire, Candace patted him on the back. This would be the second of her sons to venture south, into the unknown. Cal took his place beside Evan, his hands clasped in front of him, tensing the muscles in his thick arms.

"Cal was the very first one to say he wanted to go," Evan explained. "He's spent more than half of his life out here in the bush. He's one of our great young hunters. And he has always followed good in his brother's footsteps. They were raised in a good way. Miigwech, Candace, for allowing your sons to lead us."

"Hoo-ah," boomed Walter in agreement, and others echoed the same sentiment with whoops and cheers.

"And of course," Evan continued, "wherever Cal goes, Amber goes, and vice versa. These two have been attached at the hip since we moved out here, and now they're attached for life."

He nodded at her, and her eyes squeezed tight as she smiled widely. She took her place next to Cal, standing a half a head shorter than him, but her wide shoulders and strong arms no less imposing, even under a loose grey T-shirt that hung over her long, faded black skirt.

"She is one of our young medicine people, keeping the old ways strong," proclaimed Evan. "We'll need that knowledge out there. She'll keep us healthy and—"

"Don't forget I'm a better shot than this guy," Amber interjected, nudging Cal in the gut with her elbow and sticking out her tongue.

The gathering laughter resounded louder this time.

Evan continued, with more confidence than he had begun, announcing that their firekeeper, Tyler, his closest friend, would be joining them on the journey south. Taking his place next to

Evan, Tyler whispered, "We're gonna be the dynamic duo again, bro." The two joined hands by their upward thumbs and pulled each other close to slap the other's back. "Love you, man," Evan whispered back. They broke and Evan faced the group again. "We need another old guy to guide us down there," he said. "Someone who remembers the old days, and how to dial a phone, in case we find one that works."

The next to be called was Walter's nephew, J.C. Only five years older than Evan, J.C. had the soul of an elder, and Evan had always looked up to him. He knew the old stories and how to read the stars and leaves. He would be the oldest of the walkers. Born James Charles, he had been given the lovable nickname Jimmy Chuck as a child, and it had evolved to the more serious J.C. in his teen years.

The onlooking crowd was loose now. As J.C. took his place, Evan could sense their approval of the friends and family who would journey for months and find them a route to a new and ancient home.

But there was one more name to call. Evan shuffled his feet as his nerves threatened to overtake him for the first time since he'd begun speaking. "Maajaan maampii, ndaanis," he spoke, inviting his daughter to come forward.

As Nangohns strode calmly and confidently to her father's side, the crowd murmured with surprise. Nicole lifted her head in pride, disguising any trepidation.

"You all know our girl as one of the best archers this land has ever seen," Evan said. "That deer we've been eating is her kill. When Walter asked us to prepare for this trip, this one insisted on coming with us. I was against it at first. But when I look at this young woman"—his voice began to crack—"I know that she's a born leader. She's already taught me and her mother so much."

Nangohns tightened her lips and stood proudly with him and the other four, looking out at their fellow community members.

The crowd continued to quiver at the revelation, and some of the older ones turned to each other, whispering. Nicole felt their brief gazes bearing down on her. Taller than most of them, she responded by returning an assured gaze of her own around and behind her, and the uneasy murmur fell quiet.

"That's it," Evan said simply in closing. "Mii iw."

"Miigwech, Evan," said Walter. "Well?" He raised his palm to the sky, gesturing to the crowd for a response.

They erupted in cheers and whoops, and the walkers before them humbly hung their heads and smiled, holding out their palms to their friends and relatives. The singers picked up their drums again, and Gloria struck the hide four times to commence a travelling song. The crowd formed a line to one side of the fire to form a procession. One by one, community members hugged each of the walkers, offering well wishes and thanks.

Nangohns couldn't help but beam as her relatives and friends danced their way through to greet her. She looked to the end of the line. Among the handful of people left was Meghan, walking stiffly and stoically, smiling, but with a look of apprehension that gave Nangohns pause. Nangohns tracked Meghan as she hugged and thanked Evan, J.C., and the rest.

When Meghan reached Nangohns at the end of the line, she stopped square in front of the girl, putting her hands on her shoulders. Meghan's lip trembled, triggering a flash of panic in Nangohns. Meghan pulled her closer and squeezed tightly. She felt the older woman's hot breath on her earlobe. "You be safe down there," Meghan whispered. Nangohns heard her voice shake. Meghan paused, then repeated, "Be safe," and released her grasp before returning her hands to Nangohns's shoulders, smiling now.

"Miigwech" was all Nangohns could muster, her eyes fixed on the tears in Meghan's blue eyes.

Meghan bowed her head and turned. Nangohns watched her shuffle slowly away until another well-wisher approached.

The song repeated until all were done hailing the walkers. The early-morning sun burned higher in the blue sky, and the introduction was done.

That evening, Nicole and Evan walked along the shore on the far side of the lake. They had told the kids they wanted to check on the rice beds. Flies swarmed thickly around them as they stepped carefully along the large grey stones, looking out into the tall green grass shooting up from the water. By the look of it, the rice would be ready to harvest by late summer. If all went well on the trip south, Evan would be back in time to help.

The couple took a seat on a pair of large, flat rocks as the setting sun painted the surface of the lake a shimmering pink.

"So, today went pretty good, then, eh?" said Nicole.

"I'd say so," replied Evan. "Still, I'm glad that's over."

"Same here," said Nicole. "I could feel some of the women watching me when you called Nangohns up."

"But then they knew. They understood," said Evan.

"They know that she's your daughter too," Nicole replied, wrapping an arm around her husband. "She's a leader. And no one shoots an arrow like her."

"I had to understand too," admitted Evan. "She's pretty much an adult now, even though it's hard for us to see her that way. She might be having babies eventually too. We gotta do this move for her and the other young ones."

Nicole looked out over the water. "Yeah, they deserve that chance. They're our future."

There was a quavering in her voice, and Evan pulled her closer, seeing tears welling up in her eyes.

"You know, I'm trying really hard to stay strong for you both right now. But I can't help worrying," she said. "I'm trying not to go there in my head, because I believe in you both, and I know you'll keep each other safe. But if you don't make it back, I could be losing half of my family."

Evan took her in his arms and kissed the top of her head. He could feel the strength in her shoulders. She let herself relax into his embrace and squeezed in closer to him.

"When we're out there, we'll still be here with you," he assured her. "We'll always be here."

She took a deep breath through her nose, managing to keep back the tears. Evan could almost feel the warmth of her beating heart being passed to him. The day's heat had persisted into the evening. Nicole reached out and touched his thigh and nuzzled into the side of his neck. Their hands explored each other with increasing intensity. They moved to face one another and kissed, and absorbed each other, as they had so many times before.

FIVE

THE SUN HAD RISEN twelve more times since the ceremony announcing to the community the group that would be walking south, and now they were ready to leave. Late spring had quickly became early summer, according to the sun. Abundant rains had helped the strawberry crops rebound—enough that some of the fruit could be harvested to send with the walkers on their journey.

Two days prior to departure, they had met in the main lodge, where they had gathered everything they would need for a round trip of well over a thousand kilometres over the course of roughly two months. In addition to the supplies to camp and cook and hunt—like tents, small pots, and a .22 calibre rifle and two boxes of bullets—Amber packed a mortar and pestle to grind and prepare medicines from the land. Evan would carry the pouches of tobacco and sage in his pack. Cedar and sweetgrass would be easy to find along the way. Small hand-held shakers were carefully wrapped in hide and placed among clothing and small plastic food storage containers.

The night before they left, the six walkers, along with their partners, Dan, Walter, and a few other elders, entered a sweat lodge for a final cleansing. The ceremony stretched well into the night, with songs of healing and gratitude sung together, along with epic stories and prayers for good health and safe passage. In the fierce heat of the ritual, tears and sweat fell from faces onto folded arms and legs and the cedar boughs that lined the ground. They emerged from the ceremony refreshed and temporarily relieved, empowered to seek yet another renewal for their community in a faraway land their ancestors had respected and loved.

The morning of their decampment, a faint smell of wood smoke lingered around the big lake as members of the community gathered once more on the shore. Maiingan was tending the fire burning in the stone circle, as the usual firekeeper, Tyler, was about to depart. A few steps away, Tyler and Nick held each other tightly in a long embrace. The formal opening prayer and medicine offerings had already been made, and now those staying behind waited as the walkers drew out their final moments with their loved ones. J.C. and Amanda laughed together, while she dabbed at her eyes with a torn white rag. He would leave no children waiting; they were among the few childless adults in the new village. Cal and Amber stood surrounded by family members, keeping up a jovial facade over their buzzing trepidation.

Nangohns sat on the grass across from her father, holding Waawaaskone, whose wide brown eyes were alert to the bustling activity around her. Her neck still wasn't strong enough to hold up her head of thick black hair, so her aunt cradled her in her elbow.

"Did you grab that flint?" Evan asked Nangohns.

"Enh," she replied. "It's in that side pocket." She indicated her full blue backpack.

"The tarp?"

"You watched me pack it!" Nangohns replied.

A slow pulse of four beats reverberated ceremonially once again through the loose gathering, signalling the beginning of the travelling song. Nangohns stood and handed the baby back to Pichi. The two young women embraced for a long moment. They parted, and looked into each other's teary eyes and smiled. Nangohns turned to her mother, and both sobbed loudly over the sound of the farewell song. Nicole spoke into her ear, and the girl nodded. Evan hugged Pichi and then kissed his granddaughter's tiny round cheek. They said their farewells, and Evan turned to Nicole.

He held her hands in his, feeling the lines of her palms. He rubbed his thumbs atop her fingers and noticed her pupils dilating, even in the morning brightness, as her eyes peered deeply into his.

"Come back to me," she said.

"I will," he replied.

They kissed once more and broke.

"Aambe maajaa-daa, let's get going," said Nangohns, as she pulled her pack onto her shoulders and looped the rope of her quiver through her right arm. She adjusted her baggy T-shirt under all the straps.

Evan picked up his backpack and hoisted it onto his shoulders. He pulled his two braids from under the straps and let them fall onto his chest.

As the song pushed into its fourth round, there were no more farewells to make. Walter belted out a loud "Hoo-ah" and widened his hands in a parting motion. The crowd followed his cue and created two lines pointing east. As they lined up, they danced, tapping each foot twice on the ground to the beat as they stepped forward, like dancing at a powwow.

The six chosen walkers lined up, starting with Evan, stomping in rhythm as he approached the end of the line. Nangohns followed behind him and moved in sync, as did Tyler, J.C., Amber, and Cal, all in single file.

The crowd hollered and cheered, their yells getting louder as the walkers proceeded through, heading east towards the old reserve site. Evan cleared the last two in line on either side—his mother and father. He shut his eyes and bellowed out to the horizon in front of him, as if to prepare the animals and plants before him. When he opened his eyes, he could no longer hear anything, his eyes fixed on the bush straight ahead.

They walked all morning down a familiar trail until the sun blazed high above them, the heat nearing its peak on this early-summer day. They followed faded trail markings tied on the low branches of the trees that closed in around them. Two years after the permanent power failure, Evan had tied these in roughly ten-metre intervals to mark the path from the old reserve site to the new camp. The orange tape was fraying at the ends, and some had lost nearly all colour.

Evan had told the others that he wanted to stop at the old reserve first, but hadn't said why. Nangohns assumed he wanted to scavenge for anything that might be of use on their trek. The route they had settled upon followed the big river south, and to get there, they had to walk east first, through the former rez. It had been years since most of them had seen their old houses and the buildings in which they once worked, lived, and played.

"We gotta be getting close, eh?" Cal asked no one in particular. They had walked mostly in solemn silence all morning, but by now they had reached the anonymity and neutrality of the deep forest.

"Just up this way is the far end of the rez, the west side," confirmed Evan.

They continued in single file, Evan in the lead. The trail became wider as they approached the old rez, but they maintained the formation they had set as they left their home, their short line snaking through evergreen trees and down a slight ridge as the land opened to a wide glade. The green grass stood high and thick, and lush foliage enveloped everything they could see. The trees lined the immediate horizon in verdant shades, obscuring the landmarks and gravel road they expected to lead them into their old home. From this vantage point on the western edge of town, most of the structures had been visible in the time before. But the reclamation of these ruins by the land was nearly complete.

Evan led them through the tall grass in search of the grey gravel of the road, but it had yet to appear below their feet. They took high strides over the thick growth, the ones in the lead stamping down the grass to make an easier path for the ones following. They soon felt the hard edges of the pebbles beneath them, and the straight line to their former home, once clear of all vegetation, came into view.

The simple vinyl-sided and asphalt-shingled homes were familiar to Nangohns but also foreign. Weather and time had cracked and torn the outer walls and roofs. The faded blue, green, and beige siding accentuated the broken windows and gaping doorways of the houses. Approaching the dwellings that lined this road, they noticed maturing trees bursting through the foundations of several houses and penetrating smaller outbuildings and sheds. Yards and driveways were completely covered with saplings and brush, with some rusted cars and trucks resting on deflated tires—parked forever, overtaken by time.

Each house had been stripped of outside stairs, porches, and decks. The ones who stayed behind had begun that process, and the sight of a lone square concrete footing reminded Evan of when he came back years later to get the rest of the lumber. Human life had all but vanished from the place by then. He remembered pulling a four-by-four pillar out of the factory-moulded grey stone after Tyler and Isaiah knocked down what was left of the deck. He had looked for the other footings, but they'd been swallowed up by the long grass. At other homes they had disassembled steps and porches one by one, and carried the wood back to the new settlement. It had been their final task here, after a few earlier visits to raid closets, drawers, cupboards, and sheds for supplies. All who had remained had either fled to the new village, were known to be dead, or had disappeared. So they scavenged what was still useful to them.

On this return, the place felt even more like a graveyard, and Evan realized that he was wearing the black nylon shorts of one of the dead or missing—he couldn't remember who.

Silently they approached Evan and Nicole's old house. Nangohns walked a half-step behind her father. Evan remembered holding her hand when she was a toddler, taking some of her first steps on their short walks from the road back to their driveway. He felt a void open in his chest, knowing those memories were all that lived in their first family home. His feet remembered the path, and pulled him left onto the grassy driveway. The baby-blue siding had now faded to near white, and was peeling away from years of harsh winds. The steps and windows were gone.

Tyler's feet stuttered when he realized precisely where they were, and the others slowed their pace. Without turning to look at them, Evan said he had to get something and moved towards the far side of the house. The shed, where he used to butcher moose and deer, was wide open and looked empty.

Once inside, Evan raised his hands to the upper framing and pulled a shovel down. He came out as quickly as he'd gone in, and directed the others to follow him around back. The wide yard opened to another vast clearing. His four-wheeler was still where he'd parked it for the last time, but its tires were flat and the black vinyl seat had burst open, exposing the yellow foam of the cushion. The racks he'd used to clean hides were gone. A smaller brown plastic shed remained upright beside the dilapidated four-wheeler. Evan walked up to give it a nudge.

"Cal, Tyler, can youse guys move this?" he asked. The two stepped over and easily lifted the structure, barely taller than them. They walked a few steps to the side and let it drop. Evan studied the imprint left on the ground. The grass was flattened and brown where the shed had been. He walked over to a patch of dirt about a metre wide in one corner. The other five watched in silence as he drove the shovel into the dark-brown earth. After just a few strikes and scoops, the metal blade thudded against something hard. The black top of a sturdy plastic box became exposed with just a bit more digging, and Evan started scraping away at the sides to clear more space. He tossed the shovel aside and squatted down to lift the case out of the ground. The rest watched as Evan rested it beside the hole and popped the side handles open. He lifted the lid to show a full black garbage bag, which he yanked down, revealing a white wool blanket with green, yellow, red, and black stripes. He unrolled it on the grass in front of him. Another plastic bag, this one white and wrapped in clear packing tape, lay at the end of the roll. Sharp corners and lumps protruded from the untaped bits of plastic.

Evan picked up the strange package and cradled it in his left elbow and forearm. He reached into his front pocket for his smallest knife. He pinched the grey handle and unfolded the blade, and then carefully slit the tape in even spots around the bag. The others watched silently, observing Evan's careful peeling away of the protective covering to expose shiny black metal beneath.

Evan grabbed the first handgun by the muzzle. He placed it carefully on the blanket, and tore away the rest of the plastic bag as he extracted three more, all black and of a similar make. He laid them neatly beside each other and shook out the rest of the contents. Four extra magazines fell onto the blanket, along with four clear plastic boxes of 9-millimetre bullets. He lined up the ammunition neatly beside the guns and ran his fingers along the bumpy grip of one of the gun's handles.

"So, we have four pieces here," he said to the group. "And we have four extra clips for each of them. Each of these bullet cases holds forty, so we have 160 rounds of ammo altogether."

No one responded. The silence prompted Evan to look up at each of them. He noticed Tyler's mouth agape.

"I'd be lying if I said I never wondered what became of them guns," said Tyler, with more than a hint of disapproval.

"Which guns?" asked Cal, pushing his way closer to see.

Evan shot Tyler a harsh look as if to say "Knock it off"— to which Tyler stood firm. Raising two palms, he reminded Evan that this was his unscheduled stop. "Hey, man, you can't blame us for wondering what's up."

Crouched down, questioning eyes all around him, Evan looked cornered.

Cal's eyes widened, making him look even younger than usual. "Are those his guns? Really?" Cal asked breathlessly.

Amber brushed a hand against his arm. "Cal, c'mon."

A wave of understanding passed over Nangohns, who had been silently looking on, unsure how to interpret what was transpiring in front of her.

When she was seven or eight, Cal had told her a story about her father and the stranger called Justin Scott—a mammoth, bald white man who had appeared on their rez a few weeks into the first winter without power. He had come by snowmobile, bringing with him booze and drugs (things the younger kids knew only by name and reputation)—and guns. Cal said he had heard his uncles talking and they said Scott had tried to take over the old band council and eventually lured people under his influence, including Evan's younger brother, Cam, Nangohns's uncle. Cal told her that when everyone was starving and dying off that first winter, Scott had promised them food, but when Evan and the others found out that what they were eating was the bodies of the dead, there was a fight, Evan got shot, and the white lady, Meghan, had finished it by shooting Justin Scott in the head.

Nangohns had suspected that Cal, as one of the older kids back then, was trying to scare her, but the story would still creep into her mind at night. The few times she asked her mom and dad about it, they said it wasn't Cal's or his uncles' place to tell tales about the bad old days. Often, Evan would become stern and gloomy to the point where Nangohns was afraid he'd never look at her again. He also wouldn't talk about his brother, Cam, who survived Scott's rule but was never the same, and disappeared one night the following winter. Evan's cold responses eventually deterred her from asking. It was generally known that there had been violence that first winter, and that Evan had taken a bullet. And it was, in a way, a source of pride. But in their household, it wasn't something they discussed.

Twelve years on, the violence of that time haunted them all in different ways. For the younger ones, it was a ghost story pieced together through fragments. A story tinged not only with horror but also with their elders' shame—for allowing a monster into their midsts, and for what they had to do to destroy it.

Nangohns looked from Cal back to her father, visualizing the small, round scar underneath his black sleeveless shirt where a bullet fired from one of these guns had struck him just below his collarbone, more than twelve years ago.

"I think it's important we each have a weapon on us," Evan announced matter-of-factly, breaking the tension somewhat with practical considerations. J.C. and Tyler seemed content to press on. "Nang's got her bow. Cal's carrying that rifle. The rest of us will each take one of these."

They determined that they'd have to test the guns, which hadn't been fired in over a decade. Cal, Tyler, and Nangohns knelt down to watch how Evan cleaned the pistols and learn how to load the bullets into the magazines.

Amber remained standing, and after a moment asked if she could trade guns with Cal.

Evan looked up. "If that's cool with Cal," he said.

Cal shrugged in assent.

They each loaded ten bullets into a magazine, then slid them back into the handles. Nangohns rarely used a gun to hunt, and studied the strange device in her hand, startled slightly by the sharp snaps as the ammo locked into place.

Evan stood, and the other three followed his lead. He walked away from the group and faced the forest. "Stand back," he warned, looking over his shoulder. He wrapped both hands around the handle, and the steel and plastic of the grip warmed from his sweating palms. He inserted his right finger into the trigger ring and planted his feet firmly into the ground. As he exhaled a deep breath, he squeezed the trigger, and a loud bang exploded from the chamber and echoed through the backyard. The bullet sped into the bush, and a small plume of gun smoke lingered in the air and crept into their nostrils. Evan lowered the gun and released the magazine into his hand.

"That one works," remarked Tyler.

Evan stood back, and Tyler took his place to fire his weapon into the bush. A branch fell in the distance. Nangohns and Cal followed, shooting the third and fourth rounds into the green horizon. When this test was complete, they removed the clips, and Nangohns handed the firearm she'd tested to J.C., who packed it carefully into his bag, as did the others.

Evan put the wool blanket back into the plastic bin and placed it inside the shed. The blanket was too big for any of them to pack away, and Evan didn't want to stay at their old house any longer than they had to. He hoisted his pack onto his shoulders again and made his way around the shell of his old home to the front.

Nangohns walked after her father. She looked up the outside wall to one of the darkened, hollow windows, and wondered whose bedroom that had been. She recalled, albeit imperfectly, this building with its sharp lines and angles as her first home. She hesitated for a half-step, trying to jog another memory of her first few years in this place, but couldn't. This wasn't the time to remember, she thought, as the rest moved out in single file once again.

Tyler gave a brief glance over his shoulder. Neither Evan nor Nangohns looked back.

The summer humidity and afternoon heat fell upon them, and beads of sweat formed on their brows and shoulders. Shoots of grass burst up through the road, some up to their waist. The overgrown ditches seemed to close in on the former roadways.

Evan's nose picked up a hint of sweetgrass as they approached the former centre of town, where major buildings like the outdoor hockey rink, band office, school, and gymnasium still stood. The grey metal roof of the rink to their right was intact, but the thick white plastic boards that enclosed the ice surface had mostly collapsed. Ahead, the brown outer walls of the band office were faded, and scorched in some places. Trees and bushes grew high around the school and gym, and most of the windows of all the buildings were broken.

Evan had not planned to stop anywhere else here; anything useful had been picked clean long ago. The crunch of gravel below the soles of his boots evoked a haunted memory of the place as he led them eastward, past the familiar sites—the baseball field and jumping rocks on the shore of the big lake. The grey gravel infield of the ball diamond had become green with weeds, and the outfield grass was as high as the chain-link fencing that enclosed the play area. The wooden bleachers were long gone.

They approached the community store on their left.

"Remember this fuckin' place," grumbled J.C. Nangohns did, vaguely. It had been part of a chain of grocers servicing First Nations in the north that sold food at inflated prices to the people who lived there. Nangohns remembered pleading with her mother to buy her something from the colourful candy display at the checkout counter, but being told it cost too much money—a common refrain from the other grown-ups about that store. Now, the front door stood open, but it was too dark inside to see if the shelves were still there. In the first days of the blackout, panicked shoppers had ransacked the place. Evan thought back to scanning the near-empty shelves that day in astonishment. He realized now, that had been just the beginning.

Down the road beyond the store there was a long slope, heavily overgrown. This was where the ploughs had dumped what they cleared from the roads every winter, creating an enormous snowbank—yet another grim landmark from that first winter. According to the scattered stories Nangohns had picked up over the years, this was where Tyler and Isaiah had dumped the body of the man called Justin Scott, whose handguns they had come for and now carried. They had dragged his corpse there on a sled, his body drained of blood from the bullet hole in his head. They rolled the intruder's nearly three-hundred-pound frame down the bank and left it there to freeze: a warning to any other potential trespassers. By spring, his remains were gone, eaten up and carried away by the birds and animals.

If the tangled slope had stirred these memories in Evan and Tyler, they did not let on. They fixed their eyes on the bush ahead, steering them east, with hopes of reaching the river by the late afternoon, where they'd set up camp for the night. As expected, the service road along the hydro lines that led south was completely grown over and unreliable for passage or guidance. They knew the river would lead them south and eventually to the city of Gibson—the next major stop on their trek. It was a route their people had followed since long before wires cut through the land.

Evan led them into the thick brush, and they swatted at flies as they walked for hours until it was time to settle by the river and rest for the night.

SIX

THE MUDDY BANKS OF the big river forced them to traverse higher ground as they headed south. The water was running high for early summer, higher than Evan remembered from the last time he walked this area. The last few winters had been unseasonably long, with heavy snows, and the spring thaws came quickly, causing most waterways to swell. When the river ran fast like this, creatures on two legs and four legs alike were wise to avoid the lethal pull of the water. It was risky to stray too close in search of food or a drink, or rest and respite from the heat.

When they'd planned their walk, Evan, J.C., and Walter had counted on them being able to stick to the lowlands near the river, where they believed the brush would be less dense and the terrain more passable. They expected the water to have receded by this point in the season. Instead, the land the walkers hoped to cross remained saturated, a thick slurry of sand, rocks, and remnants of vegetation and wildlife that had been swept away in the annual spring purge. Their feet sank into sloppy mud with their first steps onto the banks, and the steady, strong current carrying debris in the other direction gave them pause. Instead of walking the shore, they continued in single file over the higher ground where the crust of the land gave way to the ancient aquatic carving.

The first two nights away from home had been relatively comfortable. They slept on knolls separating the bush from the shore, regular breezes blowing through the river basin keeping the bugs away all night.

Now, on the morning of the third day out, the sun cleared the trees and coated the walkers in a comforting orange glow from the southeast. J.C. led the way, with Amber bringing up the rear. J.C.'s soaked running shoes slurped with each step, followed by an abrasive chorus of wet footwear behind him, wildly out of rhythm.

Evan couldn't remember the last time he had been out this way. J.C. had come out with Isaiah once—seven or eight summers ago—when they were scouting routes to the dam. The annual flooding made hunting and fishing near the river unpredictable, so few made the day-long trek anymore. Getting to the river meant walking through the old reserve, and any detour around it added an extra half day to the journey. It was a landscape they were still learning, and that had already changed so much in their people's relatively short time living within it.

J.C.'s pace slowed as he turned his shoulders to look once more at the river. Nangohns followed his eyes to the swirling wrinkles on the surface, which dipped and turned in ambient chaos.

"Every time I'm around here, I always think of my mishoomis," he said, speaking loudly enough for all five walking behind him to hear. "He was born here on the land. He used to tell me about this river, and how it was something that everyone had to learn to respect. Because it was new to them.

"His parents—my great-grandparents—were some of the ones that were forced up here. They had good memories of life on that big lake with lots of fish. A lake so wide you couldn't see the other side, his parents always told him. But they never got to go back there in their lifetime.

"My mishoomis used to tell me a story about when our ancestors got moved here. The government gave them all fishing gear. Nets and rods and stuff. I guess it was the trade-off for stealing the shore on that big lake down south. 'You're fishing people,' the Indian Agent said to them. 'You come from the lake. Go fish!' And then he just let them be.

"They say the fish were plentiful around here, though, back then. Real thick, with lots of meat, and skins they could tan for whatever they needed them for."

J.C.'s voice distracted the others from the sound of their sopping-wet feet as they trudged through the mud.

"So my mishoomis said his dad and his uncles thought, well, if the fishing is this good on these lakes, let's go use the net on that river! They had to go check it out first, though, because eventually they'd need to get a boat out there somehow. One spring afternoon, they decided to take the whole day to walk out here and scope out the scene.

"The banks were flooded, though, and they didn't realize, because it was only their first spring up here. My mishoomis said his dad told him that they'd never seen water move like that. They watched it swirl and mix and flow by them. They thought the fish here must be even bigger if they had to swim all the time.

"So my grandpa said his uncle—his dad's middle brother—wanted to cast some lines just to check it out. He got his gear all lined up and put on his hip waders. I guess they thought it was a good idea. So he took a few steps out and felt the water push against his calves. It took him a little by surprise, but he righted himself. Planted his feet and kept low. He wanted to go out a little farther, my uncle, so he took another step.

"By now, though, the others were shouting to him to come back. They were getting worried. They were higher up on the bank, and from where they were standing the moving water looked and sounded dangerous. He went farther in, but was no match for that strong current. The river slammed against his thighs and knocked him over. He went right under. His head came up again just a little ways downstream, and they watched him take his last gasps for air. The water pulled him back down, and they never saw him again."

J.C. paused and looked again to the river.

"So that's why my mishoomis told me," he said, "to always respect the water. Especially that river. It can take you if you don't show it the respect it deserves."

Nangohns looked back at the river. A long, jagged branch drifted along on the strong current.

"So, how's everyone's feet doing?" asked J.C. They grumbled and laughed as they pushed forward, waiting for the sun to reach its peak before stopping to eat.

Over the next few days, as they followed the river southward, they settled into a routine of walking, eating, sleeping, and getting up early to set out again. The flies became more tenacious and abundant the farther south they went. The trees were taller and more luscious in foliage. Their daily diet consisted primarily of small game like rabbit and partridge, shot here and there by Amber with the rifle or Nangohns with the bow, and blueberries, raspberries, and strawberries foraged along the way. The blackberries were still tiny, white on thorny stems. It would be several weeks still before they were plump and ready to harvest. They'd be handy on the way back, they told themselves optimistically. They occasionally ate the dried meat they had packed, but made sure to eat fresh when they could, in case they needed the deer jerky and smoked fish farther along in their journey.

Eventually, the river bent around rocky banks and they came to more elevated terrain. It narrowed and widened unpredictably, creating rapids along the waterway below. This land was unfamiliar to most of them. Evan knew the Anishinaabek shared these homelands with their Mushkego Cree relatives, whom they hadn't seen or heard from since Jibwaa. The closest community had been more than a hundred kilometres to the north of them, on the other side of the hydroelectric dam that had been built to bring them closer together.

But now the land appeared empty, devoid of human life.

In the early evening on the fifth day of walking, a familiar orange wash came over them through the higher trees as the sun lowered towards the horizon. Cal was leading, and he swivelled his head from side to side, scanning for a place to camp for the night. He saw a patch of pine trees ahead and led the walkers to it, hoping for a soft bed of fallen brown and orange needles to sleep on. Evan followed Cal and felt his feet sink into the soft ground under the green pine awning. Nangohns walked behind him, with three dead partridges shot earlier in the afternoon dangling from ropes tied to her packs. The other three took their time approaching, savouring the evergreen scent. One by one, they peeled their packs from their shoulders and let them bounce on the natural mattress of thin, pointy dead leaves.

Amber leaned the small of her back against her blue backpack and untied her shoes. She pulled each off forcefully and set them down neatly in front of her, resting her pale, blistered feet on them. "Goddamn," she said. "My feet are taking a beating."

"No one wants to look at your gross-ass feet," said Cal beside her. He had already removed his shoes and laid his blanket on the cushiony ground.

"If you're not used to them by now, you better *get* used to them. You're in it for the long haul."

Tyler snorted, amused.

"Never mind, you," said Amber. "I hear you snoring every night. It's a miracle Nick hasn't given you the boot yet! He's probably getting the best sleep he's had in years now."

"As if," responded Tyler.

"Lucky you there's no other single dudes up there to swoop in and hide their mocs under your sleeping bag!"

Nangohns noticed Tyler's smirk slowly fade and his eyes soften in affectionate longing. He missed his partner. Before he could notice her gaze, she looked away and caught Amber nuzzling her small tanned nose into Cal's bare bicep. He smiled and pulled his arm from his side to wrap around her shoulders.

Something pulsed through Nangohns and she suddenly felt outside of herself. She leaned forward to retie her running shoes, stained darker now by dirt and mud. She knew of love and romance, and saw how they survived and thrived all around her, but in recent years had started wondering if and when her life would suit any kind of partnership. The few young people she had grown up with were like family to her, and she found it difficult to consider love or lust with any of them. As they ventured deeper into this unfamiliar land, she considered the possibility of awakening that part of her in Zhaawnong. Perhaps something new was waiting for her there.

"Let's take a breather," announced Evan. Her father's voice broke her out of her momentary reverie. "Then we'll go get some firewood. We should cook up those birds quick."

Evening came swiftly under the pine cover, and they soon set out to gather the deadfall of the forest. Nangohns, Cal, Tyler, Evan, and J.C. dispersed in different directions in the twilight, leaving Amber behind to keep watch over their belongings and pluck the partridges. When enough dry wood was gathered, Evan sparked a mixture of birch strips and dry pine needles beneath a small stand of kindling, and before long strips of partridge meat hung from roasting sticks pulled from nearby saplings.

"Think there are any restaurants up and running still somehow?" Cal asked after their meal. "I haven't had a pizza in thirteen years. That's the first thing on my list!"

"You know how much shit goes into making pizza?" said Tyler. "You need cows for the cheese. Mills for the flour to make the dough. A butcher to slaughter that cow for ground beef on top."

"Okay, tell you what, if all that's still there, the first slice is on you."

Tyler laughed. It had been a while since they'd thought about money—something that had always seemed in short supply in the days before.

Noticing Nangohns's pensive expression, Cal turned to her. "You don't remember pizza?" he asked her, mildly surprised.

"I was three when all that stuff went away," she reminded him.

Her sternness surprised her father. "Nang," said Evan, "pizza was this bad food that gave our people a disease that made their feet and legs fall off before they died. It tasted pretty good. But most of the food that tasted good was bad for us."

"Hmmm," Nangohns said. "What was it made of?"

"What wasn't it made of!" exclaimed Cal. "Cheese, pineapple, tomato sauce, pepperoni—"

"We'll worry about pizza when we get to the city," Evan interrupted.

The companions, ranged about the fire, stared into the fading embers before them. J.C. cleared his throat, as if preparing to speak—as he had at so many campfires over the years. His black hair with grey streaks hung down the sides of his face, obscuring his ears and accentuating his narrow eyes. The reflection of the flames danced in his dark-brown irises. He fixed his gaze on Cal, nearly young enough to be his son, and the younger but taller man, feeling J.C.'s gaze on him, shrunk into himself humbly.

"Really, Cal?" exclaimed J.C. after a tense pause. "Pineapple on pizza? That's fuckin' disgusting, bro."

Laughter followed again, and the older walkers eased into their spots on the ground, leaning their heads on packs or resting on their elbows to straighten their legs. Nangohns remained hunched forward, hugging her bare knees. Even among her own people, the recent and distant past and the land to the south all seemed like a haze of half knowing. She'd become accustomed to shaking off the more impenetrable questions and focusing on the tangible, on the living world around her— the one she knew better and better and could move through more adeptly the older and stronger she became. From what they'd seen so far, the way things were, Jibwaa, hardly mattered. She would soon know more about the world as it was now than anybody back home, even Walter. She raised her head from her forearms, clutched around her knees, looked at the fire, and finally straightened her back to recline.

The night was cool and free of bugs, so they decided to forgo tents. The clamour of their voices gradually dimmed to a murmur, and they each nestled into their blankets on the soft bed of pine needles. One by one, all but Nangohns fell asleep in the open air, and the fire smouldered into darkness. She lay on her back and watched the few brilliant stars that penetrated the lush awning above their encampment. The outlines of the leaves made a jagged frame for the twinkling lights in the dark ceiling.

Her eyes adjusted to the shadows of vegetation around her as she awaited sleep. The embers of the fire slowed to a dull hiss, and the deep, languid breaths of the others in the camp emerged above it. She turned onto her side and adjusted her head on her makeshift pillow of a backpack to try to dull her senses to the faint sights and sounds around her, which were keeping her awake.

She gazed into the darkness of the forest. Her eyelids were pulling slowly together when she heard the snap of a branch somewhere away from the campsite. Her mind jolted awake, and she tilted her head up to free her ear from the nylon bag. She struggled to listen over her pounding heart. After a dozen or so beats, she heard another snap and a faint rustling. The sound was far enough away to echo in the expanse around them, and seemed farther off this time. She propped herself up on her elbows and glanced at the others, still asleep, and then turned to where the sound had come from, trying to make out anything through the silhouettes of tree trunks in the immediate vicinity.

Minutes passed and her heart slowed. She heard nothing else. She lowered back to the ground and stared up at the stars, watching them twinkle through the opening in the canopy until she finally drifted to sleep.

SEVEN

THE SIX WALKERS TRUDGED for three more days through thick, hot weather. The imposing presence of the river gave way to an abundance of lakes big and small, full of pure, cold water, which they bottled at every stop. Each time, Nangohns thought of what her mother used to tell them when she and her cousins were younger, reminding them to think of the water as it flowed into their cores, and then out to their extremities, all part of a grand life cycle. The reflection was an exercise in gratitude, Nicole always said.

When they stopped at sandy beaches, they would take turns bathing. Nangohns liked to wait until the peak heat of the afternoon and then submerge herself in the shallow water of a wide, calm lake. She would cup sand in her callused palms and scrub her skin clean, removing dirt and grime and exfoliating her peeling summer hide.

The strange midnight noises from a few days earlier had faded from her mind after a few peaceful nights of sleep. Now, the marvel of new land and lakes was unfolding before her.

A few nights before they expected to arrive at the outskirts of Gibson, once the third-largest city in the region, they watched the clouds roll in. Thick white billows lay low in the sky. Rain was imminent.

It started as a light shower the next morning, and within moments erupted into a boisterous downpour, flooding out the coals of the fire as the walkers set forth, their packs already wrapped around their glistening tanned shoulders.

The steady, low hiss of the rainfall made talking while walking in single file futile. Whoever was taking the lead occasionally barked orders to those behind them, warning of slippery rocks, jagged outcrops, fallen logs, and other hazardous obstacles in their path. Long, thin clumps of dark hair streaked across their wet faces, and drips of water fell through their eyebrows. Their sleeveless cotton and nylon shirts were soaked through, right down to the pants or shorts they wore. By this point, they were used to wet shoes, and walking in a summer storm didn't bother them.

The rain continued into the late afternoon, the darkness of the incoming evening accelerated by the overcast sky. Evan suggested finding shelter for the night to wait out the weather, and the others agreed and began looking for a place to camp. At the top of a ridge they found a small plateau surrounded by high maple and oak trees, and once at the summit they removed their packs.

Tyler and Evan went to find dry firewood, while J.C. and Amber unpacked the blue and green nylon tarps to string up amongst the branches of the deciduous shelter. Under the tarps, they unpacked the nylon tents and set up the poles. They hadn't been able to hunt any game throughout the day, so Nangohns rationed out dark-purple moose jerky and plump strawberries picked the day before.

Raindrops rapped against the tarp as Cal worked with the flint to spark a fire. A small plastic container was set aside to keep birchbark and wood shavings dry for moments like this. Smoke soon streamed up to the bottom of the tarps and spread across the wrinkled blue and green material, finding its way out into the rain, where it was pounded back down to the earth.

After eating, they warmed their feet around the blaze, six pairs of pale soles painted a vibrant clementine. The rain calmed to a slow, soothing trickle as their clothing dried on makeshift racks of sticks set near the fire.

The light of the day had almost completely faded when Evan sat up and began rummaging through his pack. Nangohns heard the crinkle of a plastic bag and looked over to see her father hunched over his pack in the darkness. He stood and slowly moved closer to the fire, his round face and full cheeks illuminated from below, obscuring his eyes, making the sockets look to Nangohns like small, dark caves. Scratching his sparse beard with dirty fingernails, he reached into the bag to pull out a rectangular fold of paper. He pulled it apart and crouched near J.C. to lay it out before them. The creases of the big sheet had given way to holes, and the map was close to coming apart into pieces. Evan carefully smoothed the folds flat on the dry ground near the fire, ensuring the light of the fire spilled evenly across the greens and blues of the paper.

It was an older map, charted decades before the outage. Nangohns had seen it before. She watched her father and J.C. scan it silently. Evan indicated the X that marked Shki-dnakiiwin, just to the west of another smaller X for the old reserve site, which wasn't printed on the map.

"I'd say we're probably about here now, eh?" J.C. used his index finger to circle a large area in the basin to the south of the big river.

"This must be that big lake we passed yesterday," Evan

replied, pointing to a crescent-shaped body of water that Nangohns noticed was the largest in the area.

"So if we keep south for about another day, then go hard west, we should hit that road." J.C. pointed to a line with a three-digit number marking it that abruptly ended at another lake. Slowly tracing it to the south, J.C.'s finger connected it with the main highway that led into the city. "It looks like this is probably our easiest way into Gibson," he added.

"But is it the safest?" replied Evan.

By now the rest had snapped back from their moment of relaxation around the fire.

"The other option," J.C. said, "is to find the hydro line and follow that down. It shouldn't be too far west of us."

"If there's anybody left out here," chimed in Amber from her spot on the ground, drawing in her legs to sit upright, "they may be trying to keep things together. If we get to the hydro line and it's clear, maybe there's our answer. If not—"

"You saw back home how fast the bush can grow over," Tyler interjected. "It takes everything back. There are trees almost as high as those lines now. And that service road they made for us to drive down here is useless. It's been more than a decade now."

"We keep going south tomorrow, then," Evan said. "Then, on the next day, we'll go look for the hydro line. If it's clear, we'll stick to it. If not, we'll go to the road."

"Sounds like a plan," said J.C. "What does everyone else think?"

"What else we gonna say?" mused Cal. "Nah, I'm gonna go back?"

The group laughed easily—they were agreed. The city was roughly the halfway point on the map to their final destination: the north shore of Georgian Bay.

The fire faded to smouldering ashes as they retired to the tents to sleep through the wet summer night. The faint patter of rain on the thick tarps overhead eased them into rest.

Evan awoke to the splatter of what sounded like rainfall on the tarp above him. Jolting at the sudden cacophony, he lifted his head from his pack and listened. Nothing followed, and as his mind sharpened, he thought it must have been lingering moisture blown down from the leaves above by the wind, although the weather had passed and the air outside seemed still. He held his breath to try to hear any activity outside the tent, his heartbeat accelerating in the silence.

He twisted around to feel for his half-empty pack in the darkness, and patted his palm against the hard handle of the gun from the outside, gently tapping the outline of the weapon before lowering his head to the pack's softer side.

Facing away from Evan, and unbeknownst to him, Nangohns lay awake, eyes wide open to the darkened wall of the tent. The splash had triggered a memory of the bustle she'd heard a few nights prior. This time she thought she heard the snap of another branch and what sounded like a snort after the splash from above, but she wasn't sure. Her pulse pounding in her ears drowned out any other sounds, and the rumble of her father's snoring returned, and was enough to calm her back to sleep.

In the morning they stuffed their dried clothes into their packs, laced up their shoes, and departed, descending into the slight canyon of another rushing river, south into the green hillsides. The flies returned with the early afternoon, and they tied cloth T-shirts around their heads to protect their scalps from bites.

They had decided to make their next camp on the shore of another one of the big lakes they had seen on the map, and by mid-afternoon they had arrived. There was a generous amount of daylight left to rest and relax on the warm brown sand of a beach that curved along the lake's northern shore as far as they could see. They set up a few dozen steps from a large orange rock that sloped into the water, creating a clearing amid the thick green reeds that circled the beach. The shore on the other side appeared to be a kilometre away, and the high, tree-lined hills above enclosed them in a safe refuge.

Nangohns and J.C. hunted while Amber scoured the nearby woods for medicines and berries. Evan unrolled the tents on the sand to dry them, but they agreed not to assemble them and to sleep under the night sky again instead. Cal returned from collecting firewood and announced that he was going to try fishing; he was getting tired of moose jerky and rabbit. This was a big, cold lake. He was bound to get some bites in there.

While he was preparing his line to throw in the water, with jerky as bait, a sharp pop sounded from farther down the beach and into the hills above. One shot was followed by another shortly after. The sound echoed mildly across the water. Evan wondered just how far the sound carried, and who or what else could hear it.

Cal shouted in excitement, and yanked his fishing stick upward. He pulled the line in hand over hand until a long northern pike flopped up onto the rock. As it twitched at his feet, he picked up a rock beside him and bashed its head. "They're biting today!" he shouted towards the firepit before walking back to get more bait.

Nangohns and J.C. returned with four rabbits. Cal managed to hook two more pike, for a total of three. This haul would last them for days, on top of the modest stores they still had in their packs. They were thinking now of what lay south of the city, and they estimated their food would last for a few days' walk beyond it.

After supper, Evan noticed Nangohns sitting on the big rock overlooking the camp, her long arms wrapped around her knees as she looked out over the water. Tyler and Amber were busily wrapping and packing the meat they had just cooked while the rest dried in the sun and smoke. They shoved the containers, tightly wrapped in cloth, into one of the backpacks, and then tossed a rope over the high branch of a nearby oak tree to suspend the pack out of the reach of bears or raccoons.

Evan walked over to his daughter, his bare feet sinking smoothly into the cooling sand as twilight crept in. He enjoyed the feeling of the grains between his toes; there weren't any beaches this big back home. They would mark this lake on the map so they could return on the way back. If everything went smoothly, he thought, they could catch the tail end of summer here.

Nangohns saw her father climb from the sand up onto the rock to join her and smiled. Her long black hair was untied and draped down around her face and across her shoulders and back. Evan sat down beside her and they both looked out to the lake. The glass surface of the water in the still early evening reflected the emerging stars above. The sky would soon explode into the thick celestial strip of the Milky Way—known by many of their ancestors as Jiibay Miikan, or the Spirit Road.

"Looks like the stars are coming out already," she said.

"Your namesake."

"Hmmm," she sighed, and smiled again in recognition.

"I remember when me and your mom found out you were coming. It was late in the fall. I was coming home from a hunt. I didn't get nothing, so I figured it was time to go home."

Nangohns had heard the origin story of her name countless times in her young life, but she let her father tell it again. He'd been out on foot in the bush and got turned around, so he tried to reorient himself by the stars.

"There was one little star sitting just above the trees on the horizon," he said. "Something told me to go in the direction of that little star. It wasn't as bright as the other ones that were coming out, and it flickered just so—I just knew I had to walk towards it." It led him to one of the main roads, and he walked home from there. "I came home and told your mother about it. It was late by then, and she had been worried. I told her there was this little star I followed out of the bush. And she said, 'Well, I'm glad you made it, because I have some news,' and she showed me the pregnancy test with the two lines. And then I knew, that light was you, guiding me home."

"So you asked all your grandparents if you could name me that, and they said yeah," Nangohns interrupted, finishing the story for him. "And nine months later you flew in to that hospital, and when I came out, you called me Nangohns."

Evan smiled and nodded. The quiet of the evening carried the voices over from the beach.

"I love that story," Nangohns said. "Miigwech, Noos."

They both looked up at the stars and watched them reveal themselves one at a time.

"It's nice to have a different view," Evan said.

"The stars seem brighter down here," Nangohns said in agreement. "They're in different spots too, looks like." She craned her neck to look straight above.

"We're a ways south from home," said Evan. "There's different kind of light the farther you go, up or down. Gonna be a nice night, I think."

Nangohns gave a subtle nod and exhaled. She could hear Cal shouting something indistinguishable to J.C. on the beach below. For a moment she wished she had found a more secluded spot.

"How you doing out here?" Evan asked.

"I can't believe we're finally doing this," she replied. "I miss Ngashi and Maiingan and Pichi and little Waawaaskone. I bet she's gonna be pretty big by the time we get back."

"For the first couple of months, babies don't really do anything," Evan said, almost conspiratorially. "They're kinda boring. By the time we get back, she'll be looking around and making noise and everything."

"Are you saying I was boring for the first couple of months?"

"Yeah."

"As if!" She elbowed him in the ribs, and he laughed gently.

They continued to look out over the water, which darkened slowly as twilight faded. They heard the splash of a fish jumping, and could see a ripple emanating outward before flattening again into the surface of the lake.

"You're a natural out here," Evan added. "We wouldn't have made it this far without you."

She shrugged. "I learned it all from you," she replied. "I guess you should be proud of yourself."

Smiling, Evan looked back up to the transitioning evening sky.

"How much farther Zhaawnong do we gotta go, Noos?" Nangohns asked.

"I think we're about halfway."

"What are we gonna see down there?"

"I don't know, my girl. I don't know." He let out a long, deep breath. "As long as we stay together, we'll be okay." He looked at his daughter. She saw both conviction and uncertainty in his eyes.

"I believe you," Nangohns said, wrapping her arms around Evan's shoulders and pulling him close. He placed his hand on hers, and they were still for a moment longer before getting up to return to the others around the fire. As they descended, Nangohns said, "This is a good spot. We should mark it on the map and be sure to stop here on the way back."

Late that night, Nangohns was the first to awaken to the rustling sound. It took half a second for her to home in on where they were. And then she smelled the unmistakable spoor. Bolting up from under her red wool blanket, her eyes adjusting to the pre-dawn darkness, she spun her head about, frantically scanning the ground around them. Just a few feet beyond the sleeping bodies that lay before her, she saw a hulking black mass moving on the beach. It was repeatedly lunging downward and then rearing up, like it was digging at something. The sound of its snorting grunts sent a chill up her spine.

"Guys," she called out, her voice a bit choked but rising in volume as she drew out the word. "Guys, wake up!"

She grabbed her bow and three arrows and silently doubled back from and around their huddled sleeping bags to get an unobstructed view of the animal. The rest of them jerked awake unevenly. Now with a clear line of sight, Nangohns squinted through the faint grey light to see a bear tearing at one of the backpacks with its teeth and front claws.

"Oh shit!" yelled Cal, emerging from sleep. He was positioned closest to the animal. He felt about the ground for his backpack, soon realizing it was in the massive paws of the beast. He jumped up and stepped carefully backwards to where the others huddled together.

"He's got my pack!" Cal exclaimed.

The bear seemed unfazed by the commotion. It continued to tear at the nylon bag with its sharp claws, probing for the meat and berries it smelled. Evan shoved Cal aside and stepped in front of the group. He cleared the loose hair from his eyes with one hand and raised his other arm straight up, pointing the handgun at the shadowy mass on the beach. The shape of the weapon in the dim light surprised Nangohns from her vantage just down the beach and behind the rest of them.

"What you waiting for, Ev?" Cal whispered harshly. "Shoot it!"

"Those bullets aren't gonna do shit to that thing," responded Tyler.

"Relax, both of you," Evan said. "Nang, don't shoot. I don't think we can take it down quickly, so we better try to scare it off."

"Yep!" Nangohns shouted back. She lowered her bow and ran back to stand behind Evan and the rest.

"Maybe keep that thing handy, just in case," J.C. whispered.

Meanwhile, Evan moved out in front of them, pulling the gun closer to his chest and moving his free hand up to hold it with two hands. He shouted to try to scare the bear off, but it ignored him altogether. By now some of Cal's extra clothes were scattered over the sand. The brightening dawn brought the scene more into focus with each passing breath.

Evan aimed the gun higher, above the bear's head, and squeezed the trigger once. A loud bang thundered through the forest. The sound was enough to jolt the bear upright. It froze for a second before bounding away into the trees behind their campsite. As it ran, Nangohns could see the remnants of Cal's pack in its mouth.

Once the animal was out of sight, Cal darted over to what was left of his belongings to assess the damage while the rest of them caught their breath. Evan thumbed the lever to release the clip and dropped it into his palm. He stepped away from the group to his own pack and shoved the gun and ammo inside.

"So, you sleeping with that thing or what?" asked J.C.

"Fully loaded and ready to shoot too," added Nangohns.

Evan zipped up his bag. "For the last couple nights I've been keeping it loaded under my backpack," he admitted. "I thought I was hearing things at night. We're getting closer to the city. And we just don't know what's out there."

"You were hearing things too?" exclaimed Nangohns. "I thought I was losing my mind."

"The weird thing is," Evan continued, "the things I was hearing didn't sound like any bear. This guy was on a mission."

"You think it could have been something else? Someone—" began Tyler.

"Always making sounds at night, wherever we happen to be camped out?" snapped Cal, flushed and visibly angry. "If you thought it was dangerous enough to keep that gun loaded, why the fuck didn't you say anything to us?"

Amber reached out for his arm to pull him in, but he shook her off gently. Tyler raised a palm to Cal and, with a stern look, urged him to be calm. Cal glared at him, his jaw clenched tight, but after a few seconds turned away, cursing under his breath.

The rest of the group turned their attention back to Evan.

"Do you think we should all be locked and loaded?" asked Tyler.

"No," replied Evan. "But I think when we get closer, one of us is gonna have to keep watch through the night." He paused for a breath. "I'm sorry I didn't tell youse guys."

By now Cal's temper had cooled, and he and Amber were moving back towards the group.

"It's okay, Noos," said Nangohns. "I didn't know what I was hearing either. And as for Gibson, we'll figure out what we gotta do when we get there."

"Goddamn makwa!" Cal moaned, cursing the black bear and looking over the remnants of his supplies. "Where am I supposed to put all this now?" He knelt on the ground and held up some tattered shirts and a pair of jeans.

Amber walked over to him. "What all did he get?" she asked.

"Looks like most of my clothes fell out." He sighed. "Still got my blanket here. I thought I didn't have any food containers in there, but he musta smelled something. And . . ." He paused.

"What?" she asked.

The others came closer.

"My gun. There was a box of .22 bullets in the side pocket too."

Cal recited an inventory of some of the smaller supplies left in the backpack's many pockets. Some rope, a flint, a fishing line, one of the two rolls of duct tape. He checked the side pocket of his cargo pants to make sure his knife was still there.

His eyes widened, and he looked at the others anxiously. "We gotta find that gun!" he said.

"If it's still in the pack hanging from the bear's mouth, it's long gone, man," J.C. informed him.

"The sun's coming up," said Evan. "Nangohns could try to track the bear a ways into the trees and see if it dropped anything, but we're going the other way."

"We'll get by," Tyler said to Cal in a reassuring tone. "We still got a lotta those same essentials. Amber, how many of them rifle bullets are left?"

"Well, we had two boxes of fifty, and now one's gone," she said. "We only used about a dozen so far to hunt those rabbits and partridges. But we're gonna have to be a little more careful with them. We still got a long way to go, eh?"

Evan reckoned they were holding to a steady pace of about thirty kilometres per day. They were still a day out from Gibson, and another dozen—maybe more, if they kept up their pace—from their final destination on the north shore of the big lake.

"I'd say at least another night before we're on the outskirts of the city," he said.

"I still think this whole bear thing is weird," said Cal. "Why wasn't it scared of us?"

"It musta been hungry," said J.C. "When they're used to humans, they'll walk right up and take food from them."

"What humans do you think it's used to?" asked Amber. "We haven't seen anyone else in more than twelve winters."

Evan replied, "Either this is an older one with a good memory, or it's been near people recently. I couldn't tell how old it was in the dark. It was pretty big, though."

"Think it knew gunfire too?" asked J.C.

"Any animal is gonna be scared by a noise that loud," Nangohns interjected.

"Bastard took my shit!" muttered Cal.

"Speaking of shit, I gotta check my shorts," said Tyler. "I haven't been woken up like that in a while!"

Nangohns wrinkled her nose, and Evan let out a deep, raspy laugh.

Feeling like order had been restored, they revived the fire to cook breakfast while Nangohns went out in the glow of the morning light to see if she could find the bear's tracks and salvage anything he might have dropped. By the time she got back, empty-handed, a breakfast of wild rice and blueberries was waiting for her. When everyone was done, they took turns braiding each other's hair for another long day of walking in the hot sun. By mid-morning, they hoisted their backpacks, and Amber led them southwest.

EIGHT

AS THEY TREKKED WEST in search of the road, the landscape smoothed into a more tolerable grade to tread along, but
a scratchy thicket emerged. Tyler took the lead, hacking away
at the wiry branches with a machete, clearing the path for the
other five behind him. Burrs clung to their pants and shirts and
snagged their exposed flesh.

Eleven days south of where they had started, nearly a fort-
night deeper into the early summer, the heat had intensified,
and in the low brush the heat pummelled their scalps and
shoulders. They had to be careful not to empty their water bottles too quickly. Since they'd left the lake, the only water they'd
passed all morning was in swamps, which they decided was
best to avoid drinking for now.

It was about midday when Nangohns looked up from the
path in front of her. Peering over the heads of her companions,
she detected the slightest colour change in the bush ahead. The
shrubbery remained thick, but seemed a bit brighter. Through
the trees, she noticed a wider trunk that stood out from those
around it. The straight pole bore no branches nor bark, and
she recognized its shape and colour from ones they had passed
en route through the old rez.

"I think we found the hydro line," Nangohns deadpanned to the group.

Tyler picked up his pace, easing his cutting and stomping on and over the layer of brush.

The pole stood erect, still strung with black and grey wires on the arms at the top. The wires connected to other, equidistant poles, running in both directions as far as they could see.

"I guess we have our answer," said Amber, looking back and forth along the line. "No one's been through here with a weed whacker in a long time."

Tyler concurred, assuring Evan that with no apparent maintenance, there could be no charge in the wires. A few more years of growth and the surrounding trees would succeed in taking the whole line down.

The hydro line had powered a resort on the lake at the end of the road up ahead of them. J.C. had worked a whole summer there once when he was about sixteen, pumping gas and cleaning the cabins and the shithouses. He thought he remembered some cottages dotting the land nearby, but couldn't recall with certainty.

J.C. determined that the main road couldn't be more than ten clicks away, just a couple hours' walk at most. Evan patted the thick pole one more time. Taking the machete from Tyler, he moved to the front of the line and aimed them perpendicular to the cables above.

Before long, the sound of a stream babbling up ahead signalled an approach to their potential new route.

"Hear that?" He turned his head to speak behind him. "That water's probably culverted from under the road. That's usually how they made these bush roads, to keep them from washing out."

They soon found a shallow, two-metre-wide stream that ran through the detritus of the forest. The clear, cold water strained through brown leaves and grey twigs beneath their soaked feet as they trudged directly through the runnel. Evan was eager to climb the ditch, which stood roughly as tall as he was, to catch a glimpse of the road above. He darted up the side with a few quick steps, careful not to slip on the loose gravel, and the others followed.

At the top, Evan found himself looking out over a long straightaway of gravel road. To the north, it disappeared gradually down a hill in the direction of what he assumed was the old resort. The road bending off to the south was, to his surprise, largely intact and free of any green overgrowth.

One by one, all six walkers scrambled up, and gathered in the middle of the road.

"That way, I guess, eh?" gestured Cal with an upward palm to his right, southward.

"We'll find the big highway down that way," said J.C.

"We need water," objected Tyler. "Maybe we should go up that way first. We know there's a lake there." He indicated the road to the north. "It can't be too far, right?"

"But there'll be lakes for sure down that way too, without going out of our way," declared Evan.

Cal, Amber, and Nangohns watched the debate keenly. One of the men knew this place, and the other two knew survival.

"What if there's someone there?" J.C. asked Tyler. "Are we ready for that?"

At the mention of not what but who they might find, the hairs on Nangohns's arm stood up. She was the only one of the group to have never seen anyone outside of their community. Until the bear, they had been so focused on making it

91

through the bush that they hadn't discussed a plan yet for interacting with other humans.

Evan, who had been gazing down the northern path, turned to address the group. "Ready or not, this is why we left. I don't know how you get ready for fuck knows what, but we can't just shut up every time we think we might not be alone out here."

He maintained eye contact with each of them equally as he delivered this reminder.

"We gotta walk with pride and hope. We gotta believe that there are other people in Zhaawnong that are just like us, who just wanna make sure they bring up the next generations in a good way."

They stood in silence for a moment before J.C. reiterated the need to find water and assured them there'd be plenty of lakes southward. The light above was tinted from a white-yellow to a gradually darkening orange, and the air cooled as the eldest of the group led the way south.

They soon came to a rectangular green sign marking the upcoming junction with the highway. It stood upright and level, its right angles and symmetry out of place against the medley of branches and leaves in the backdrop. Nangohns scanned the letters and numbers in large white font, the characters bigger than her hands and any other text she'd ever seen. J.C. estimated they were only about a kilometre from what had been the main route through the region, a highway known simply by its number, popularized in songs Nangohns had heard the older guys sing back home. Now she was there. She was seeing it for herself.

J.C. stopped just beyond the sign and asked Evan for the map.

"Alright, so we're right about here," J.C. said, tapping on a rectangular panel about a third of the way down from the top of the map. The others crowded around for a closer look. J.C. raised his head and looked around at their surroundings, and like a litter of wolf pups, their heads swivelled to mimic the motion of their current leader. His eyes went back down to the map, where he located the city, Gibson, about a thumb's length from their spot.

"I'd say we're about forty clicks out," he announced, and then paused.

A pair of crows bellowed overhead. Their black wings fluttered in the still air. Nangohns twisted her head to look.

J.C. and Evan silently locked eyes.

Cal shuffled his feet. "So, we gonna go, then?" he asked.

"Looks like there's a small lake just a little ways to the west here. Right in that direction." J.C. pointed into the bush behind him. "It should only be a couple clicks. Let's go fill our water bottles and have something to eat."

Nangohns had almost forgotten about the growing hunger in her belly. They were about to complete another full day of walking through some of the thickest landscape they'd seen yet, on little rest. If the roads they hoped to follow were still mostly intact, the way ahead would be a bit easier. But what loomed in her mind was what they might find living along the old roads, what could be left in the settlements these massive arteries once tied together.

They walked quietly. Evan thought back over their journey. He was beginning to lose count of the days and nights, and marked their passage only by the landmarks and events along the way. The swollen river. The big, clear lake. The sounds in the night and the thieving bear. They had been walking through bush mostly, with no passage through towns and villages, no evidence of human life. He pictured in his mind the handgun tucked away in his backpack.

As they descended down the ditch and into the bush, the dense woodland awning sheltered them from the swiftly setting sun. Evan felt the moisture of the nearby lake, and soon they were stopped at a rocky shoreline overlooking a small, secluded lake—tiny compared to the reservoirs of their past breaks, but wide and deep enough to drink from.

As the afternoon waned, they sat, quenching their thirst and nibbling on dried meat and fish laid out on the rocks before them. J.C. stood up and proposed that they rest by the lake until sundown. They could sleep if they wanted, but they should embark after dark and make the roughly forty-kilometre trek into Gibson under cover of night.

"You want to walk through the night?" asked Tyler, his forehead creasing.

"We can't tell from here if anyone is around," said J.C. "If we come in at night, we're less likely to be seen."

"The road is our surest way in," Evan said evenly. "But J.C. is right. We have to keep quiet. We don't know who might be living around here still."

"So we'll be going pretty soon, then?" asked Nangohns.

"Sooner than usual, yeah," her father replied. "But you have time now to rest. Sleep. I don't think we should stray too far from here, or shoot any guns."

"We got enough meat for a few more days," J.C. added. "We can't count on finding food in the city. We'll look for some meat once we clear the city on the south side."

Cal stood and surveyed the ground around them for the flattest space. He pulled a dull-pink blanket out of Amber's pack and flapped it out to let it fall to a flat bit of ground nearby. Nangohns and Tyler each found their own spot to nap. J.C. got up to walk around the lake, and Evan ambled over to a thick pine tree up from the shore and sat against it. He closed his eyes, and his breath soon became long and drawn out as his chin dropped to his chest.

The sound of a splash snapped Evan from his brief slumber. His eyes opened, in slits at first, but a sharp pain shooting up his crooked neck stretched them awake. He blinked hard a couple of times and straightened his head, looking out at the lake. J.C. came into focus, walking naked towards the shore. His wet hair slithered down the sides of his chest, revealing the paler skin that was usually shielded by a shirt. The lighter, untanned complexion stopped in solid lines at his shoulders and knees. J.C. took a seat on the boulder in front of Evan to drip-dry in the calm evening warmth. The other four were scattered on the forest floor away from them, still asleep.

"How's the water? I might jump in."

"I was feeling a little grimy from that walk through the bush this morning. Those goddamn burrs."

J.C. leaned his forearms on his knees. He looked out to the water and back to Evan. "You feeling okay to leave tonight?" J.C. asked.

"We don't really got any other choice, eh?" Evan replied.

J.C. was unconvinced. "Man, I really doubt we'll see anyone or anything," he replied. "We're this close already and there's no sign anywhere. Can't be too sure, though. May as well sneak in."

"Make sure you keep your shirt on, then," Evan said. "You probably glow in the dark with them tan lines!"

They both laughed.

"Shit, man, yours are worse than mine!" J.C. joked.

"Too bad we can't stay here another day and even out our tans," Evan chuckled.

J.C. stood up from the rock to step to another one where his red tank top and cargo shorts lay splayed in the sun. He got dressed and returned to his seat. His eyes hardened when he looked back to Evan. "You gonna carry that gun in?" he asked.

Evan scraped the dirt out of his thumbnail with the opposite finger. "Yeah, I am."

J.C. nodded slowly. "Should we tell them to?"

"Let's just wait and see what we find," said Evan. "But one of us should always be in front and behind."

"Mmm-hmm," murmured J.C. He pulled his wet hair to his chest and wrung it out with both hands, then shook his head to expel a few more drops.

They talked quietly there by the water for a while, about family back home, about the trail so far.

"We're making good ground," J.C. said, looking his friend in the eye. "Thanks to you, and that daughter of yours. We're holding our own, for sure. We'll be back before you know it."

Evan smiled, and they noticed Cal and Amber stirring on the ground between the trees about twenty steps away. Soon the rest would be up and they would be on their way back to the road and eastward, in the blue-white glow of the half moon.

NINE

THEY WALKED IN SILENCE. The only audible sounds were the soft rubber of their shoes against the hard asphalt and the occasional unscrewing of water bottles. The pavement had cracked, and occasionally fell away into small potholes from years of freezing and thawing, forcing them into single file once again, with Evan in the front, scanning through the darkness to look for hazards. Like the gravel road they had come from, there was no vegetation yet squeezing through the surface, but it would be only a matter of time before Mother Earth reclaimed this scar once again. The arches of Evan's feet ached, and there was a tightness in his calves as his gait adjusted to the hard surface.

The glowing semicircle above elevated slightly as the night went on, and moved in a more horizontal trajectory across the dim atmosphere above. Their dilated pupils adjusted to the darkness, and even the faded lines of the highway became discernible on the hard grey asphalt. The cracks and holes became more visible, and the single-file formation loosened. They followed long bends and straightaways, looking into the uneven treeline of the horizon.

They reached the junction of a paved road that intersected with the highway, similar to the one they'd emerged from just as night fell. Evan, still in the lead, could see a rectangular marker standing on two posts about a hundred metres from the intersection. He walked up close to it and could make out the faded white letters on the green metal sheet: *Gibson*, it read. Followed by a *10*.

"It's not long now," he whispered as he rejoined the other five standing in the middle of the road. "Probably another hour and a half until we're there."

As they walked, they passed more intersections and driveways, leading to buildings they couldn't quite see in the darkness. The walkers vowed not to stray from the path until they could see better. The details of the homes on either side of the road were impossible to make out, but Evan noticed that there were no vehicles anywhere.

The unmistakable overhang of a gas station roof loomed up ahead of them, the silhouette of the tall sign that would have pierced the horizon, displaying the chain's logo and the price of fuel. Most of the pumps had been toppled, and the shop appeared ransacked and broken. Indistinguishable dark debris was scattered on the ground. Nangohns wanted to ask what these structures used to be, but she kept quiet, along with the rest.

Finally, the pre-dawn glow emanated in the east. The stars ahead began to fade, and the black of night turned deep-blue. They pushed into the outskirts of the modest northern urban sprawl. More structures lined both sides of the road. Building features like shingles and siding material were increasingly visible in the emerging daylight. Nangohns could make out a single-storey structure with a small paved lot where the overgrowth thinned out. She could distinguish a row of tall letters running along a sign above the main entrance: NOBEL PET FOODS. Ranged on the opposite side of the road were two lines of similarly squat structures, connected and fronted with rows of identical rectangular entranceways and square window frames. A tall metal post still stood, with a square sign at the top that read MOTEL. The tall, booming letters on the signs seemed to shout at her, unlike the finer print she'd learned to read in the tattered books of her childhood.

She looked ahead towards her father walking at the front of the group. He turned to face them and stepped backwards. Backlit, with the sun's emerging glow behind him, his face was still mostly cast in shadow, the hollows of his eye sockets and patches of beard providing the only contrast. He fanned his hands outwards, instructing them to spread out.

Nangohns held her bow in her left hand at hip level, ready. Evan noticed her grip on her weapon and slowed his backwards stroll as she approached him.

"How you doing, my girl?" he whispered.

"Good?" she whispered back, nodding as if to indicate the strange surroundings. She felt her body buzzing. Curiosity was squeezing the nervous tension out of her chest as these new, hard angles of urbanity arose on either side of them.

"Okay, then." He offered an assuring smile back, and returned to the front.

The road leading into the city had crumbled and succumbed to weeds and grass much more than the more elevated highway they had come in on. Tall stems sprouted from wide cracks in the asphalt, and deeper potholes pocked the way. Along the cracked line of curb, young trees claimed their place, blasting through the grey concrete and towering above. Shrubs burst through the drains that were built at periodic intervals along the curb, concealing the rusted metal grates that once kept road debris from falling through. If there was once a sidewalk this far out, it had been obliterated by the deciduous trees that now thrived in its place.

The vegetation had also uprooted street signs and obscured traffic lights, toppling some onto the roadway. Other natural and human-made debris lay scattered across the tumbledown road as well, including dead branches, dented and rusted mailboxes, tires, discarded manhole covers, and other relics of city life. The main path into town was totally impassible by vehicle, and as far as the walkers could tell, it had been for a very long time.

As they passed over these obstacles, the rising sun painted the ruins around them in a shimmering fiery glow. Evan looked into the hollow remains of an auto body shop on his right. The big bay doors stood agape and the interior was empty. On the left, trees sprouted through the hard surface of the massive parking lot of a department store. The blue walls of the building were faded and chipping, and all that endured of its wide glass entrance were jagged shards along twisted metal frames.

Another lot on the other side of the street was totally overgrown, as was the interior of a restaurant that was recognizable only by the large single letter that stood high on a sign beside it. They all strained their eyes to peer through the empty windowpanes, trying to make out the menu board. Nangohns had no memory of this place, but Cal and Amber both remembered eating here as children on shopping trips and family outings to the big city.

The blooming radiance of dawn exposed not just the extent of the collapse, but also the depravity that had followed. They could see clearly into every building now, and the ones that hadn't been overtaken by the bush were stripped bare. The shelves and racks of an outdoor sports store were empty. Evan squinted to look into a coffee shop, where it looked like even the sinks behind the front counter had been removed. Some stores looked charred by fire, and others were levelled completely, with only hints of blackened remnants left on the ground.

Finally, the group came to the city's major intersection, where the hockey arena and a big hotel stood kitty-corner from each other. The electronic sign outside the arena was dark, cracked, and dormant, but above the front entrance a torn banner draped across the sloped roof. It celebrated the junior hockey team's provincial championship the season before the lights went out. A mild morning breeze moved through the open air of the crossroads, flapping the bottom corner of the banner.

Evan stopped at the corner of the arena, and the rest gathered near him. He waited for the wind to die down before whispering, "If there's anyone here, I think they'd be in the arena or in that hotel over there." He pointed to the building across the street. Most of the windows of the six-storey building remained intact.

"If there's anyone here," J.C. repeated. "I'm not so sure about that, though."

The shadows of the tall buildings and remaining traffic lights shortened as the morning light elevated. The quiet that surrounded them amplified everything else they sensed. The wind carried the scent of the new vegetation of the parking lots and the streets to them, and the thickening humidity coated their skin once the wind eased.

They set off east once again. Stretching past the arena and the restaurants and hotels clustered around it was a residential area of mostly bungalows and some townhouses. The homes here lay in even more appalling ruins than the torn-up shops and ramshackle former big-box stores and fast-food restaurants that had greeted them upon their arrival. Some of the houses had clearly succumbed to the elements and to nesting creatures that had taken over the insulated outer walls. The roof of a baby-blue bungalow had caved in, folding in the closest walls with it. Grey shingles spilled into the room and were scattered over the floor, visible through the crooked window frame. Its neighbour had completely toppled to the right, exposing mouldy insulation and drywall, splintered wall studs, and rusty nails.

Most of the houses were still upright, though. A sturdier red brick split-level stood on the other side of the road. The words NO FOOD HERE were spray-painted in black across the red bricks under the empty picture window of the street-facing wall. The front door was gone, and the white garage door lay crumpled in the driveway, with weeds growing around it. One house down, the charred shell of a four-door sport utility vehicle rested on its rims in a driveway. The beige two-storey home behind it appeared emptied of all contents and life. Every door and window was gone.

Evan looked closely at the grey vinyl siding of a bungalow on the left and noticed small black holes peppered around one of the bedroom windows. He tapped J.C., walking on his right, and motioned his head to the evidence of a gunfight. J.C. nodded.

The taller grey and brown buildings of the modest downtown skyline neared. They walked along the broken street, observing the last lines of decayed homes. The far side of one residence was charred and melted, and a handful of homes had been burned entirely to the ground. Nothing but empty concrete foundations indicated that structures once stood there. The debris had broken down completely or been washed away by more than a decade of snow and wind and rain.

"Probably gonna be slim pickin's here, eh?" mused Cal.

"I ain't ready to go look," said Tyler.

"Me neither," added Amber.

Death had swept through this place so long ago that its scent had dissipated. Their nostrils filled with the fresh smells of summer, of knee-high clover that had overtaken lawns and boulevards, or of the yellow bunches of black-eyed Susans that crowded over the cracked sidewalks.

Evan realized he had only ever driven this route when visiting Gibson. He remembered looking out the truck window at the brick homes with wide driveways and multiple cars parked outside, marvelling at the luxury. Passing through much more slowly now on foot, the emptiness was overwhelming. He could see from the sidewalk all the way down a long corridor, lined by the ruins of taller buildings, to the city centre.

"What do you want to do?" He turned to J.C. "You know this ground best outta all of us."

"May as well stop up there at city hall," J.C. replied. "We can take a breather in that shade." He pointed to the overhang at the front entrance of the brown, cubic municipal building straight ahead.

The strip leading into the heart of downtown was once a mix of bars, restaurants, boutiques, a police station, a mall, and other formerly necessary establishments like insurance brokers and real estate offices. Those details were discernible only by the signs overhead; each storefront had been hollowed out. In those naked, cavernous spaces, Evan saw no trace of humanity. No chairs to remind them of where people sat. No photos on the walls. No telephones that once carried people's voices around the world. If these buildings had served as shelters in the immediate aftermath of the blackout, Evan thought, there was no evidence left that people had sought refuge under their ceilings and behind their walls. He looked for blankets or sleeping bags where they would have slept. He scanned the bare floors for empty cans of food. He saw no shred of cloth-ing. A lifeless place.

Tyler led the way through the small concrete plaza and up the long steps to the front door of city hall. Evan remembered seeing announcements and other events taking place here on the TV news. The stairs ended at a wide platform that sprawled towards the front entrance, where the thick glass walls had been destroyed for access to the big building. On the concrete walls on either side of the entrance, SMOKING AREA signs were posted. Evan recalled standing there once, shivering through drags off a cigarette during a mid-winter trip to the city to renew his driver's licence. They walked into the depths of the shadow under the awning of the floor above them, and Tyler stopped short of the door. They gazed into the main foyer of city hall.

"Goddamn," Tyler said. "Look at that."

Handwriting of various sizes, in black, blue, red, and green ink, covered the white walls of the lobby. From what they could read, the scrawls were desperate final messages to loved ones, either instructions or farewells.

Brenda Chabot go to the cabin

Mike Miller I took the kids to my mom's I have the car I'll come back for you I love you

The scribbles were written around an empty rectangular white space on the wall, where a bulletin board once hung. The board and the paper posted to it were combustible material and had probably been removed sometime after all these notes were written. The notes went only as high as someone could reach while straining upward on their toes.

"This is where they all must have gathered," said Amber, raising her hand up to the wall as if to touch the words embla-zoned there, but pulling back at the last second.

"Or where they hoped everyone would come back to," Evan said.

"Looks like lots of them lost hope," Cal added. "Some of those look like their last goodbyes."

It appeared that when all the space on the centre wall had been covered, the ones who came after wrote their messages on the other walls of the lobby. Any artwork or decoration had been removed to make more space.

Monica I love you I hope you're safe
I love you Omar we will see each other again someday
Sean I will always be with you I love you
You are loved May you find peace God bless us all

J.C. turned away. "Jesus," he whispered. "I can't read any more of that." He walked out to the line of the shadow, but the others lingered. Nangohns had trouble making out most of the handwriting. She had learned to read only by the printed words in the few dozen books they'd salvaged from their old reserve, and she had rarely seen anyone use their hands to write letters into words. She understood the spirit of these writings, though, which was evident in the hasty scribbles and smears in and around each letter, crammed into what was a quickly shrinking space, a last resort to relay something meaningful, to hope for survival.

Without a word, Nangohns began exploring the doorways leading from the main entry hall deeper into the building. By a pair of heavy doors that opened onto a large central stairwell, she noticed an old framed map of the region. An engraved plaque affixed to the bottom of the brassy metal frame listed the names of the patrons who had donated the map. It was dated 1981. The map itself was the size of a picnic table, Nangohns thought, and she was impressed that it remained mounted, nailed somehow to the concrete wall. The lines on the map didn't resemble the motorways Nangohns had become familiar with from their tattered old road map. And someone had scrawled over the original chart with heavy red lines.

Light shone in through a window in the stairwell, and Nangohns recognized the geographical shapes beneath the red markings, which charted the land down from Gibson to where three Great Lakes converged. The north shore of the body of water called Georgian Bay was low enough on the map that she could put her finger on it. Glancing from the point marked *Gibson*, near the top of the map, back to the relatively short line demarking the north shore, she couldn't help but feel that they had so much farther to go. Her heart sank.

Then a violent cross-hatching of red scrawl to the east of the three lakes caught her eye. Six unevenly shaped overlapping circles with x's drawn through them dotted the land south and to the east of the lake called Huron. The lakes in these areas, rendered in blue elsewhere on the map, had been coloured in a dark, inky red. Written in between the ominous red circles were words Nangohns struggled to decipher: DEAD LAND. DO NOT ENTER.

Next to one of the reddened lakes, she noticed in smaller script: DEAD LAKE. STAY OUT.

The creak of the hinges of the main hall doors startled her, and she discerned Cal's silhouette re-entering.

"You coming?" he asked.

"I . . . I think this might be something," Nangohns replied. "Can you tell my dad he should see this?"

Cal paused for a moment, his mouth agape, but with his hand still holding the front door open, he popped his head out and called the rest in.

Evan, Tyler, and Cal made their way to where the map hung. Amber and J.C. were hanging back, Tyler explained.

Nangohns, who hadn't broken her gaze from the tall chart, nodded towards it. "Look at those red markings," she said.

Evan and Tyler stepped closer.

"It's like they were closing off certain areas," observed Tyler.

"And certain lakes," said Nangohns, pointing to the red splotches working their way up the eastern flank of the map.

"'Dead land'—that can't be good," mused Evan, as he pulled their folded map from his pack. He flattened out the relevant panels on the wall next to the larger map, and looked from one to the other, Nangohns and Tyler peering over his shoulder.

Cal tugged at the mounted map's heavy metal frame, as if he wanted to yank it off the wall.

"Hey, stop that," said Tyler.

"Sorry," replied Cal.

"These marked-off zones are closer to the big cities down south, but this map doesn't go very far east," said Evan.

"You think we'd have known if we were walking through 'dead land'?" Tyler asked Evan.

"I mean . . ." said Evan, not knowing what to extrapolate from the strange markings. "I kind of wish we could take a picture."

"Well, the top and middle of this map aren't touched, and we're trying to get here," said Nangohns, returning her finger to the line indicating the north shore of the big lake.

"Is J.C. out there?" said Tyler.

"He really doesn't want to come in," said Cal. "I tried."

Tyler raised his palms. "Fair enough." He turned to Evan. "I think we chalk this up as another big fuckin' question mark and get out of here."

Evan agreed, and after giving the map a final look up and down, the four of them walked out into the sunlight to meet Amber and J.C. Evan was the last one out.

Looking down at the ground and then back up, letting the sun warm his face, he eased himself down onto the hard step and set his backpack on the concrete. None of them had rested their legs since their pre-dawn procession into the city limits, and the sun was now many lengths clear of the horizon. Cal dropped a backpack onto the concrete floor and crouched to lay down, lowering his head to the bag as a pillow. The rest took their seats in a circle along the staggered rectangular stones. They took turns breathing deeply and sipping the last of their water to relax themselves. There were no dogs or birds or any other living things nearby to distract them from the sorrow and tragedy that hung in this empty space.

"What was so interesting in there?" said Amber.

"More creepy scribbling, basically," Cal assured her.

"One hundred thousand people," proclaimed J.C., harshly enunciating every syllable. "One hundred thousand people. A hundred thousand people lived in this city. Now they're all gone." He shook his head in bewilderment, his eyes opened wide in confusion and fear. He ran a palm across his grey-streaked scalp.

His wavering demeanour worried Evan, who hadn't seen J.C. tremble like this yet on their journey.

"That's a lot of people," J.C. continued. "This was the biggest city around. One of the biggest in northern Ontario. Whatever happened sucked the life out of this place. Or pushed it out. I can't believe it. And look—it must have happened so fast."

"We've only been on one road," said Evan. "Only seen one part of the city. There's lots of different neighbourhoods here."

"Well, I don't wanna go looking," said Tyler. "If it was bad back home in that first little while, it woulda been some real survival of the fittest shit down here after a few months. Who knows who or what we'd find."

"No birds," said Nangohns in a low, steady voice.

They all turned to look at their youngest member.

"There's no birds flying around. No vultures, no gulls, no crows, no nothing. There's nothing for them to eat. They're the ones that eat the dead things. There are no dead things here. Hasn't been nothing alive for a long time."

Evan nodded and they all looked at the sky, blue and shimmering in the half horizon in front of them.

"We could go looking through some other parts of town," Evan said, following his daughter's lead. "If we walked to one end and back, it could take all day."

"Even if there's no one left, we're not gonna find food," Tyler said. "The last ones here probably walked this city a thousand times over, taking every last can until they left or died. We're talking a decade ago now. What food would even be any good?"

Amber sniffled and looked down at her lap. "I dunno if I can keep going," she told the group. There was a long pause. "I wanna go home."

Cal bolted upright and moved across the loose circle they had been sitting in to comfort her. She planted her face in his chest and let out a muffled sob.

"What else do you think we'll find?" Tyler asked, looking at Evan and J.C. "What do we want to find?"

"We didn't just come looking for answers. We don't have to hang around here. But we have to keep going," Evan said.

"Because Walter said we have to?" said Tyler.

"Brother"—Evan put a hand out, appealing to his friend of more than thirty years—"how many times do we have to say it? We're picking that place clean. If we stay up there, we're gonna starve."

"How do we know that for sure? We've survived there for a long time. Didn't always have a plan, either. We know how to survive. All the more reason to honour our ancestors who survived there. What do we owe them?"

"What about us?" Nangohns's raised voice cut through the emptiness of the space.

Everyone, including J.C., twisted their necks in her direction.

"The young ones. The next generation. The future. We didn't choose where we got to be born. But we trusted you to care for us. To love us. To make the right decisions for us. And you did. We're alive today because of you. You found a way to make a good life for us. Nmiigwechiwendam. I am thankful." She cast her long, slender face down to the ground before she continued. "But for a long time, you didn't tell us everything about what happened when we were little kids," she spoke slowly, looking them each in the eyes.

Amber held on to Cal's torso while looking over at the younger woman.

"We asked you, over and over. But you ignored us. Or you didn't tell us the whole story. I know you were trying to protect us. But did you forget what it's like? Didn't you think we'd outgrow that little place? I love it there, and I respect that land. But you all know we were supposed to disappear there. They sent us there to disappear. They didn't want us to survive on that land. They wanted us to die."

Evan swallowed hard as he felt tears well at the corners of his eyes. J.C. rubbed his forehead.

"Now look around you," continued Nangohns. "Who survived? Who is left? We still don't know. But we're here. We should be proud of that. Look at these buildings. They're falling apart. Soon they're all gonna fall to the ground, and Mother

Earth is gonna take this place back. She's already grabbed hold. Soon she's gonna start over. And she's doing that for all of us. So yeah, we owe our next steps to our ancestors."

Nangohns began to conclude her speech. "We're here because of them, and we respect them. But we have to think about the future. We'll still be here after you're gone. And we deserve a say in the world we're going to live in. I say we keep going."

A warm gust floated in across the plaza. Tyler's face had settled into a stare, and Nangohns couldn't tell what he was thinking. Amber emerged from Cal's arms, continuing to wipe tears but sitting straight up. She picked up her pack from the cracked concrete.

Tyler broke out of his thousand-metre stare and looked around the circle at his fellow walkers, his eyebrows raised. He looked at Evan and gave his friend's bicep a reassuring pat. He turned to Nangohns and nodded respectfully. "Maybe it's how much we've put into building up what we have up at Shkidnakiiwin. That place feels like home, maybe more than the rez ever did. Maybe it's 'cus making little ones isn't something my old ass has to worry about. But I think about you and the little ones to come. And when you're right, little cuz, you're right. Not because an elder had a dream; not because of ancestors or what was taken from anyone. Not even because it burns us up not knowing if we're the only ones left—how can we be? But for youse and yours. Whether we turn back now or keep on to the big lake where the birch trees grow tall, I'm with you."

"I believe in you too, and us," Amber chimed in.

Evan moved closer to Nangohns and put his hand on her shoulder. "Miigwech, ndaanis," he said, looking into her eyes. "Gzaagi'in."

"Gzaagi'in, Noos," she replied.

III

Teary-eyed, J.C. suggested that they smudge. Amber opened her pack to dig out a small abalone shell in which to burn the medicine. The iridescent concave inside of the shell shimmered in the morning sun, bouncing pink, purple, green, and blue sparkles into their eyes.

When the ceremony was complete, the walkers sat in tranquility for a few minutes. Then J.C. stood slowly, grimacing from his sore knees and back. He looked around the concrete plaza, overrun by plants through the cracks between the massive stones. He tapped his palms against his thighs and nodded his head as if remembering a rhythm from a song his ears hadn't heard in more than twelve years.

"Well," he said, facing out to the commercial hub in front of city hall. "They sure fucked this place up, didn't they?"

They allowed themselves to laugh once more, reminiscing about city amenities like nail salons and discount stores that they ultimately never actually needed. They would go south from here, all agreed. Neither Evan nor J.C. needed to consult the map. They remembered the roads well enough. On paper, the rest of the walk to the north shore of the big lake was fairly straightforward. "Can't miss it," J.C. joked.

Evan estimated that it would take them most of the afternoon to get out of the city. When Tyler suggested they find a safe place within city limits to camp, Cal, Nangohns, and J.C. refused outright.

"We're gonna need more of a rest at some point, though." Tyler insisted. "We've been walking since last night."

"We should be clear of the city and back into some bush by dusk," J.C. assured him. "There are lots more lakes down this way. We'll go until we find someplace to get water."

"Alright, 'sgo den," said Cal.

They descended the wide steps to the street and turned east again, glancing back only to memorize the landmarks along their route for the journey back. As the older buildings of the downtown core shrank behind them, the former main street aligned again with the boxier buildings they had seen on their approach. This close to the heart of the city, the colours of the brands and chains recognizable to Evan had either faded or been burned or smashed away, the gouged-out structures indistinguishable. To Nangohns, the dilapidated, discoloured signs and banners were ruins all the same: strange and useless shapes and patterns that indicated nothing practical in terms of reaching their destination.

On the south side of the road, though, the ramshackle properties fell away entirely to greenery, and up ahead, they noticed a big gap in the road. Soon, the north side of the road was empty of anything human-made, and they were surrounded by trees, wildflowers, thick bushes, and the sounds of small birds chirping. The faint rush of water resounded from where the pavement fell away.

"I'm pretty sure this was a park," said J.C.

"Yeah, I've definitely been here before," said Evan.

"But there were big fields here. Looks like it's all totally grown in."

"Whenever we'd come down here in the summertime when I was a kid, we'd get a bucket of chicken and eat it at the picnic tables. I think they used to be over there." Evan pointed to his right.

"Jesus, it doesn't take long for everything to grow over, eh?" said Cal.

"Nope. I bet this whole city will be covered by trees and bush in, like, fifty years," said J.C. "Ever seen pictures of those

Mayan pyramids down in Guatemala? They got dug out from the bush after being abandoned for hundreds of years. Those big buildings downtown aren't built to last like that, though. They'll probably collapse and disappear in no time."

The cracks in the old pavement multiplied and grew closer together as they neared the washout. The road eventually fell away in chunks, revealing the layers of asphalt and dirt underneath. Tyler led them cautiously down into the crevasse, which was about as deep as he was tall. The stream flowed about three metres wide and about half a metre deep. The water moved steadily over the ground from the higher side of the parkland on the left down to a wider pond on the right, which had been carved out by the flow itself after the road went untouched and unmaintained for a long time.

The sight of the clear moving stream was triggering. Nangohns felt her dry tongue in her mouth, swollen from thirst. Her throat scratched. "Aapji ngaasknaabaagwe," she declared her thirst. "Can we drink that?"

"Kaa, no, I don't think so," said J.C. "Better wait until we get out of town a bit. You never know what's in the ground here."

Tyler waded into the stream to gauge its speed and the stability of the ground beneath. He planted his foot in the mud and took another step forward. The passage was sound, and he walked a few strides to the other side. Everyone else followed, and they climbed up to get their footing on the crumbling asphalt once again.

The sun had reached its peak at this latitude for this time of year. The midday radiance forced their eyes to pinch closer, but the heat relented slightly. A gust came up behind them, relief blowing in from the west, with high clouds rolling in behind it. By the time they reached the southern road, the western horizon was completely cloud-covered.

The shadows that walked in front of them softened, and they stopped at the crossroads. More skeletal structures surrounded them. They estimated this was the right intersection, given the size of the road and the wreckage of what looked like gas stations and restaurants around them.

A handful of billboards were scattered amidst the low commercial skyline; the few large signs that weren't torched or torn down advertised phone companies, and automobiles with smiling white faces inside, and the digits of phone numbers and letters of websites—markings that were all foreign to Nangohns, and even Cal and Amber couldn't quite decipher them. The group paused for a few moments to observe the nearby decrepitude.

The remains of the gas station on the southeast corner of the intersection still included a roof above where the pumps once stood, but the colours of the ubiquitous national petroleum company were faded along the edges, and the logo was missing, likely blown off after years of intense howling winds that no one heard. The white-painted pillars that held up the roof had rusted and decayed. The fuelling bay itself lay in chaotic disarray. A panic had obviously ensued here, with the pumps either knocked over or missing. All of the brown, rusty covers to the underground tanks had been removed, leaving the concrete around the openings badly damaged, likely smashed open by sledgehammers or other large implements. A green garden hose lay on the ground, with one end dipping into the one tank that had somehow been pried open.

"Can you siphon gas with a garden hose?" Tyler turned to ask Evan.

"I dunno, never tried it," he said. "Looks like they were desperate, anyways."

Cars of various makes and models were parked randomly in and around the gas station. One on the far side of the lot was scorched and stood on corroded rims.

"It obviously didn't work for some of them," said Cal.

"Nope. They were either too late, or . . ." Evan's voice trailed off as he narrowed his eyes on the burnt car. He thought he could make out a blackened figure in the back.

"Why did they burn so many things?" asked Amber from behind him.

"Let's just get going," said J.C.

The other five silently agreed, and they set their course south on a city road that would eventually become highway, like the east-west road they'd come from. The commercial stretches once again became residential, with dismantled homes of fading colours lining the road. As on the other route, some had collapsed, others were singed black, and others appeared mere shells of properties, raw building materials exposed to daylight.

Cal suggested they take a look inside one of the burnt-out dwellings, and J.C. concurred.

"I'm not going," said Amber. "I'll wait here."

"I'll wait with you," said Evan. "Don't be long," he commanded the others.

"Lead the way, Cal," said Nangohns.

He scanned the row on his right, and then the left. He homed in on a red brick house with a grey shingled roof. "That one looks sturdy enough," he said. "It probably won't fall in on us."

He walked towards the driveway. Nangohns followed, and then J.C. and Tyler. They stepped over and around the bushes that had grown through the interlocking stones of the empty parking spots in front of the house.

Just like almost every other house, the door was gone. They stepped across the threshold. The walls were bare, except for a row of three white hooks on the painted blue drywall to their right. The stairs of the split-level home were gone, as was most of the flooring.

"Looks like any kind of wood was a pretty hot item, eh?" said J.C.

"I wonder where they took it all to," said Cal.

"Maybe camps or settlements away from the city. Kinda like we did."

"Think they'd still be at places like that?" Nangohns asked.

"Maybe, if they really knew how to hunt and stuff," replied J.C. "I guess we won't know until we actually see them."

They hoisted themselves to the upper level one at a time, careful not to catch their torsos or legs on the exposed nails on the floor. They walked into a large, bright room that appeared to be a sitting area with an adjacent kitchen. The room was bare, except for a pile of shattered electronics in a corner. Black speaker casings, a heavily dented amplifier, and the empty metal shell of a DVD player lay piled against a cracked medium-sized TV screen. No furniture remained. No family pictures or artwork hung on the walls. The high, wide hole where the picture window used to be let in the afternoon glow.

J.C. stepped over to the kitchen, devoid of all counters and cabinets. An open refrigerator and an askew, dented electric stove stood lonely in the bright space. Splinters, drywall fragments, and other debris were scattered on the floor. No cookware or utensils were left behind.

J.C. put his hands on his hips and scanned the rooms once more. "Well, I think whoever lived here got the fuck out of Dodge as soon as there was trouble," he said. "They probably loaded up their cars with as much as they could. It's hard to say if they had a plan, though. Most people around here probably just took off once things got hairy. Who knows where they woulda went. I bet other people moved in here after they were gone. And then once those ones were gone, others came in. We're talking years of different survivors here."

Nangohns moved past the kitchen area to peer out the big sliding door that used to open to a deck. All that wood was gone too, and the backyard was shoulder-deep in brush that snuggled against the growing trunks of trees.

Cal went down the hallway beyond the living room. Beams of sunlight coming in through the gaping doorways lit the way. Tyler followed, with Nangohns walking slowly behind him. J.C. went back to the foyer to see if it was worth jumping down into the lower level to investigate.

Back on the second level, the first door on the right opened to a bathroom, where the only items left were a knocked-over toilet and a cracked yellow bathtub. A rectangular imprint on the floor near the door marked the place where the vanity had been, now missing along with the mirror and medicine cabinet.

They peered into the remaining rooms along the hallway. The first was an empty bedroom stripped of the top layers of flooring. The next room was the same. Even the closet doors and the trim had been ripped away. Cal stopped suddenly at the end of the hallway as he looked into the last room on the left, then calmly entered. The other two approached slowly. They stepped onto the carpet, stained with dirt, their eyes fixed on the floor on the far side of the room, under the window. On a single mattress lay a human skull, a collapsed ribcage, and the skeletal remnants of the limbs. The mattress was stained brown and purple. They couldn't see clothing or any recognizable items among the grey bones. Only about half of the upper and lower teeth were left in the skull. There was no odor from the remains.

"Maybe they were sick and got left behind," Tyler murmured.

"Weird that there's just a pile of bones, though," noted Cal. "No clothes, no nothing."

"Nice of them to leave a mattress," said Nangohns without thinking.

"I don't think we need to see anything else," Tyler said, and turned and left the room.

The other two followed him out of the house. J.C. was already standing out on the road with Evan and Amber.

"So?" Evan raised his eyebrows at Cal.

"The place got totally cleaned out," he responded matter-of-factly. "There's nothing here."

No one mentioned the human remains.

"Alright, then," said J.C., and they walked south again, stepping over and around the stems that shot out of the cracked and broken four-lane road, which led straight out of the city.

In the distance ahead they noticed a mass of wreckage across the road. As they approached, they made out three SUV-sized vehicles, lined up tightly together, with their tires flat or gone entirely. The glass was gone too, and they could peer right into and through the vehicles, even from about a hundred metres away.

"Some kinda roadblock?" asked Amber.

"I guess when you're raiding and stealing to live, you expect it to happen to you too," said J.C.

"What's that on the roof of the one in the middle?" asked Cal.

They neared the dented and rusted blue four-door family vehicle in the centre of the roadblock. Three small, round silhouettes jutted from the roof. The shapes quickly became unmistakable. The cracks in the backs of the three skulls came into focus even in their shadows. Sunlight had bleached the domes white, yet somehow nothing had knocked them from their perch.

The walkers momentarily ignored these dismal beacons and went to inspect the vehicles. Anything usable in the three large SUVs had been ripped out: the bucket front seats, the foam filling of the back seats, the strong woven straps of the seatbelts, the mirrors. The jawless, mostly toothless skulls atop the middle car made Nangohns think this roadblock was more of a warning than a practical barrier.

"They musta been trying to scare off outsiders, eh?" Cal remarked.

J.C. only hummed in acknowledgement. Evan looked back once more. The three older men shared a quick glance. In the desperate early months after the blackout first struck, they'd dumped the bodies of unwanted invaders at the edge of their community for the same reason. They kept this truth from the younger ones.

They walked past one more stretch of plazas, fast-food restaurants, and gas stations before clearing what had been the city limits. *The lines drawn on maps didn't matter at all to anything anymore*, thought Nangohns, who had never relied on maps until this journey south. The imaginary boundaries she saw her father and the others referring to had dissolved, along with the people who had created them. The land itself had wiped the temporary lines from collective memory, leaving only the boundaries that mattered most: the weaving rivers, the zigzagging shorelines, and the subtle, irregular slopes of the hills and valleys.

Evan walked out in front again, and they set forth in silence, looking straight ahead. No one looked back.

TEN

THE SIX TRAVELLERS SPENT the night on a lake just south of the dead city. They got up before dawn and walked until midday, passing abandoned cars buried in the ditches and on the narrow shoulders of the weaving highway. The farther south they pressed, the more deer they noticed through the trees and around the roadway.

That evening they gathered on the beach of another small lake. A fire burned in the middle of a circle of rocks as the daylight faded. J.C. was spearing long green branches through thick fillets of trout.

Amber joined them shortly before mealtime with a satchel full of medicinal supplies. She had spent the better part of the afternoon ranging the bush, looking for flowers, leaves, roots, and bark, harvesting what she could in return for modest offerings of semaa to each plant and tree.

"Wegnesh gaa-debnaman?" J.C. asked her as she joined them on the sand, looking at the green canvas bag that rested against her torso.

"Baakwaan zhinkaade maanda mshkiki," she smiled, proudly identifying the plant within.

"What the zhaagnaashak call sumac," J.C explained to Cal.

She pulled a long cluster of the red berries from the satchel. They had never seen anything quite like it growing up north.

"Ev's mom and Nicole told me to look out for it," Amber explained. "They said they'd only seen it a couple times before, but it was one of the medicines Auntie Aileen wanted them to know. She made sure they remembered it."

Since leaving the city, they had all been on high alert and were reluctant to pitch their tents for the night. So they laid their blankets out on the soft sand and put on long sleeves and pants to prepare for the overnight drop in temperature. The fire dimmed to glowing red embers as the stars burst alive in the night sky above, splashing the faint ivory of their home galaxy from horizon to horizon. They slept until the chill of the morning and the burgeoning shine in the east stirred them awake.

Nangohns set out early with her bow, heading around the south side of the lake. Cal went off with the rifle in the direction of the opposite shore, while Amber and Tyler walked back to the bushes growing along the road. It was warmer down here, and the blackberries were especially ripe. J.C. and Evan stayed near the beach to gather wood for a day-long fire and the long logs they would need to build a high tripod to string strips of meat through to smoke.

Just as they tied the tops of the thin logs together, J.C. and Evan heard a sharp whistle echo across the water. They scanned the shoreline and saw Nangohns standing on the rocks far down the left side. She waved them over, successful. As they walked along the rocks of the shore, stepping around fallen trees and carefully navigating slippery moss on some of the submerged stone surfaces, they heard a distant gunshot from the far shore.

"Sounds like Cal mighta got lucky," said J.C.

Nangohns was out of sight now, but they heard another whistle as they walked into the cove where they had seen her emerge. They looked up into the dense canopy. About twenty or so metres up, Nangohns waved a red palm at them before hunching back over a young buck splayed out on the ground. J.C. and Evan climbed the slight hill to join the girl as she separated the flesh from the bones.

Nangohns had already removed the arrow from the buck's side and started butchering one of the hind legs. Evan handed J.C. a small pouch of semaa, and the men closed their eyes and stood silently to offer thanks for the animal. Nangohns looked up from her work and paused as her father and then J.C. placed the specks of tobacco on the ground in front of the animal before each taking a limb. All three worked quietly, slicing and tearing through hide, muscle, and tendon until they were joined by Cal, who had circumnavigated the lake on his search for food. He held a dead brown rabbit in one hand and the rifle in the other.

The hunters returned to the beach to finish their work. The plan was to have the entire deer cooked, smoked, and dried by the end of the day. Evan estimated the young deer would yield about fifty pounds of meat, which could be easily distributed in the space among the five backpacks they still carried.

Amber returned with full containers of berries. Soon after, Tyler also brought back a full bounty of fruit. They placed their hauls near the packs where they'd be stored.

"Check this out," Tyler said, commanding the attention of those who were working on the meat. "I found something when I was out picking by the road."

He dug into a pocket of his cargo shorts, making a crinkling sound. The others watched silently. He pulled out a crumpled silver-coloured ball of debris. He unfolded it, and its shiny surface glistened in the sun as he revealed its rectangular shape. He tugged it taut and held it upright for the others to see. The letters MRE were printed in large, bold font in the centre of the package.

"MRE?" Amber asked. "What does that mean?"

"Meal, Ready-to-Eat," answered J.C. "It's an army ration."

Evan inspected the wrapper. "We had some boxes of these to feed people back home when the power went out," he explained to the younger ones. He took the foil from Tyler's hands. The edges were still straight and showed no sign of fraying in the elements. The lettering on the front was clear. He flipped it around to see the tear in the back seam, and could still read the ingredients. No trace of the food remained inside, though.

Evan handed it to J.C., now beside him, who gave it a once-over then stuffed it in his pocket. They shared a guarded look.

"Those packages are made to last," J.C. told the rest. "They stay around for a long time. It's just old garbage."

Leaving it behind, the older men returned to the food preparation.

By early evening, grey clouds had formed across the sky. By sunset, the dome above had been completely obscured, the curtain closed on the celestial spectacle. Enough wood was left over from the day's cooking and smoking to let the fire burn all night, and with the smell of meat strong around them, they decided to stand watch through the night in case of bears, raccoons, or other sniffing, hungry animals. Each of them took a turn, waking up someone else when they got tired.

Evan took the last watch as the cloaked horizon began to brighten softly. He sat hunched forward on his blanket, with his covered arms resting on his bent knees. He looked up from the small flames to the sharpening treeline on the other side of the lake and silently reviewed their progress in Zhaawnong. More than halfway through their journey, they finally had evidence of the chaos Nick and Kevin had witnessed right after the blackout, and of the eventual deadly result. They'd seen proof that waves of survivors had struggled to persist in a devastated world, but it was clear that no living human had passed through the streets and dwellings of Gibson in years.

Any opportunity for salvaging or scavenging useful supplies to take back home seemed long gone. Evan accepted that this was no longer part of their mission. But their journey south had been bountiful in other ways. The land here was healthy and full of life. The air and water were clean. Maybe they could resettle among these generous lakes, he thought. If they went back north now to get everyone, they might have time to return south and establish a new encampment in a place like this before winter set in.

But when the others arose, they came to a consensus that they would continue their trek south. They'd mostly follow the path of the main highway, for at least ten more days. Wherever possible, they'd seek parallel bush roads and paths, cutting over derelict motorways that once ran east to west. They would scout a few of the larger towns that stood in between along the way, but the group was resolved to let the dead stay buried and, barring any signs of life, would stick to the backcountry routes.

Over those next few days after Gibson, in the evenings before dark, Evan, Cal, Nangohns, and J.C. formulated the route they'd take when they brought the others down, fixing in their memory landmarks, the time between stops, hazardous terrain to be avoided, and favourable stops for water, hunting, and shelter.

On the twentieth day of their journey, the overcast sky yielded no shadows on the land around them, and the trees and brush that closed in on either side became more striking. The brown lines in the white skin of the birch trees and the bumpy crevices of the pine bark danced in their periphery, while the flowers and buds of the weeds they walked through on the road brushed against their bare legs and arms.

The organic scent of the corridor was augmented by rain in the afternoon, and darkness seemed to come earlier under clouds and with the thick bush around them. They pushed through in the rain as far as they could before finally retreating from the road to stop and build a shelter. Soon the fire burned steadily while they ate the softer pieces of cooked deer meat. They decided again to keep the fire going all night, the over-night watch now a regular routine.

In the morning, J.C. and Nangohns volunteered to replen-ish their water supply while the others broke camp. They found a ridge leading down to a small lake. The foliage above thinned the farther they descended, brightening their way to the lake, and the dead leaves and branches that littered the forest floor along the slope gave way to large boulders at the shore.

J.C. stepped high onto one of the big grey rocks. A few paces behind him, Nangohns heard it shift slightly under his weight. He steadied his feet and looked back at her.

"Watch your step," J.C. said with a wink.

Nangohns followed J.C.'s cautious feet down the natural steps to the water. There, J.C. squatted to get to water level and let out a groan. Nangohns knew the pain in his joints that he often complained about was aggravated by long days on the road and the humid weather of late. One by one, Nangohns unscrewed the lid of each bottle and handed it to J.C., who dipped it into the clear lake to refill it. Nangohns heard the deep pulses of the water filling the large vessels as she watched him from behind. His head was sunk below his shoulders, his loose hair hanging low over the rocks to the water. After filling the third bottle, he stood slowly, groaning again. "Fuckin' knees," Nangohns heard him mutter under his breath. "Your turn," he said, turning around and moving past her slowly.

She crouched on the rock the same way he had and dipped her hand into the water to fill a grey bottle that had once been blue, stripped of all its paint after years of use. She screwed the top on and began to fill the next one. Her mind wandered as she immersed it in the clear reservoir, thinking of home, her mother, her brother, his partner, and her new niece. She pictured their faces as she wanted to remember them: not glimpses of the day they'd left, but rather snapshots of family times in their compound, smiling, eating, laughing, dancing, and more. Nangohns looked softly at the tranquil lake in front of her and smiled at the memory. She swallowed the escalating sadness that crept up her throat and into her eyes.

"Uh, I think that one's full, Nang," she heard J.C. say behind her. She snapped to, lifted the bottle out of the lake, and hastily screwed the lid back on. "Sorry," she said. "Was just looking at the water. It's so flat."

"Yeah, kinda like a mirror."

When they finished, J.C. retraced his steps up the glistening rocks, and Nangohns stood to follow. In her haste, she forgot to transfer one of the wet bottles from the pit of her elbow to her hand. She took a wide step to her right to manoeuvre the jagged path, and the glistening aluminum bottle slipped from the smooth skin of her bare arm and fell to the hard surface below with a loud clang. The sound startled J.C., and he spun his head around to look mid-step, his back foot slipping on the damp stone. He threw his other foot forward to stabilize himself but overstepped the edge of the boulder, and his entire body lunged forward. His long arms flailed and the heavy bottles flew into the air as his front leg fell into a crack between the rocks. Nangohns heard a dull *snap*. The bottles crashed onto the craggy shore with loud bangs as J.C. screamed in agony. Nangohns dropped the other bottles and carefully rushed to him. He shrieked again, and again, and caught his breath.

"Aaaahhh, goddamn it, I think my fuckin' leg's broke!" he shouted. He awkwardly leaned back onto the dark-grey stone he'd fallen from, to try to steady his body. He gritted his teeth, squeezed his eyes shut, and clenched his fists as he drove his elbows into the boulder to try to hoist himself up. It was futile.

Nangohns's heart raced. "Tell me what to do," she stammered in between deep breaths.

J.C. let out a low growl, then gasped. "I'm stuck," he said. "Go get everyone else."

She bolted up, adrenaline surging through her, and bounded over the rocks that led to a higher, firmer grade. In a few long strides she was halfway up the hill, and when she raised her head to look at the peak above, she saw her father and Tyler rushing towards her, with Amber and Cal close behind. "He's hurt!" she blurted out, and all five ran down the hill to J.C.

His breath had calmed, but his lips were pulled tight against his teeth. His eyes squinted with pain.

"Jesus Christ, bud," said Evan. "What the hell happened?"

"Just slipped," J.C. replied, wincing, still leaning back on the massive rock. "Wasn't paying good enough attention to my feet."

Evan lay flat to get a good look at the leg stuck between the rock. What he saw made the thin hairs on his forearm stand on end. The leg was clearly broken.

"Can you get it out?" he asked.

"Nah, it's fuckin' lodged right in there." J.C. gritted his teeth again.

Evan scanned the stony shore around them. The rock to the left of J.C.'s broken left leg was about hip high, but there was a big gap on the other side of it.

"Alright," Evan said. "Let's push that one over."

The gap above was wide enough for him to plant his feet on the inside of the smaller boulder and shove it with his legs. As he got into place, Tyler, Cal, and Amber put their hands on the side they could reach. The contact with the rock nudged it slightly, and J.C. grimaced with a rough moan. Nangohns moved behind him to prepare to lift him out of the mess.

"Okay, ready? On three," Evan commanded.

He counted to three and thrust against the rock with his legs. The three on the ground forced it clear enough for Nangohns to shove her forearms under J.C.'s armpits and pull him backwards out of the crevasse. J.C. screamed again as Nangohns drove her feet into the rock to straighten her legs and lift him out. She set him down gently on his butt on the wet rock.

J.C.'s face went pale when he finally got a look at his leg. His toe pointed upward, and from the side, his snapped tibia made the entire limb zigzag at the heel, the break, and the knee. Amber gasped when she came closer, and the blood rushed from Tyler's face as well.

Their injured partner calmed himself again with a few long, deep breaths and closed his eyes. The others stood or sat in stunned silence.

"Well, I guess we know for sure it's broken," J.C. mused.

No one laughed.

"We can splint that no problem," Amber blurted out to break the awkward worry that had befallen them all. She looked at his face, trying to make eye contact. "It's just gonna hurt when we set it."

"Let's get to it, then," J.C. said, now the calmest of them all.

"Do you want to do it here, or somewhere a little more comfortable?"

J.C. allowed his mind to slow, attempting to ground himself. "Let's go back up there," he said, nodding to where they'd slept the night before. "Tyler, get me a wheelchair!" he joked through clenched teeth.

Tyler chuckled.

"Good thing you lost that beer gut a while back," said Evan. "At least now we'll be able to carry you."

Tyler hopped up onto the rock behind J.C. and squatted to hook his long arms under his injured friend's armpits. Evan and Cal moved behind Tyler to support J.C.'s weight once he was up on their level.

"Okay, I'm gonna lift," Tyler warned them all, and with a quick heave and a howl, J.C. was up. He wrapped his arms around Tyler's and Cal's shoulders, and they took careful steps to the edge of the line of boulders. Evan walked ahead of them to guide J.C. to the ground. He grunted with each forward movement, and asked for a rest against the rock before they pushed on up the hill to their campsite.

His cheeks puffed out as he exhaled, then he nodded, signalling Cal and Tyler to hoist him up again. Sweat beaded across his forehead as he hooked his arms tightly around the younger men's necks. His fists clenched in pain, and his gritted yellow teeth formed a rigid, wretched rectangle on his face. His carriers stabilized their shoulders and straightened their backs to ensure his broken leg didn't touch the ground. Evan guided them up the slope with careful instructions about stones and fallen logs. Amber and Nangohns followed.

The walk back took twice as long as it would have on twelve legs. They placed J.C. gently on the ground, and he let out one last pronounced breath and covered his eyes with his palms. They all looked down and away to give him a private moment with his suffering.

Amber instructed Nangohns to find wood for a splint, and set to making sumac tea mixed with some dogwood bark to help with the pain. J.C. looked like he was about to be sick. Tyler had already sparked a fire with the leftover wood, which had stayed dry under the tarp.

When Nangohns returned, the water was boiling in the little pot atop the fire. It turned a translucent red, and Amber took it off to let it cool on the ground. She diluted it with a bit of cold water. J.C.'s leg lay crooked on the blanket beside her. Amber dipped a small tin cup into the pot and passed it to him to drink. He sipped slowly. When it cooled, he gulped down the rest.

"I don't know how much that will help," Amber admitted, "because this is really gonna hurt. You ready?"

"Yeah. Gimme a stick," he said.

Evan scanned the ground for a branch about as thick as a thumb. He found one right at his feet and handed it to J.C., who shoved it between his teeth. J.C. gave Amber a nod, and she sidestepped to crouch in front of his broken leg.

Evan leaned down behind her to watch closely. "You ever done this before?" he whispered.

She shook her head subtly, not wanting J.C. to see or hear the exchange.

"Okay, you ready?" she asked again.

He drew a deep breath through his nostrils and nodded nervously. She cupped his heel with one hand, gripping the rubber sole of his shoe, and wrapped her other fingers around the toe. He grunted and crammed his eyes shut. She slowly pulled the foot towards her. The stick in his mouth stifled his scream, but his head kicked back in agony. He bit down harder as she straightened the broken limb and attempted to set it in place.

Evan patted Amber on the shoulder and squeezed the top of her trapezius muscle to assure her of a job well done. She turned her head and looked up at him, eyes wide and anxious. J.C. lay splayed out on the ground, gasping for air. His lower leg appeared straighter than before. They could all only hope it was set properly and would heal.

"How you doing, bud?" Evan asked him.

"I'd love a smoke," he said.

"Maybe we'll find a stash of them somewhere down the road."

J.C. grinned and snickered. He wiped his forehead with his bare palm and then rubbed it on his shirt, which was damp with sweat.

Amber opened her backpack to take out the extra cloth they'd packed for treating injuries. She tore an old T-shirt into strips. She warned J.C. of her next steps, then placed the two long tree limbs Nangohns had brought on either side of his

133

broken leg. He grimaced again as she tied them tightly together. With the splint firmly in place, she felt for a pulse in his foot and asked him to wiggle his toes. Then the procedure was done, and all six stood quietly for a moment.

"Chi-miigwech kina wiya," J.C. finally said. His breathing had returned to a normal pace, and the adrenaline of the injury and the splinting was wearing off. His agape mouth dragged the rest of his discoloured face down, and his wide hazel eyes revealed a daze of realization.

J.C.'s shin was swelling quickly, and although Amber had straightened his leg, it was impossible to ignore the severity of the break. She inspected it once more, noticing the cuts and scrapes from the fall, then shifted her gaze to his distraught frown.

"Have a rest," she told him. "That took a lot out of you."

After a time, J.C.'s eyes finally closed. Amber remained at his side, preparing medicine to clean his wounds. The others whispered about what to do next. All Evan could say was that they wouldn't be walking anymore that day.

ELEVEN

THE FIRST NIGHT AFTER J.C.'s injury passed uneventfully, and the second one did too. The other walkers tried to engage him in idle conversation to lift his spirits, but most of his responses were monosyllabic. His physical reactions barely extended beyond a smile that seemed forced and disingenuous.

They let him be for most of those first two days, except to carefully help him up to relieve himself when he needed to. The broken leg was stable in the splints, but walking on his own seemed like a distant, desperate possibility.

By the third day, J.C.'s shinbone had puffed out as wide as a softball at the break. They could only hope that Amber had aligned it properly and that it would heal enough for him to eventually walk on his own again. But they all knew that would likely take until the end of the summer, potentially pushing their return home far later into the fall, when the nights would be much colder, with the fruit of the land either long fallen or dormant.

On the third night, Evan came to his old friend's side by the fire. He brought in his outstretched legs and tucked them under his thighs to prepare to talk. He cleared his throat, prompting everyone milling around to turn in his direction.

"We're gonna have to make a plan for the next little bit," he began. "Looks like we might be staying put for a while."

J.C. sat stoic while the other four acknowledged the situation with tightened lips and subtle nods.

Evan articulated what they all knew. They could afford to stay a bit longer, but if more bad weather set in, it could be dangerous. The winds down this way could get pretty fierce; even under the trees, they were still out in the open, and movement to and from the camp had been proving difficult.

"I think we need to either build something or try to find something better," concluded Evan.

"What do you mean by find something?" Cal asked.

"Well, there's gotta be some old cabins around here. There's plenty around the lakes farther south. Or maybe that old gas station on the map isn't too far down the road. Just anything to get a roof over us and walls around us while we hang out."

A couple of them should head back north on the highway to see what they might have missed, proposed Evan. It had been cloudy and foggy on their approach; there might have been driveways or smaller roads leading off. Another couple of them, he continued, should walk south, looking for the same thing. Some kind of shelter. No one would go too far—walk until the sun peaks and then make their way back.

Cal volunteered himself and Amber to go south. It was decided that Evan would stay behind to work out plans for the road ahead. Meanwhile, Tyler and Nangohns would double back north.

The fire popped as a thick branch crumbled into glowing embers. The six of them stared into the hot orange and black pile for a moment, sitting with the plan for the morning.

J.C. cleared his throat. "I wanna sing," he said.

Evan smiled, but Nangohns detected sadness in her father's eyes. "What do you want to sing, my boy?" Evan asked his friend.

J.C. suggested a travelling song. "We gotta get this show back on the road somehow," he said.

Tyler and Nangohns dug out the three small hide shakers they'd packed among the various backpacks and passed them around. J.C. took one, and Nangohns and Cal took the others. Evan picked up a branch off the ground in front of him to tap a beat on a small log piled by the fire. J.C. shook the instrument four times, and the dried kernels of corn knocked against the rough inner hide of the bulb. The others joined in rhythm, and J.C. began to sing the ancient song about the eagle seeing travellers on their path.

He closed his eyes and pushed the words and the notes out into the forest around them, and the rest joined him in a comforting chorus. As his voice trailed off into the night, he beat the shaker four more times to end the song. The others hollered, the release of their lungs pushing their voices through the trees and across the lake below.

The next morning there was little to prepare for the half-day walk out and back, so they packed small satchels with food and water. Cal carried the small rifle and Nangohns her bow. If they saw an animal to eat, they'd shoot it, but not if it was too big. They were well supplied for the moment.

"Youse guys look out for each other, eh?" J.C. said to them as they loaded up and prepared to depart. "Be safe. Weweni sago."

"Think they'll actually find anything?" Evan asked.

"Nah, I doubt there'll be anything too close to the highway," J.C. replied. "I remember this stretch being pretty bare back in the day. But it's worth a look. Plus, I wanted to give them a chance to get away from me for a bit. This whole deal is probably bumming them out."

"They care about you a lot," replied Evan.

"Yeah, I know. But a change of scenery for a few hours is never a bad idea."

Evan quietly agreed. Both men sat, not exactly facing head on, but not looking away from each other, either. They wore their hair loose on this summer morning, not needing to keep it braided or tied back as they did when they were trekking through the bush. Evan removed his boots in solidarity with his friend, who hadn't worn anything on his feet since the fall.

Suddenly a low, serious rumble came from J.C.'s throat, and Evan's gut sank. He knew what that meant.

"Ev," J.C. said.

"Yeah?" responded Evan.

"Youse guys need to go on without me."

"C'mon, man, you know we're not gonna do that." Evan had worried this was coming. "We're gonna wait here with you until you're good enough to walk again. We got everything we need out here. And if we find a shack or something, you'll get healed up in no time."

J.C. sighed, and his eyes shot up to the wide green leaves above them. Evan saw him swallow. Deep down, he knew J.C.'s mind was made up.

"Evan, my brother, you know that don't make sense. It's gonna be at least a month until I can walk again. Summer's gonna be more than half over by then. And we don't even know how much farther we gotta go."

"But maybe we'll find something that'll help. Like maybe there's a wheelbarrow or a trailer or something you can sit in, and we can go sooner."

J.C. chuckled, but Evan looked distraught. He refused to consider departing without him.

"You saw that city." J.C. put up his hand. "That whole place was stripped bare." He paused. "I'm just gonna hold you all back. And if we don't leave here until I'm healed, and we're still walking when fall comes? What then? You gotta get them kids back home."

"We know the way back, though. And you said yourself we're more than halfway there now. We can do it." Evan felt his eyes water and his throat tighten.

"It's too big of a risk, Ev. I can't even tell how this leg is gonna heal. Maybe it's fucked for good. I can feel a sickness coming for me. Amber's done all she can, but I can feel it. I'm gonna get weaker just sitting here until I can stand on it again. I'll just be eating up all your food. And wasting all your time."

"What would we tell Amanda when we got back home?" Evan focused on every syllable he spoke to keep his voice from wavering.

Instead, it was J.C. who broke. He sniffled and looked to the ground. His bottom lip trembled. "Tell her that I'm back with Mother Earth. That I've been returned. That I live on in the land. I'll be here forever. And I'll be with her, and all of you, as long as your hearts beat strongly. Tell her I was full of love, and happiness, even though my life was over. That I didn't regret nothing. Tell her that I was smiling."

J.C. smiled at Evan. Tears ran from his cheeks over the corners of his upturned lips. Evan buried his face in his palms and sobbed. He jumped to his feet and shuffled over to his friend and wrapped his arms around his shoulders. Each man nestled his face into the other's shoulder and wept.

Once the tense sadness left his face and chest, Evan took a deep breath and broke from J.C.'s tender embrace.

"What the fuck, man, we're already talking like you're dead!" he let out with a snicker.

"Shit, you've seen me survive worse." J.C. continued the laughter.

Evan pulled the collar of his shirt up to his nose to wipe it, and J.C. did the same with the back of his hand. Evan squeezed his shoulder once more, then returned to the conversation. He knew there was no changing his friend's mind. He also didn't want to meddle with his wishes. In this new era, few had the opportunity to decide their own fate peacefully. Evan wanted to respect J.C.'s desire to determine his final days on his own.

They agreed they shouldn't tell the others right away. They'd have to be careful about it. Evan would tell Tyler when they found a moment alone. He would take it hard, they both knew. J.C. suggested they give it two or three days, but no more; if they found a good spot for him to hole up, and harvested supplies to last him the next couple of weeks, it was possible they could check in on him on their way back. But that was feeling more and more like a fantasy.

"Two or three days." Evan let out a long breath. "Jesus, that's pretty soon."

"It's more time than you can afford, really."

"Let me sit with this tonight. And we'll talk to the others together tomorrow."

A peaceful quiet fell upon them again. A breeze rustled the leaves that sheltered them, then lowered to rouse specks of ashes from the dead fire. The grey dust blew into Evan's face, carrying a strong scent of charred and combusted wood.

J.C. picked up the weathered metal water bottle beside him and shook it. Faint notes of droplets reverberated from within.

"I'm out," he proclaimed. "Can you get me a refill?"

"Here, empty mine for now," Evan answered.

Evan picked his up off the ground and unscrewed the shiny top. He handed it to J.C. to down the few gulps left. J.C. closed his eyes as he tipped back the bottle, holding it vertical for a few seconds longer to savour the last few drops. He passed it back to Evan and wiped his chin and lips with the back of his hand.

"Damn, that water down here tastes pretty clean, eh?" he said.

"The rain musta been pretty pure," noted Evan.

"Make sure you say thanks to the lake again. From me."

Evan agreed, and with an uneasy feeling stepped away from the campsite with a bottle in either hand. He felt J.C.'s eyes on him as he walked towards the ridge that descended down to the lake. He turned back to check on J.C., whose visage had softened. J.C. relayed an easy grin. *This has to be hard on him*, Evan thought. The fatigue in J.C.'s body and spirit was strikingly revealed through his drooping eyes and his now permanently creased forehead. But Evan did see a glimmer of relief in that last non-verbal exchange.

Evan made his way cautiously down the hill and then onto the big, crooked rocks on the shore. He stepped along the flat surfaces, now thoroughly dry. His feet went surely along the stable stones, but he made sure to plant his bare soles and test each step, not making any sudden moves. At the edge of the craggy shore, he set the two bottles down on the grey stone beside him. He sat and dangled his feet in the pristine lake. The water felt cooler this morning, a noticeable change since the warm rainfall. He opened J.C.'s bottle first and reached forward to submerge it in the lake. The deep gurgle of the air escaping was the only sound. And then he heard a sharp *pop* up the hill behind him.

Evan let go of the bottle, and it sank to the bottom as he bolted up to his feet. Abandoning the other water bottle on the rocks below, he bounded across the pass and up the hill.

"Jimmy!" he cried. "Jimmy, goddamn it, don't do anything stupid!"

His feet pounded into the rocks and jagged roots on the ground, tearing the skin, but Evan couldn't feel anything. His vision blurred as he raced faster than he had in a long time.

He arrived at the campsite seconds later to find J.C. lying on his back, with his blue blanket draping the top half of his body, covering his head. Evan's heart pounded as he plodded slowly towards the prone figure. The broken leg lay static in the same spot as before, toes upright. The other had fallen to the side. Something inside Evan wanted to believe J.C. was napping, a dubious sense of denial to protect himself against the reality of death.

At first, the blood stain was barely noticeable on the dark-blue wool, but as the purple blotch grew, Evan could see clearly that it came from J.C.'s head. He had draped the blanket over himself to spare Evan the sight. Evan's hands trembled violently as he reached down to pull the blanket back. A storm of grief and shock heaved through him before he could, and he snatched his hands back.

"Goddamn it, Jimmy! Fuck!" he shouted again. The ends of his long black hair shook as his body quaked with loss. His head swivelled back to his friend's body, and then away again. The disbelief evaporated every time he gazed upon the lifeless figure, and his misery increased with each passing moment.

Evan collapsed to the ground, covering his eyes with his dirty palms. He writhed in fits of mourning that burgeoned from his chest out to the ends of his limbs until finally, lying on his back, he caught his breath. He stared up at the greenery that muffled his cries and sheltered him from the intensifying rays of the morning sun. His swollen tongue and burning throat told him he needed water. Still heaving with grief, he got to his feet to make the short walk back to the lake to get his bottle.

Evan returned with his and J.C.'s water containers in either hand, water dripping down his face. He had dunked his head in the lake, and his soaked hair clung to his back. He set the bottles on the ground by J.C.'s feet and squatted beside his torso.

He had seen and transported his share of dead bodies. But he never got used to preparing and carrying the inanimate body of someone he loved.

Evan placed his hand on his friend's chest. He felt only faint body heat through the blanket. The wool fabric creased on the corpse's right side, where J.C.'s arm had extended and stiffened after firing. Evan took another deep breath and pulled down the blanket. The drying blood pasted the wool to J.C.'s head, so Evan gave it a tug to free it from the wound. A thickening crimson blotch covered the temple and part of the cheek. *At least his eyes are closed*, Evan thought.

On the ground to the left of J.C.'s head was one of the handguns. To the right, where J.C.'s head finally faced, was a thick pool of blood from the exit wound, mixed with dirt and long hair.

He appeared at peace. His spirit was getting ready to travel now, Evan told himself, so it was their duty to help prepare him for the next world. He placed his hand once more on J.C.'s chest, to feel where his heart used to beat.

Evan covered him back up and began to build a sacred fire. He arranged dried wood in the fire circle and used one of the flints to spark it into flames. The fire grew as he stood in front of it, praying for his friend to make a safe journey.

He cleaned the blanket in the lake and gathered more firewood, though it was scarce after their already days-long stay. They'd have to expand their perimeter to find enough to keep the fire burning for at least three more nights of funeral rites, their custom since returning to the bush.

Cal and Amber were the first to return. Evan heard Cal's voice well before he saw them, and he walked up to meet them on the edge of the clearing. He wanted to tell them himself, before they saw the damp blue blanket shrouding their friend's stiffening body. The heartbreak was evident on his face, and they knew immediately something was amiss. As he told them, he guided them gently to the ground, where they sat for a while to catch their breath.

Evan led them back to the site, where they cried again, and mumbled words of their own, making tobacco offerings and praying over the body. Amber set about cleaning the fatal wounds, dousing a ragged shirt in water and wiping J.C.'s head and face clean.

When Tyler and Nangohns descended into the clearing, the other three wore the news on their faces, though none of them could find the right words to begin. Tyler asked what had happened, and Evan said in a choked voice that J.C. had decided to walk on.

Evan led them all back to the campsite, where Nangohns and Tyler offered their prayers and they all sat to visit with J.C.'s body.

As the eldest now, it was Evan's responsibility to advise and direct. He announced that he wanted to give J.C. the right send-off—that the fire burning now would burn long enough to guide him home.

"Four days, then?" Tyler asked.

"Today is day one," confirmed Evan. "On the fourth day, we'll let the fire go out. And he'll be home."

Cal and Amber exchanged a nervous glance. They hadn't found anything on their walk to the south, including game to hunt, and the shelter of the gas station had little to offer. They were worried about spending more time in one place, eating up their supply of deer meat. Tyler felt the same; they hadn't found anything back north, either.

Evan resisted their objections, unwilling to leave J.C.'s body for the buzzards. Tyler and Cal were pleading with him sympathetically when Nangohns silenced them.

"He led us this far," she said. "Now we have to help lead him to the Spirit World. It's important."

No one disputed the girl's statement.

"He sang us that travelling song last night," Nangohns noted. "Maybe he knew then. But I wanna sing it again."

Amber agreed. And the others nodded. The shakers were passed around and the song began. The ensemble was missing a voice, but their cries echoed through the forest and pierced the thick sunshade above. They closed their eyes and danced where they stood, their mouths open to release breath and sound into the air that cycled back through their lungs and then out again.

The song concluded, they moved J.C.'s body from the death site, cleaned the blood, and set to work. The pit they managed to empty was only half as deep as a standard burial site back home, given the rocky underlayer, so they gathered large rocks to fortify the tomb after burial.

On that first night, they feasted to honour J.C.'s spirit. They set aside small chunks of meat and berries in a tiny wooden bowl Tyler had carved from a thick, dry branch. They also

145

placed some of their feast, along with tobacco, cedar, sage, and sweetgrass, in the bundle that would be buried with J.C. They each cut a small lock from their hair to send with him, as part of their individual grief rites. They chorused into the night, singing songs about creation, the eagle, the water, and travelling. They took turns feeding and stoking the fire through the night. They would let it extinguish on its own on the fourth day. Evan took the first shift, sitting beside his dead friend and peering into the gaps in the orange flames as darkness surrounded the camp.

In the afternoon of the third day of mourning, a day before the burial and their departure, they resumed planning for the rest of the walk south. They emptied J.C.'s backpack and divided up his clothes and supplies. Cal inherited most of them, including the pack itself, along with the handgun and some of the other gear. He found a small pouch at the bottom of the bag, filled with items they assumed were mementos. He handed it to Evan, who placed it in the red blanket that wrapped J.C.'s bundle, along with a shaker, a utility knife, and pinches of sumac and bark harvested by Amber. J.C.'s body would be sent to the Spirit World with the necessities for a safe passage.

Each took a turn bathing one more time, and as dusk fell, another feast commenced. The bounty from the deer was nearly half gone now.

As dawn illuminated the forest on the fourth day, Cal, the final firekeeper, let the flames dwindle.

Evan addressed the other four as they prepared to depart. "Well, I'm no elder, so I don't really know what we're supposed to do here. I don't know what I'm supposed to say."

Tyler, who'd been by Evan's side for so many deaths in their young lives, looked at the body and up to his friend. "Don't worry, Ev. You don't have to say anything. We've honoured him. Let's put him to rest."

They gently laid their friend's body in his final resting place and buried him with his bundle. When the last stones were in place, they picked up their packs and walked away, singing him off one last time.

TWELVE

THEY'D SMELLED THE CHARRED remains of the forest long before they saw it. After burying J.C., they'd walked south on the broken and overgrown road well into the afternoon. Just a few kilometres past the ramshackle gas station, the air around them became stale and ominous. As the yellow light of day transmuted to the dense orange of early evening, they walked into an impoverished grey-scale landscape. The rolling hills off each side of the highway had been stripped of summer greenery. Many of the black tree trunks left over stood much shorter than the lively northern forests the walkers had grown accustomed to on their trek. The long branches of the trees that stayed upright had been reduced to bare, crooked limbs. Fire had completely razed this land, leaving the ground dark with carbonized branches and chunks of ash. The orange sun to the west silhouetted dead trees as far as they could see.

With no deadfall on the ground anywhere around them for a fire, the walkers bundled up in layers that evening. The absence of vegetation left nowhere for the heat and humidity of the day to linger into the night, and they prepared to endure one of their coldest sleeps of the trek thus far. None would have a restful night.

In the stillness of the next morning, Nangohns sat on the scorched ground, staring through the gaps in the blackened forest around them, her father kneeling behind her, running a fish spine through her long, silky black hair, working free the knots. The sheen of her hair glimmered in the early-morning sun as Evan palmed the tangled clumps with one hand and worked them free with the other. Nearby, Amber packed up their dwindling food supply, Tyler rolled blankets, and Cal sipped water. They were breaking camp in a bare landscape, temporarily removed of vegetation by a ruinous, renewing forest fire that had raged during a previous summer.

Evan separated his daughter's hair into three bulky ropes to braid together. As he did every time he tied her hair this way, he reminded himself of the unity of body, mind, and spirit, which each of the clusters represented. He'd learned that from his mother, but not until he decided to finally grow his hair long in his mid-twenties, after regular haircuts became irrelevant. He weaved the three bunches together, one over the other in a rhythmic sequence. He pinched the end of the braid between his index finger and thumb, and took the thin strip of deer hide from his teeth to tie the end secure. He tapped her on the shoulder and rested his palm there to let her know he was done, and she squeezed his fingers gently. Their family ritual brought her home in the midst of their bleak, blackened surroundings.

When they set off down the road later that morning, walkable hills rolled on either side of them, giving way to streams and small lakes in the valleys. The reflection of the blue sky in the water was the only colour in the disfigured and sullied terrain. Nothing budded from the trees or ground for game to graze upon. If the fire had torn through here as recently as last year, it would be another full cycle before anything emerged from the ground again.

❦

They spent another night amid the charred trees near a small lake, and moved on at first light. Nangohns knew they would reach the next landmark in the next few days. Arriving at the intersection with the major east-west highway would mean they were in the home stretch to the north shore of the big water to the east. But the endless vistas of singed countryside made orientation and progress difficult to gauge. The damaged land all looked the same, only taking on slightly different tones in the varying brightness of the sun. Any road signs or markers had been either incinerated in the fire or pulled up from the shoulder long before the natural devastation. Roadside billboards advertising lodges, hotels, and restaurants had also been wiped out. The heat and the flames had even plucked away the weeds burgeoning through the asphalt.

They had been walking through the burnt land for nearly two days when, while stopped to rest and eat, they heard a sharp *caw* pierce the warming air overhead. They looked up to see two crows flying southeast. The air was now so still they could hear their wings flap as they passed overhead.

"Aanii Aandegok! Aapiish epzayek?" Cal asked the crows.

"Looks like they're heading where we're going," noted Amber.

"No matter where they're going," Tyler added, "that's a good sign. They know where the food is, anyways."

Evan nodded, and Nangohns grew more hopeful.

"Let's go follow them, then," she said, and they finished their last bites and got up to walk again.

Around a slight bend in the road, a long stretch opened before them, gradually inclining up one of the bigger hills they'd

150

seen on this leg of the walk. The horizon ahead looked as sparse and burned as the topography they'd traversed for two days now. The forest fire had been much bigger than they'd imagined.

They climbed the long hill in the spread formation they had adopted the night before they entered the city. Nangohns's feet picked up the pace as she followed Cal to crest the modest northern summit. The peak overlooked a broad valley, and in the distance, they saw the usual greenery of the warmer season emerging.

The highway lay straight before them, then disappeared in a bend into the trees on the far side of the valley. The charred ground and stumps gave way to recovering maple, ash, and birch trees. The latter bore the scattered scars of the fire along their white trunks. But just a few steps beyond the line where the fire had gone out, life was returning to the forest.

Nangohns felt her feet step higher, her strides longer, as she moved through this land she was seeing for the first time. As the road twisted along, she imagined the settlers who had built these routes around cliffs and lakes, to and from mining sites and logging roads. The trees stood taller the farther south they voyaged, and the ones close to the old highway shaded them from the sun. Streams babbled on either side, flowing through culverts underneath them. Birds of various species—from scavengers to songbirds—fluttered above them from tree to tree, calling to each other in the growing heat. It was a welcome return to warmth and moisture after several days of walking through nothingness.

Nangohns closed her eyes and raised her lean face to the sun. She stretched her arms out to relax her shoulders. Her eyelids filtered the sunlight into a bright redness. She rolled her head slowly to stretch her neck, and when she allowed her eyes to open, she spotted a strange gleam ahead.

"Hey, what's that up there?" Nangohns pointed to the road ahead. A small, piercing light poked through the bush on the east side of the road, forcing her to squint. She stopped in the middle of the road as the rest came to a halt.

Amber came to her side, lifting a flat hand to her brow to shield her eyes. "Where?" she asked.

The others squinted in the brilliant daylight to scan the space before them. Nangohns pointed to a clump of trees just ahead of them. Amber trained her gaze on the spot and took a few slow steps forward, then stopped in her tracks and let out a faint gasp. The men behind them mumbled as they peered ahead. Then Evan saw it: a small white light beaming from just above a low, umber rock cut. It looked out of place among the tree trunks. He felt a tingle at the back of his neck.

Tyler's and Cal's heads locked into place as they finally located it as well.

"That's weird," said Cal.

"Looks like some kind of reflector," Tyler said. "It's bouncing the sun right back at us."

Evan moved slowly forward around Nangohns and Amber to investigate. The others cautiously followed. The strange, piercing light flickered and dimmed as they approached, but Evan kept his eyes fixed on the grey trunks of the maple trees a couple of metres back from the tip of the outcropping that jutted over the shallow ditch. He heard the others whispering behind him, and his gut twisted as his mind ran over the few traces of humanity they had come upon in recent days, from scribbles on walls to skulls to a ration wrapper. Stopping on the edge of the pavement, in front of the stone platform and the tall, lush maples, Evan considered retrieving his handgun. He noticed that Nangohns had her bow at the ready.

"Looked like it came from somewhere in that bunch," whispered Cal over his shoulder.

Evan stepped carefully down into the ditch and then hoisted himself up onto the rock, which was about a metre higher than the road surface. He got to his feet and dusted his hands off on his cargo shorts.

Nangohns crouched as she watched him walk up to the trees, scanning the bush behind him. The other three were fanned out around her, Tyler looking south, down the road. Amber stood frozen, her fists clenched. Even after so long in the emptied-out landscape of their journey so far, Nangohns couldn't shake the feeling that the reflector was some kind of lure.

"Aangwaamzin," Nangohns whispered to herself. She wanted to urge her father to approach more carefully.

He froze in front of the split trunk on the left. "Holy fuck," he muttered to himself, but loud enough for the others still on the road to hear.

"What is it?" Tyler asked.

Evan's head shook in disbelief, his top bun bobbing from side to side. He stepped to the side and turned to face the others. "It's a fuckin' cellphone," he proclaimed, pointing at the small, shiny black rectangle lodged in the Y of the trunk.

"What?" Tyler squinted to try to focus on the object, but could only make out a small obstruction in the tree. Needing to see more, he jumped into the ditch and then up onto the rock cut.

Cal rushed up after him. Equally mesmerized, Amber followed slowly. But Nangohns held back, and raised her hand to hover over the bow on her opposite shoulder. She looked around again, silently discouraged by the loud chatter of her elders, but when no hazard emerged from the forest in front of them, she relented and joined them at the discovery.

They gathered around the tree. At roughly waist high, the maple trunk forked, and lodged there was an oblong piece of smooth plastic with a cracked glass front, almost as wide as a palm, and twice as long. It sat at an angle facing the road, bouncing light to the north.

Evan reached down to pull it from its perch. He froze in astonishment as soon as he touched it. "Holy fuck," he repeated.

Nangohns watched him grasp the gadget and attempt a gentle tug. It remained firmly lodged in place. Evan said nothing and jiggled the phone from its spot in the fork of the tree. It popped out of a cleft that Nangohns realized was carved. A person had installed it there. Her father raised the shiny black object higher for a closer look, and turned it over in his hand to reveal a blue case emblazoned with a white leaf on the back.

"This is Izzy's phone," he said, staring at the logo.

"No way," said Tyler.

"I helped him pack before he left," Evan affirmed. "He insisted on taking it in case he found some place to plug it in." A hollow sound escaped his lungs. Almost a laugh.

"What's it doing here?" asked Cal.

Evan inhaled sharply, rousing himself out of his disbelief. "No idea," he said, "but it looks like he—or whoever had it— put it here on purpose."

Evan pointed at the small indents carved into the tree. Cal leaned in to look closer, and the others took turns inspecting the spot.

Amber wondered out loud if it had been left here to be retrieved later.

"No, it's a marker," Tyler said. "See how it was pointed out that way? He . . . they . . . whoever left it wanted us to see it."

Cal turned around and looked up and down the highway. "Why did he want to mark this spot?" he wondered.

Tyler peered over his shoulder and into the bush.

"There must be something here," Evan said. "Or there was at some point."

Tyler asked if they should split up and look around. Evan balked and said they should stay together. This was, for sure, a sign. But not necessarily a good one.

"Izzy knew the bush. So did Kevin. Maybe they wanted us to go back that way." Evan pointed at the thick forest behind the forked tree. The evergreen trees that punctuated and shaded the ground were tall, and the underbrush looked passable enough; they wouldn't even need to cut a path.

Soon they were moving steadily through the woods in single file, brown leaves rustling as they went. The shaded woodland sloped up to a dirt ridge lined with more evergreen trees. Grey and white rocks bulged from the ground, and the five walkers watched their feet as they navigated the new terrain.

Nangohns's faded blue running shoes kicked up leaves and twigs. They hadn't been walking long when she looked up at the trees in front of her and noticed something light-red wrapped around a pine tree off to the right. Calling out for the others to stop, she ran up to the tree.

Evan was soon at her elbow. He gasped in disbelief. He stopped and clasped the back of his head with both hands.

A thick strip of faded, stained fabric was wrapped around the trunk of the tree at shoulder height. It was some kind of cloth or garment, thought Nangohns, noticing the stitching on the material that wove into the knot.

Evan dropped his hands, and then reached around the trunk to untie it, pulling loose the long arms of a nylon shirt. He turned to hold it out in front of the others. "This was Izzy's," he said. "Well, it was mine. I lent it to him because it stays pretty dry and he didn't have nothing like that."

Evan cupped his hands behind the faded red polyester and brought it to his face to smell it. He held the sweater tight to his face and, before he could process what it might mean, he lowered himself to the ground and began to weep. Cal and Tyler knelt by him, and Nangohns and Amber moved behind them to place their hands on their shoulders in comfort. There had been no final farewell for Isaiah and Kevin, and their spirits loomed large in the hearts and minds of the walkers. In stunned silence, they wept for their friends.

After catching his breath, Evan stood up and weighed the possibilities, still shaken by what they had found. Could Isaiah have been marking off a trail from the main road? It quickly dawned on him that this was the only option that didn't make his stomach churn. The alternative was that someone had got a hold of their friends' things.

"Why would someone just put his shit in the trees like that?" asked Tyler.

Evan raised his eyebrows and pulled his lips together. He cast a glance back towards the road, trying to picture the landmarks along the path they'd taken in. Nangohns walked up behind him and placed a hand on his shoulder. Evan started at the touch, but recognizing his daughter, he reached for her hand and squeezed it, then turned around to face her and the group.

"We have to keep going," he said.

"I think so too," said Tyler. "Let's see how far we can go, anyways."

They had followed a straight line from the phone to the shirt, and resolved to keep going in that direction. In about a hundred metres they found another garment, this time a T-shirt, wrapped around a thick oak branch. Farther in, they found a thick strip of faded green cloth, likely from a cotton sweatshirt, tied to a branch close to a maple trunk. They continued in a straight line, under the shade of the high leaves and through the natural detritus that blanketed the forest floor, and found another of the green rags wrapped in a similar way on another branch. All the markers they passed were tied at roughly shoulder level, and now that they'd noticed a trend, they kept their eyes peeled for the faded green scraps of cotton.

The pillars of the forest spread farther apart as they walked, under a sun that moved swiftly westward. Wide gaps opened in the awning above as they gradually approached the outskirts of the heavier woodland. They saw one more green marker on a thin birch tree, and stopped to assess their surroundings. Through the shorter and narrower birch trees on the edge of the bush, they saw a wide glade shimmer in the late-day sun. If Izzy, or whoever left this trail, had ripped apart the entire sweater, Evan deduced, there would still be a ways to go. But from the clearing they couldn't find a trace of it in any direction. The trail seemed to end there.

Before they could consider what to do next, Nangohns suddenly held up her hand and shushed them. "Wait," she whispered. "Do you hear that?"

"What is it this time?" Tyler whispered, half as a joke, half in disbelief.

They stood still and strained their ears, their eyes darting through the trees. Nangohns heard the high-pitched voices again, but couldn't quite make out any words. She closed her eyes to focus, and the others watched her intently as they analyzed every sound of the mainly silent woods. She waited for the faint murmurs to resume, and this time she recognized the sound: it was children talking. Her heart beat loudly in her chest and in her ears, drowning out the voices. Her eyes widened in shock and excitement. "It's kids!" she exclaimed through her teeth in a pronounced whisper. "I can hear kids talking."

"Are you sure?" whispered Amber. Her forehead creased as she leaned in closer.

The rest huddled in to hear more.

Nangohns was sure. And without a word, she pointed to a field just beyond the clearing. They all turned to look at the bright-green grass bending in the orange sunshine. At the next ripple of sound, Amber jolted. Evan, Tyler, and Cal were still straining to make it out.

"They're speaking the language," Nangohns said with continued astonishment. "I could hear 'maajaan.' I think they're playing around."

"I hear it now," whispered Cal. "Sounds like just two voices."

Nangohns nodded agreement. It was enough for Evan to signal them to move in for a closer look.

"Be real quiet, though," he cautioned.

They descended into the meadow. Nangohns felt her hands tremble and balled them into fists. If this was a trap, they were walking right into it, like a rabbit into a snare.

Stopping at a thick pine tree, they huddled together. Nangohns crouched behind Evan, placing her hand on the rough bark and squinting into the meadow on the far side of the red tree trunk. There, in front of another line of trees, she saw two heads of black hair bouncing up through the tall grass. The children spoke in rapid-fire, high-pitched squeals, punctuated by giggles and laughter. She couldn't make out any more of their words, but she estimated they were roughly half her age—not even ten years old. Her pulse accelerated at this glimpse of other humans, the first they'd seen since leaving home. She unconsciously gripped her father's shoulder, not realizing it until he patted the top of her hand in reassurance.

Evan rose slightly and crept forward, careful to stay in the shade. The others stepped up to flank him on either side, but stayed crouching.

"Don't move," he said. "We don't want to scare them. We don't know who else may be around."

They all nodded in agreement, their hearts fluttering nervously in their chests.

Evan slowly stood up to survey the field and the trees on the other side. He tried to stay rigid, but his slight movement was enough to catch the children's attention. Their heads turned in the group's direction, and their eyes widened at the sight of the unfamiliar grown-up.

"They look Anishinaabe," whispered Amber.

Nangohns couldn't tell if the kids had spotted the rest of them crouching in the bush.

"Say something, Ev," said Cal.

"Aanii!" Evan blurted out, awkwardly waving an arm in the air.

The children turned and ran. The grass opened as they darted through the field, swaying behind them as they made their escape. The walkers stood and watched the kids bound up the hill and into the shade of the trees.

"We follow them?" asked Tyler.

"Let's wait a bit," replied Nangohns. "Let them get home first."

But as soon as she had spoken, she realized the light was fading fast.

THIRTEEN

DUSK HAD FALLEN IN the forest, and the walkers, following the path the two children had made, had passed two more green cloth markers by the time Tyler spotted smoke in the distance. They hadn't stopped for food, afraid of losing the trail, and none of them were sure what they would do when they reached the end of it. They were deliberating in anxious whispers whether they should find cover and wait for the morning light when a low voice boomed from somewhere in the nearby wilds.

"N'gaasek!"

Stunned, Nangohns strained to hear over her pounding heartbeat, but couldn't place the source of the command.

"We all heard that, right?" Cal whispered.

Evan hushed him. Their necks jerked in panic as they peered in all directions around them.

"Gwaabminim," the man spoke again. "Gego gjib'iwe-kego."

They froze. The mysterious nearby voice was warning them, in the old language, not to run away.

"Gii-biidoonaawaan na baashkzignan?" he continued.

Evan fixed his eyes straight ahead. Behind him, Nangohns homed in on where the voice was emanating from. It echoed loudly enough for them to hear, but was somehow muffled, as if spoken from a ways off into the expanse they faced.

"Is he asking us something?" whispered Cal again.

Amber shushed him.

"Guns," said Tyler. "He's asking—"

"Shut up," the voice said. "I'll make this easier for you. I'm gonna talk in Zhaagnaashmowin, in English, so you understand. Are you armed?"

The baritone sounded clearer now, although its source remained hidden. Each passing moment brought another degree of nightfall.

"Don't tell me you don't understand English, either." The voice became audibly agitated. "Do I have to repeat myself?"

"No, no, you don't." Evan's voice trembled as he finally responded.

"Well? What is it, then? Did you bring guns or what?"

"Yes, we have guns."

"What do you have?"

"A rifle. And three handguns."

"Where are they?"

"The handguns are in our packs. We're carrying the rifle."

"Is that all?"

"I have a bow," Nangohns spoke up.

Evan swivelled his head in her direction, startled by her voice.

"Ooooh, a real Indian!" the voice joked.

Now it sounded to her like it came from behind the thick trunk about twenty metres in front of them. Her right knee trembled. A hush fell over the strange standoff.

"Why are you following those kids?" the voice asked after a moment.

Evan cleared his throat. "We've been walking all summer. We haven't seen anyone since we left home. We just wanted to see who's here."

"Aapiish wenjibaayek?" He switched back to Anishinaabemowin to ask where they came from.

"Gaawaandagoong," Evan replied.

"Gaawaandagoong?" The man's tone softened.

Nangohns felt sweat form in her armpits despite the chill of night. Nervous perspiration beaded below her nostrils too. Finally, a silhouette slipped out from behind a tree several metres in front of them, causing her to catch her breath. Two more figures emerged from wide trunks behind him. All three stood with their arms tensed at their sides.

"Here's how it's gonna go," said the one in the front, who had been questioning them. "If you wanna come with us, you're gonna leave your backpacks here. And that rifle and that bow. We'll come back for all that later."

Evan raised his arms outward, showing that his hands were empty, hoping the trio could see. With an exaggerated upward gesture, he indicated for the others to do the same. "We're not here to hurt anybody," he said. "We followed a trail. We think our kin may have been through here." He slid the straps of his pack off his shoulders. It landed on the ground with a thud and a rustle of twigs and decomposing leaves.

With no choice but to comply, the others silently placed their backpacks on the ground in the darkness.

"Okay, follow us," the leader of the trio said to them. "Keep quiet for as long as we're walking. When we get there, you'll be asked to talk. Is that clear?"

"Yeah," replied Evan.

"Nahaaw, aambe aabdase-daa."

Everyone but Nangohns walked forward. She rubbed her bare arms, feeling the chill of the coming night. "Uh," she said, "ndaa-biiskoonye babgiwyaan na? Ngiikach."

The man in front remained in place, in serious contemplation once again. "Nahaaw," he replied affirmatively, and urged her to hurry. "Wewiiptaan," he added.

She unzipped the top of her backpack, exaggerating her movements in the twilight so the onlookers could see, and quickly pulled out the sweater she packed at the top for easy access. She had tried to address them in their preferred language, hopeful that asking in that way would work in her favour, which it had. She pulled the wool sweater over her head and yanked her hands through the sleeves as fast as she could before rezipping her pack and tossing it onto the pile. "Chi-miigwech," she thanked them.

"Alright," the leader said. Although big in voice, he appeared small in stature. He hadn't moved since emerging from behind the tree. "Let's go, then."

As the line of five travellers neared, he turned and assumed the lead in front of Evan, guiding them straight through the trees where the other two waited. The first one faced away from them as they approached, and waited until Nangohns passed before joining the line at the rear. Keeping her head straight, she stole a glance at the first sidekick as she walked by. They looked about her age, she thought. But they kept their heads down, long hair obscuring their faces. After a few strides, the third member of their escort, tall and burly but otherwise indistinguishable in the evening light, finally took up the rear.

They walked in this formation until the last traces of daylight were gone and a nearly full moon cast a blue pallor on the rocky, leafy ground. For the five walkers, the trek became easier, and they settled into a steady pace. No one spoke.

The crisp, lush scent of summer night returned as they walked deeper into the bush with their new guides. Earlier, Nangohns had thought they were coming close to a camp or settlement, but now no trace of fire lingered. But after hundreds more steps, they smelled smoke again. The lead walker directed them up a ridge, and the group followed slowly and cautiously, looking for any sheen from rocks on the ground in the moonlight.

The leader with the low voice had yet to face them on this nighttime saunter. But as they ascended the slight incline, he looked over his shoulder to observe the line snaking behind him. He stood about half a head shorter than Evan and slighter in build, but exerted a commanding presence. He glanced back up to the crest and commanded them to wait while he continued to the top, where he paused to gaze upon something. He turned back to the group and ordered them forward. "Aambe."

On the other side of the hill, a small fire flickered a few hundred metres away. It burned in the middle of a wide clearing, and as they descended through the short trees that lined the small range, Nangohns noticed the dark outlines of a few buildings on the far side of the fire. They blended into the shadows of the treeline, making their size and number impossible to make out. Four figures sat on chairs around the fire.

"Stay behind me," the man in front said clearly. "And don't say anything until you're asked."

Nangohns slowed her steps and inhaled smoothly to temper her anxious excitement. The flames ahead grew larger and brighter. A low hum of discussion resounded from the small circle at the fire, but she couldn't decipher the words or make out any faces.

"Ndagshinmi," their guide called to the group ahead. Their heads all turned towards the approaching outsiders. "Ngii-mkawaanaanik," he added.

"Hooo," responded a woman's low voice. All four at the fire stood to face the arrivals.

Nangohns peered around Tyler for a better look. An older woman with grey hair and narrow eyes tucked her hands into the pouch of her hooded sweatshirt, emblazoned with *York University* in white embroidered letters. A taller, middle-aged woman stood to the right. Nangohns noticed the long, straight braids that draped down the front of her white T-shirt. Her big brown eyes flickered in the firelight, under a thick brow. Two younger people flanked her on either side, one a young man with braids and broad, thick shoulders in an old red basketball jersey. The fourth person's long black hair concealed the sides of their face, and their light-blue hoodie bulked up their torso atop torn jeans.

Their faces were impassive but not unwelcoming. There was a softness in their eyes that contrasted with the tightness in their lips.

When she saw them draw near, the woman in the varsity sweatshirt smiled widely. "Oh, boozhoo ndanwendaagnak," she said, more jovially than the monotone of her initial acknowledgement. "Aaniish ezhi-bimaadziyek?" She welcomed them, calling them relatives and asking how they were doing.

Nangohns didn't want to hesitate. "Mino bimaadis," she replied. She heard her voice waver as the last syllable left her throat.

"Oh, nishin!" The woman seemed pleased.

The three who had led them there now moved to the other side of the fire, and the leader moved in close to say something to the older woman. Her eyes remained trained on the group, but something he said dimmed her smile. She seemed to catch herself, and grinned amiably again, but this time it seemed slightly exaggerated. The messenger finished speaking and pivoted to face the group. The glow of the fire lit his acutely defined face, which settled into a serious scowl of thick, downturned eyebrows and pursed, fleshy lips.

Nangohns clasped her hands in front of her, and Evan sidestepped closer to her to let their shoulders touch. The others kept their hands at their sides. They awaited more queries in Anishinaabemowin.

"We've been waiting for you," the older woman said with a smile. "We knew you'd be coming someday."

The English was jarring, but a relief.

"Maajaak maampii," she continued. "Come closer to the fire. You must be cold and tired. Come, please."

Nangohns glanced at Evan as he moved forward. The others shuffled along with him. Their hosts tightened together on the far side of the fire to make room. The faces of the other two who had guided them to this place were still concealed in the shadows. On their side, the travellers huddled closer together for warmth.

"You've come a long way," said the grey-haired woman— apparently the leader of this small crew. She inspected all five from head to foot. "You should be proud of yourselves."

She craned her neck to direct an order over her shoulder. "Nbi," she said. She turned back to the group. "Here, have some water. You need it."

The taller, slightly younger woman took a step back and crouched down to a large black pot at the edge of the fire circle. She raised two copper mugs into the light, and the light of the flames danced off their shiny surfaces. She dipped them into the pot, and the young man in the basketball jersey walked over to help. He grabbed the cups and delivered them to Amber and Nangohns. They each offered a whispered "Miigwech," and he returned to the pot to get two more mugs for Cal and Tyler, and then a last one for Evan. They all sipped at first, and then swiftly downed the cold liquid. Nangohns could feel it rushing into her belly, and she felt immediately refreshed. She closed her eyes as she finished, relief washing over her.

"Diindiisiikwe ndizhnikaaz," the woman continued. "But if I speak to you in this way, you can call me Linda. That's how I was known before, when I lived in the city, in that other world. But even before that, when I was a little girl in my community, I was called Diindiisii. My grandmother saw a blue jay the winter my mother was pregnant with me. It came to her window every day, all winter long. When I was born in the spring, she gave me that name, because that blue jay, that diindiisii, was still there."

"Hoooo," vocalized the scowling young man beside her.

"Anyway, there'll be lots of time for getting to know us and our names. But please, tell me about you. And then we'll proceed here."

Evan introduced himself in the old language as best he could, even without an Anishinaabe name. He switched to English almost immediately and shared the names of his fellow walkers and their relationships with each other. "We left our home at the start of summer, almost a month ago. There were six of us—" he started, but Linda raised her hand to stop him.

"You can tell us all about your travels tomorrow," she assured them. For now, they should rest.

As their hosts turned to lead the way, Cal's curiosity got the better of him, and he blurted out a stream of questions.

"How many people are here? Are there other spots like this? How did you—"

Amber swiftly elbowed him in the side, hissing at him to shut up.

Linda's chest heaved gently as she chuckled. "My boy, there'll be lots of time for all of that," she repeated. "We'll show you around. But tonight, you need to rest. Biiyen here will take you to your bunks for the night."

She gestured at the short man with the booming voice who had briefed her on their arrival. Biiyen nodded, now with a slightly more affable expression. His brow looked permanently furrowed, though, making him a little more difficult to read than the others.

"Sleep as much as you need to," Linda continued. "Don't worry about getting up for sunrise. We'll give thanks for your journey on your behalf. You just sleep. We'll have breakfast for you as soon as you get up. And I think . . ." She paused to scan the five worn walkers again. "I think you'll need a sweat."

They all nodded their heads, out of sync. Nangohns felt her face flush with emotion.

"Miigwech," Evan responded, his voice cracking.

"Okay, good. And then we'll talk."

Linda closed her eyes and held her palms up to them. "Biiyen can take you to the cabin now. Sleep well, my relatives."

Biiyen raised his chin to acknowledge them, and gently tilted his head to his right shoulder, signalling them to follow. He walked in stride with Evan at first, and then moved ahead in a straight line from the fire to lead them to a small, darkened structure with a pitched roof. Its cream vinyl-sided outside walls were barely visible in the light of the fire, and as their eyes adjusted to the dark, the structure seemed lifeless and hollow. Biiyen arrived at the wooden front steps and waited for the others to gather.

"Okay, watch your step here," he said. "There's three coming up onto the porch."

He ascended the small staircase and opened the front door to the cabin. "Just wait outside for a second," he commanded. They watched him disappear into the darkness, and then heard scratchy flicks that caused small flashes of light from inside. After a few attempts, a tiny orange light faintly brightened the room behind him.

"Biindigek." His low voice echoed off the wooden walls. "Come on in."

Two sets of bunk beds nestled against the long far wall, and each shorter wall housed another set, for eight beds in total. Each bunk was made neatly with pillows, sheets, and wool blankets. The room contained little else, just a table on the near side, next to the door, with a thick yellow candle sitting on a plate in the middle and a small cigarette lighter lying beside it.

"Make yourselves at home!" Biiyen pronounced, and in the candlelight, they saw him smile for the first time. "I guess the young ones are gonna fight for the top bunks, eh?"

"Man, I'm too tired to climb all the way up there," said Cal. "Those old farts can have it!"

Tired laughter escaped their lungs. Even Biiyen seemed fatigued after a long day of tracking out and back.

"So I guess you're the joker of the bunch, eh?" he said.

"Nah, he just doesn't shut up," said Tyler. "Good thing you're the only people we've seen so far. He woulda gave us away a long time ago."

"Well—" Biiyen began, but then stopped himself. They all watched him and waited for his next words. He changed course. "It's late now. I gotta head back home. We'll leave some water on the steps for you after we shut everything down. Make sure you blow out that candle when you're ready to sleep."

Biiyen walked out the door and closed it behind him. It latched shut, a click none of the five inside had heard in a long time. They stood in a circle, stunned that they had indeed connected with survivors, and had been welcomed into their company and community. Nangohns saw disbelief in Evan's downcast eyes, and even she was struggling to accept this was all real.

FOURTEEN

A DENSE WHITE LIGHT beamed into the cabin through the rectangular window. Nangohns opened her eyes and raised herself upright on the bunk. She let her bare feet lower to the unfinished plywood floor. Her thick, callused soles probed the rough grain, and she stuck out her toes, feeling for round knots and cold nail heads. She tiptoed so as not to disturb the others.

She froze at the door, peering out at the empty field they'd come from the night before. The door hinges creaked, and Nangohns looked over her shoulder to check on the others, but they all lay still. She opened the door enough to squeeze through and shimmied out onto the porch. On the right, their five backpacks were lined up neatly beside each other, resting against the railing. A large black pot covered with a metal lid sat to the left of the door, with five copper mugs spread around it. Nangohns squatted down to lift off the lid and dipped in one of the shiny red cups. She stood to straighten her insides and poured the clear, cool water into her mouth. In four quick gulps the cup was empty, and drops streamed from the corners of her mouth and down her neck. She crouched again to refill her cup, drank, and refilled again. It tasted different from the

171

lake water she was used to on their journey. The liquid felt crisp and pure in her mouth and throat. It reminded her of the water they boiled and cooled back home. But it tasted somehow cleaner.

With her thirst quenched, she was able to focus on her surroundings. She looked to her left to see a compound of buildings, bigger than the one they'd slept in, but built in much the same way. They were basic cabins and homes with metal roofs, covered in various colours and shades of vinyl siding. She counted six structures from where she stood, but thought there were likely more behind the others.

Nothing stirred around her. Either everyone was still asleep, or the entire community was elsewhere—likely the sunrise ceremony Linda had mentioned the night before. Nangohns looked up to the grey sky, which didn't threaten rain or otherwise unsettled weather but blanketed them from the sun all the same. She bent to the water pot again and filled the rest of the copper mugs to bring inside for the others.

She found Evan sitting up in his bunk, talking to Amber. Soon they were all up, sipping the water and shaking off the daze of sleep. Evan got up to help Nangohns bring the packs inside.

"When I woke up, I thought I was still dreaming," Tyler said. "You know when your eyes open in a weird place and you kinda panic a bit? And then I remembered I was in a bed. I thought, there's no way this can be real."

"I'm still wondering if this is real," said Amber. "When I was a girl, when the blackout happened, I had the weirdest dreams. I remember not being sure what was real life and what was a dream. Now I'm having that feeling again."

A familiar low voice boomed from outside. "Gshkozik!" Biiyen called through the wall. They heard his feet stomp up the wooden stairs, and his familiar hardened brow appeared in the door window. He mockingly knocked on the door and stuck out his tongue, then opened the door and walked inside. "Do people still do that?" he asked. "Knock on doors and shit?"

"I dunno," replied Cal. "Hardly any doors where we're from."

"Didn't see many doors up there in the city, either," said Evan.

"Yeah, I noticed that too, last time I was up that way," said Biiyen.

He told them he had been up through Gibson two years ago, and had found the place as abandoned as they had. When Cal wondered aloud where all the people had gone, Biiyen pulled in his lips and scratched the back of his head.

"We'll talk about all that," he said. "Let's get you guys fed. Breakfast is ready."

He bounded down the stairs and went left, to the cluster of buildings Nangohns had spotted on her venture outside moments earlier. Noting that Biiyen was barefoot, they had also left their shoes off, and as they walked through the shin-high grass, the hardy green blades caught between their toes. Biiyen led them to what Nangohns had to assume was the largest building in the compound, two storeys high, with dark-blue siding.

"That's our gathering hall. For meetings and special occasions, especially in winter. We'll feed you in there." His tone was much more amiable than it had been the evening before, when he had escorted them in single file into the camp. "We'll give you more of a tour later. It's probably been a while since you ate, eh?" he asked them all.

"Yeah, we definitely lost track of time yesterday," Cal noted. "Aapji go nbakade!"

173

Biiyen chuckled at Cal's attempt at Anishinaabemowin. "You guys speak a bit, eh? That's good."

"The younger ones better than us," Evan said from the back.

"Well, you should know that's generally all we speak here. But we'll make a . . . how do you say that?"

"An exception?"

"Yeah, we'll make an exception for you guys while you're here. It's been a long time since I used that word!"

They reached the front of the blue building, and Biiyen led them up the few wooden stairs to a wide front deck. The building's two large picture windows reflected the full green leaves of the oak and maple trees it faced. They were soon entering a large, well-lit open space fully outfitted with furniture and artwork on the walls. The air smelled of burning sage.

Linda, sitting at the head of a large wooden dining table, stretched out her arms to welcome the group. Her grey hair was tied back in a ponytail, and her jowls tightened as she smiled. "Biindigek!" she called. "Aaniish gaa-nangwaamek? How did you sleep?"

All five ambled in and huddled together humbly, holding their hands in front of them. Biiyen went back outside.

"Please, come in," Linda said, indicating an arrangement of folding chairs around the central table. "Namadabik."

Evan peered up at the vibrant paintings hung on the finished drywall, mostly in the Woodland Ojibwe style of the Anishinaabe artists who had risen to prominence when his parents were kids. The radiant colours and thick black outlines of the animals, people, and spirits were unmistakable. Along the walls also hung drums of various sizes, from the big grandfather drum of the powwow to disc-like personal hand drums. A wooden staircase on the right led up to a loft that hung over the downstairs space. The pitched ceiling was lined with yellow wooden planks, and provided a steady echo for every sound that came from the floor.

On the far side of the main floor was a kitchen of sorts. The taller woman who had stood beside Linda the night before moved along a counter, preparing something with her back turned to them. The counter was bookended by a sink and a cooking stove, and was lined with drawers and white cupboards underneath. The cabinets above the counter were light blue, and aside from a slight discolouration, the whole ensemble looked almost like a kitchen from the before times. Evan caught himself staring at the amenities, and joined the others to sit.

"It ain't all pretty, but it's what we got," said Linda, waving her arms around the room. "You guys hungry?"

"Yeah, pretty hungry." Cal was again the first to respond.

Linda laughed. "I bet. A young man like you still needs to eat a lot."

He glanced down at the varnished tabletop in slight embarrassment.

"It's okay, my boy," she laughed again. "Melissa will bring some food over to you. You guys eat pike?"

Everyone around the table nodded.

"Good. Back in the old days, some of those fancy people down south were too good to eat pike. But holy geez, that's all we ate back on the rez when I was a little girl! Can't be picky when the pickin's are slim, my mama always used to say."

The boards under the vinyl flooring creaked as Melissa walked barefoot to the table. She lowered two plates in front of Evan and Nangohns, on Linda's left. They looked down to see the glass dishes fully loaded with fried filets of fish beside brown potato cubes and raw apple slices. Evan's mouth flooded with saliva. Nangohns inhaled the fishy, oily, warm aroma.

175

The walkers, unable to suppress their hunger any longer, dug their forks into the flakes of the pike immediately, shoving the greasy meat into their mouths. Forks clinked on the glass plates as Linda looked on.

"What, you don't say grace where you're from?" she scoffed.

All five froze. Evan slapped his fork down on the table harder than he had intended to. "We're really sorry," he mumbled, with a mouth full of fish and potatoes.

Linda scowled around the table, and only Evan and Tyler would meet her gaze.

"Ha ha, got youse!" she bellowed after a few mortifying seconds of silence, throwing her head back in laughter.

Nangohns exhaled and dropped her shoulders in relief.

"We don't say that shit around here, either. Don't worry. That god died a long time ago. Go on, eat."

While they ate, Linda went over the itinerary for the day. After breakfast, they'd rest again for a little while, and then Biiyen would come get them when the sweat lodge was ready. Later in the day, when the ceremony was complete, they'd hold a community welcoming feast. That's when they'd meet everyone else. And then they'd have time to talk. About everything.

"Diindiisiikwe," Evan said, after his last bite of fresh apple had been swallowed. "Can I ask you something?"

"Yes, my boy," she replied. "Please, go ahead."

"Last night, when you said you were waiting for us, what did you mean?"

She sighed and leaned back in her chair. She crossed her arms over her black T-shirt. "I know what you're asking, Evan. They're not here."

Evan's heart sank. Isaiah's and Kevin's faces had been living in his mind since they had stumbled upon the traces of their old friends. "When they weren't here last night—" he began.

"We haven't seen them for a long time," Linda interrupted. "They left to go south after the winter melt."

"When?" Evan asked, giving voice to the question on his companions' minds.

"They came in the fall and stayed through the winter, musta been four years ago. But we'll talk more about that later. You guys need to sweat first."

In her periphery, Nangohns saw her father look down at his plate. His sadness was palpable. Across the table, Tyler bowed his head as well. She realized that he must have been holding out hope that he'd find his younger brother, Kevin, somewhere on this quest. Cal, meanwhile, was masking the sorrow of missing his older brother, Isaiah, much better. She felt a pang of sympathy for these men. Her curiosity—her wildest hopes—about what they might find down here paled in comparison to their ongoing heartbreak.

Melissa came back from the kitchen and whispered in Linda's ear.

"The grandfathers are in the fire," Linda said, referring to the rocks that would heat the sweat lodge. "It won't be too long before they're ready. In the meantime, we'll sit in here and visit for a little while, okay?"

They all nodded, trying to shake off the sadness.

"We'll give you a good look around later. Right now, we wanna make sure everyone else knows you're here. There might be some lazy asses still sleeping that don't know you showed up last night. Can you believe, even after the end of the world, some of these goddamn Indians are still expecting handouts?" She shook her head sarcastically.

Linda's affectionate teasing reminded Nangohns of Walter and her grandfather, Dan. While the jokes seemed harsh at first, the elderly joshing was familiar, and helped her relax in this new setting with strangers. Linda was warm and welcoming, yet still commanded considerable respect from the people they'd seen interacting with her.

"Anyway . . ." she went on. "As you've probably noticed, we speak Anishinaabemowin here. And that's important for you to know. That was the whole idea behind building this Saswin, this nest, when we first started dreaming it up some twenty years ago. Almost everyone still knows English, except the kids. The littlest ones have never really heard it. So keep that in mind when you're out and about. You won't be shamed here for speaking English. But next time you come for a visit, no excuses." She winked and smiled at them all.

Evan explained that it was what they wanted for their community, when they built it. They wanted everyone to learn Anishinaabemowin, but most of their language speakers hadn't survived long after the blackout.

"You tried, my boy," said Linda. "You tried. Don't forget, it's a special blessing that we're all here today. We've made it longer than most, as far as we know."

"As far as you know?" interjected Cal.

"Geez, this guy!" Linda proclaimed, pointing her thumb at him in disbelief. "Cool your heels!" She cackled again.

"Sorry, he just doesn't have a filter," Amber said, embarrassed.

"I guess they stopped making filters when all the lights went out." Linda waved her hand reassuringly. "Don't worry, my boy. We'll tell you what we know, like I said. Now, where was I?" She squeezed her eyes shut and pressed her fingers to her forehead. "Oh yeah. About us."

Linda had grown up on the rez at Baawaating, where the two cities with the same name straddled the old border on the river called Saint Marys. Her parents had been stolen to residential school when they were kids. They weren't around much when she was a little girl, and she was raised by her noo-komis, who hid her in the woodshed when the white people came to steal her to that school.

"They musta forgot about me after a piece," said Linda, "because they never came back."

She grew up learning the language, going to ceremonies, but did well in her studies and went to university in Toronto, becoming a professor. She'd lived in the white world for almost thirty years, although she still went home regularly.

"I lived at my nookomis's house after she died. As I got older, the less I wanted to stay down there in the city. I think it was about twenty years ago or so, me and Melissa here started talking about making a language and culture camp." She twisted in her chair to acknowledge the taller and slightly younger woman now doing dishes at the counter.

"We worked together at the university," Linda went on. "She grew up in the city, but her mom was from one of the reserves on the north shore. Anyway, she can tell you her life story when she has time. We started saving up our own money, and fundraising too. We were originally going to make it like a land-based learning project through the university. 'Come to the bush and learn real Anishinaabe ways and get your master's degree at the same time' was the idea. Kinda funny, because any degree is obviously totally useless now. Anyway, every sum-mer we built a new cabin—"

"How did you get all the materials up here?" Tyler cut in. "Aren't we pretty much in the middle of nowhere?"

"Good question," said Linda, giving Tyler a wink. She explained that there used to be an old logging road just south of there. They had to clear a new trail coming north of that road to bring things in by truck.

"It took a while, and then getting all the stuff in here was a grind too. That's one of the reasons why we call it Saswin, or the nest, because we brought in the pieces a little at a time, just like a bineshii does when it makes a nest."

"We used a four-wheeler to get the stuff in on that bush trail," said Melissa, catching Tyler's eye.

"That's why we only did one cabin a year," explained Linda. "Then we did a couple greenhouses. A few other structures too, like this big gathering space, a smokehouse, a hide house, a medicine house. You'll see all that later."

"If there was a road and a trail, how did no one find you here?" asked Evan.

"Well, that's part of the other talk we'll have this afternoon. When it looked like things weren't going back to normal, we covered them up as best we could. Cut trees down. Pushed big rocks in the way. We had to hide out and keep a low profile for a while. That highway you came down on? That was the main escape route from the city up there. We built all this up over time. And we always knew it would be our hideout whenever the shit hit the fan. We just didn't expect that to happen so soon. But here we are. And here you are."

The front door creaked open, and Biiyen stepped into the room, closing the door behind him. He declared that the grandfathers should be just about ready.

"Good!" exclaimed Linda. "We'll get you all ready. Mel, can you get these guys some stuff to sweat in?"

Melissa turned from the kitchen and went to the staircase on the right side of the room to ascend to the loft, returning a few moments later with a stack of clothes and towels.

"They're all clean, just take what you need. And if you wanna get real fancy, we got some old robes kicking around too."

"Miigwech," said Evan, and the others murmured the same.

They took turns rummaging through the old, threadbare clothing and choosing what looked like it would fit. Having soaked sweat through her own cotton T-shirt and nylon shorts for several days in a row, Nangohns was relieved to peel off the layer.

"We'll wash and hang those for you," Melissa said. "And Biiyen will take you back to your cabin after the sweat to change again. We can wash everything else you brought after that. We make soap here."

Biiyen led them out of the building, down the stairs, and around the back. The yard opened onto another small clearing flanked by pine and spruce trees, whose orange needles softened the ground. In the middle stood a short structure covered with green canvas. Tending a fire at the eastern opening of the lodge were two young people, whom Biiyen introduced as Maang and Waagosh. Nangohns recalled Waagosh—slightly shorter than Maang and with lighter hair—from the small group that had welcomed them the night before. As they walked towards the lodge, the two youths said only "Aanii" and continued pushing around the burning logs, from which they'd eventually retrieve the glowing orange rocks.

The walkers placed their towels in a pile on the ground away from the fire, and Biiyen led them clockwise around it and towards the eastern entrance of the lodge. They stood in front of it for a few moments, under the overcast sky and in the steady grey smoke of the large blaze, which peaked at nearly eye level. Linda and Melissa soon arrived, and they all lined up in front of the entrance according to who would sit where on the inside. Biiyen led them in, followed by Evan and Nangohns, then Linda, who would sit at the western doorway. Tyler, Cal, and Amber went in after her. Melissa was the last inside.

When they were settled, Nangohns peered out through the low open flap and watched Maang stick a pitchfork into the fire and pull out a glowing orange stone slightly larger than a man's fist. Bright white sparks jumped from the incandescent rock as it bounced along the tines. Pivoting slowly to face the lodge, Maang guided the hot grandfather through the open flap and down into a round pit dug in the ground at the centre of the circle.

As the radiant stone landed, they all murmured "Oh, boozhoo mishoomis," and Biiyen threw a pinch of tobacco and some cedar onto it, the medicine crackling in the darkness. When Maang had brought in six more grandfather stones, they were ready to commence the ceremony. He pulled down the flap and tucked it tight to the ground, sealing them inside.

For the rest of the morning and into the early afternoon, songs resounded within the tarp to the hollow beat of a water drum, while the fire outside crackled and burned. More red-hot stones were fed inside at intervals, and copper buckets of water were passed in for regular refills.

The ceremony was nearly complete when the rain came, softly pattering against the roof of the lodge. Maang and Waagosh continued to feed chopped logs to the fire to keep it burning hot and high. Eventually, the clouds above broke, and the afternoon sun beamed down upon the ceremonial hollow. When the participants emerged, it was into the bright light of a clear day.

FIFTEEN

AFTER THE CEREMONY, BIIYEN led the walkers back to
their cabin to dress. Nangohns hadn't felt so refreshed in weeks.
There were virtually no mirrors back home at the new village,
but a small one hung on the wall of their guest cabin, and she
caught herself staring at her reflection, combing her clean dark
hair and inspecting her deeply tanned skin and pronounced
cheekbones. She and her companions were noticeably leaner
than they had been when they left home. Even after their bountiful meal that morning, the promise of the feast ahead made
her stomach rumble. Standing in front of her reflection, for the
first time in her life, Nangohns considered what she must look
like to the many strangers she was about to meet.

Once dressed, they made their way from their small cabin
on the outskirts of the permanent camp through a now bustling
community to the gathering space at the centre of the settlement. The sound of voices swelled into a cacophony as they
approached. After their weeks in the bush and along the dead
highways, it was the sound of life restored.

Fried whitefish, corn, and squash roasted on grills over
open fires. Blankets had been laid out in the arbour, and as the
descending sun pierced the clouds, children seemed everywhere

underfoot, scattered throughout the settlement, playing games in the humid summer air.

Several dozen people met them in the gathering space, standing around the freshly cooked food spread out on the blankets. Most of the adults looked about the same age as Evan and Tyler. Among them were a handful of people with grey hair, roughly the same age as Linda. The rest were much younger, either teens or young children, energetic and talkative, all chattering in the old language. Two little girls skittered up to Nangohns to get a better look, pausing briefly to smile at her before darting away.

They were led to a blanket by the fire, and the din of conversation dwindled and went silent. Linda greeted each of the walkers before turning to the crowd to introduce Evan, Nangohns, Tyler, Amber, and Cal in Anishinaabemowin. She then offered a prayer of thanks to the Creator and Mother Earth for the food, and prepared a small dish for the spirits. At the conclusion of her brief opening, she encouraged everyone to eat, and the young ones came forward to prepare plates for the elders. Nangohns thought she recognized the two children they had seen in the field the day before, only because of the slight trepidation they conveyed at first. But she could feel them warming up to these newcomers, who after all looked a lot like their own kin.

They sat on the grass and ate. The fish felt soft and tasted sweet in Nangohns's mouth. It had been carefully fried in duck fat in frying pans on the grill over the open fire and on the wood-fired stove in the kitchen. The brown and grey wild rice was soft and chewy, and tasted of home. The squash and corn balanced everything out, and she felt the fresh food settle comfortably in her belly.

Throughout the meal, several people approached to introduce themselves. Some offered basic introductions and greetings in the old language—of which Nangohns understood the fundamentals but frequently had to apologize and say "Gaawii-nnistat-zii" and repeat in English "I don't understand."

A stout boy who had come up to Cal and Amber ambled over to Nangohns to ask about their home and the lakes up north. He was younger than she was by a few years, but said he remembered living on a big lake down south, and Nangohns wanted to ask if it had a name, but a pretty girl with blue eyes cut in. She had been told that Nangohns hunted with a bow and arrow, and wanted to learn how to shoot. She said she had grown up in Toronto, the vast city in the southeast, a place Nangohns had never seen but had heard about her whole life.

The children swirled around Nangohns, Cal, and Amber while the older folks gravitated towards Evan and Tyler, who stayed close to Linda and Biiyen. The elder and the young man seemed to take responsibility for their guests' comfort in the strange new circumstances. Before long, Nangohns had met dozens of new faces.

The people of Saswin, they were learning, came from an array of backgrounds and locales, but the majority had grown up on reserves within driving distance of the cities and bigger towns of northern Ontario, to the southwest and southeast of here. There was a diversity of complexions amongst the group, from Black to freckled, but one common bond was clear, as hinted by Linda in their earlier chats: everyone was Anishinaabe.

Nangohns noticed her father chatting—as best he could in broken Anishinaabemowin—with some of the older men who reminded her of her grandfather and Walter. Evan's eyes caught hers, and he made a quick grimace as if to say "Help!" But it soon loosened into a softly mystified smile. It was hard to believe what they had found.

———

When the plates were cleared, a group of singers stood to offer a song, after which the gathering slowly broke up. Most of the crowd returned to their cabins or scattered about the compound to enjoy the setting sun. Nangohns deduced that visitors were rare but not unknown, and these kinds of gatherings weren't as novel to the people of Saswin as they were to the five newcomers.

Biiyen started a fire in the pit at the centre of the arbour. The grey smoke pumped up through the evergreen boughs that sheltered the circle. Two stacks of six folding chairs rested against either side of one of the arbour pillars, and he began unfolding and placing them around the fire. Linda walked over to take a seat, and the rest followed.

They circled the fire, which burned higher and hotter by the second. Biiyen began to feed bigger logs into it. A modest gathering now surrounded the blaze, including the five walkers from the north, Linda, Melissa, Biiyen, and the two others who had helped guide them out of the bush the day before, whose names they learned were Shkaabewis and Sage. Nangohns remembered Shkaabewis's broad shoulders in the darkness, but daylight revealed Sage's features for the first time. Their long, loose hair had cloaked their face the night before, but now it was pulled back in a braid, revealing dark eyes. They lofted a warm, toothy grin in Nangohns's direction as the newcomers sat.

Linda said a few words in the old language before settling into English. "Well, we're happy to have you here," she began. "It's been a while since we've seen anyone else. In fact, your friends were the last people we met. And they left a long time ago."

Nangohns realized that this, finally, was the time to talk and ask questions. She looked at her father and saw his shoulders and jaw relaxing.

"So they were here for a while, then?" asked Evan.

"They came just as the leaves were turning," Linda replied. "Biiyen and Shkaabewis here had taken another scouting mission out to the highway and saw them walking down. They brought them here for a rest that turned out to last a whole winter."

"I think they got used to sleeping in beds again," joked Biiyen. "They helped out a lot, though," he added. "Hunted all fall. Snared rabbits and drilled holes in the ice to fish in the winter. We were sad to see them go in the spring."

"Did they say where they were going?" asked Tyler eagerly. "They must have said something."

"They wanted to keep going south," Linda replied. "We advised against it. We want you to know that. We told them to go back home to you guys first, and then come back in another year with more of you."

"They must have marked that trail on the way out," said Tyler, looking at Evan.

"We advised against that too," admitted Biiyen. "But they thought youse would eventually come looking for them, and I guess they wanted you to find us. They were like kin to us, so we let the trail be."

"I had forgotten all about it," said Linda. "But I guess it did its job."

Linda gave Biiyen a sideways glance that made Nangohns think the trail left by Kevin and Isaiah was something the two of them had debated many times.

Looking back at Evan, and then to each of the walkers in turn, Linda continued, "Those two boys, your relatives, had questions that we didn't have answers to. We saw a lot of trouble pass down that highway in the bad old days, had to deal with trouble out here too. It's been quiet the last few years, and maybe we've let our guard down—that one would certainly say so." She indicated Biiyen, who barely acknowledged the jape, but Nangohns could see him almost imperceptibly roll his eyes. "But its hard to think back on the suffering that rolled through here, and the things that some men can do."

She paused, and everyone stared into the fire. Tyler stirred in his seat, but before he could ask anything else, Linda began again. "So, from what Izzy and Kevin told us, you all were literally left in the dark, eh?"

"Yeah." Evan exhaled out his response. "We have no idea what happened. You're the first people we've seen—the first living people we've seen—in about twelve years."

"Hmmm," she replied, and looked deeply into the fire. "Well, as they used to say in the university halls, we have a hypothesis. We saw some of it go down. And we've put this all together from stories we heard from everybody here and some of the ones who passed through."

She turned to look directly at Evan and Tyler. "Did you guys see northern lights, bigger than normal, just before everything went out?"

"I . . . I can't remember," Evan said. "We see them all the time back home."

"Well, that's okay, because I don't remember, either," Linda said. "Mel and Sage and I were actually up here when all that happened. We were getting ready to spend the rest of the winter here. Back in those days, we got cell reception here, because we're close enough to the highway, and we're not as far north as you guys. When the cell service went down, at first it didn't seem like that big of a deal. But after a couple of days we knew something was up. And then, a few weeks after that, Biiyen arrived with a group, including his brother Shkaabewis there. They'd been living in N'Swakamok—that was a big mining city. Used to be called Sudbury too."

Biiyen took his cue. "There were reports about really intense northern lights all over the world. I remember seeing it on the news that night, all these pictures and videos of skies all lit up. And people on the news kept saying how weird it was to see really wild northern lights, even down south. Like, even in the tropics they had them. But then over the next couple days, the cellphones went down, and then the power went out. Word got around that those northern lights had something to do with it. Some kind of storm in the upper atmosphere that knocked out satellites and messed up power transformers and everything else that relied on any kind of network. We waited for everything to come back on, but people in the city started losing their minds. Looting stores at first, but soon they were raiding other people's houses."

Cal cast a conspicuous glance at the other walkers, and Nangohns remembered the torn-up homes near Gibson.

"Everything was totally messed up," continued Biiyen. "The gas pumps didn't work. The police in N'Swakamok and some local government types held a few public meetings in the first couple weeks and tried to organize aid. The army drove through a few times. Only their older vehicles worked—ones that didn't need computers to run. But after a while, the government was nowhere to be seen, and no one had any way to send out messages. Then the big snow came, burying everything. Generators lasted for a few weeks, but pretty soon electric heat was useless and people started to die. So we got the fuck out of there."

"After Biiyen and that crew got here"—Linda picked up the story—"a few more started coming up over the next little while. That was always our plan. We didn't all live in the same place, but we had a network, mostly along the north shore there. We waited out the winter. There were only twenty-five of

189

us here back then. We had enough food and supplies to last us for a while. And all these buildings were already outfitted for us to actually live here. Not just in the summer. We had water filtration—big cisterns, which you probably saw on the way in. All the gardening and farming gear we'd need. We originally thought we'd just wait until the snow melted, then go back down to the cities and the reserves to see what was going on. But then the rest came to us in the spring. They walked through the mud and cold, but they made it. And they told us about all the horrors of the end of that world. The total collapse of the governments after many failed attempts to restore order. The destruction of homes and buildings. The fires. The murders, and the roving gangs of the desperate and hungry. And the sickness too. Colds and flus that were usually treatable in winter tore through homes and communities. Not everyone survived."

She paused again, letting the memory resonate with the others and then fade. The fire crackled, and the squeals and shouts of children playing into the night echoed over to them.

"It was around then we started hearing about radiation sickness," Linda resumed. "With no power and no government, the power plants farther south and east couldn't be maintained. We never got a clear picture, but something toxic got into the air and then into the land and water. For kilometres around. Because the land was sick, everything that grew got sick and died too, and the dust from dead fields blew around with the weather, poisoning everything. Folks passed through here trying to get away from it all. Some took sick and died here. Some got well enough to move on, but we ain't heard from them since."

"When your boys got here, it had been years since we'd encountered anyone, and we checked them over for signs of contamination," noted Biiyen. "When the poison gets you, you carry it on your skin, in your hair and clothes."

"Why didn't you check us?" blurted Cal.

Evan turned to Cal and put out a hand as if to silence him, before turning back to Biiyen, the same question written across his face.

"We were confident you were coming in from up north and hadn't walked through any of the dead lands," Biiyen said matter-of-factly.

"Plus, any contamination that you could have passed on should have been washed out when you sweated," added Melissa.

"You all looked healthy enough, anyway," Linda continued. "By the time you two got here, we hadn't seen much of anything in a long time. We'd covered up the trails in, and certainly didn't go looking for no one at that point, but we guess a lot of folks either found their way south, to god knows what, or got sick and died."

"All those people," murmured Amber. She looked like she was going to crumple right there.

Nangohns wanted to remind them of the map in Gibson and the strange red scrawl, but she couldn't find the nerve to interject.

"Did anybody else come and find you?" asked Tyler. "Like, anyone you wish hadn't?"

"Yes," Linda replied flatly. "There were three different visits that first summer and fall. We think the first ones found us because of the fires we had going. They saw the smoke from us cooking and smoking stuff, and came off the highway into the bush. They were a couple—a man and a woman, zhaagnaashak, probably in their thirties. They wanted to get down south to find family. We let them stay here a few days to rest. Then they left, and that was it."

Later on in the summer, Biiyen said, an older man came through, walking in the opposite direction. He had an old map of the logging roads, and they assumed that was how he had found them, even though they had tried to cover that trail. "He was one of those survival types," explained Biiyen, "all in camo and with a big knife—everything. Big, tall guy with a long beard. He seemed pretty off, but we outnumbered him. We offered him some food, and he stuck around to eat.

"The guy was talking like a mile a minute, telling all kinds of crazy stories. He wouldn't say exactly where he was from, but it sounded like he was in a city for the blackout and those first few months. He was talking about the government losing control, and gang lords taking over. He said he'd even heard about nuclear meltdowns at the power plants down there in southern Ontario, and that the main reason he was going north was to escape the radiation."

The map on the wall at Gibson's city hall flashed once again in Nangohns's mind.

In the fall, Biiyen continued, a pair of men passed through, cutting through the bush with large-headed dogs.

"What happened with them?" asked Tyler.

"We did what you did in the same situation," declared Linda.

She looked Tyler sternly in the eyes, which was all she needed to convey her meaning. But Evan noticed Biiyen staring at Linda, expectant, as if waiting for her to disclose more.

"The mood here changed for a while after that" was all she said.

The following winter was quiet, Biiyen told them, until the late spring, when a trio of men, also outfitted in survival gear, stumbled into the clearing at the southern edge of the Saswin encampment. "To this day, I have no idea how they found us," he said. "But luckily Shkaabewis saw them approach, and we headed them off at the bottom of that hill we led you down when you got here."

As Biiyen described it, they were hard cases, like the several who had come before, but these men had oozing red sores on their faces. They talked in between deep, hoarse coughs, and were clearly suffering from some kind of illness.

"They had guns and they drew on us," Shkaabewis cut in.

"So we did what we had to," Linda asserted.

"If you come across men like that, and I hope you don't, stay away," warned Biiyen. "And if you have to do what we did, leave their bodies where they fall and get out of there."

There was a heavy lull, and then Linda spoke again. "Since then, we've mostly kept to ourselves. We've been careful about going out too far in case we somehow give away our position. But some of these guys went to scout things out here and there." She pointed to Biiyen and Shkaabewis, but they didn't volunteer anything further.

Nangohns's mind raced. Answers to her questions had only raised more questions, and it seemed clear that death had wiped away any chance of knowing for sure what had really happened. Everything she had wondered about Zhaawnong was becoming clearer and muddier at the same time.

"That's enough for now," concluded Linda. "It's important to remember, though, that some things we don't know for sure. We don't know what else is out there, because we haven't really left our home. Some of what we saw on that highway and some of what found us here spooked us, so we've stayed cautious. I've had dreams, though. Dreams about the dangers still out there. The people who are still around, surviving by any means necessary. I have not seen them. I have no proof. But I believe they are out there. There's no way the whole world died off. I mean, here you are."

She paused and cued Melissa with a nod. The younger woman stood from her spot and walked into the gathering hall.

"I've had other dreams too, about good things," Linda continued. "Dreams about the places our people still inhabit. The communities they've created. Life carrying on in a beautiful way on the shore, and in the bush. I believe that is out there too. And you—you people are my proof."

Biiyen and Shkaabewis exchanged a nervous glance as Linda raised her open arms to the five walkers, who sat stunned and speechless in their seats. The old woman, on the other hand, seemed animated by a new spirit, ecstatic. She spoke more quickly than before, with more intensity. "We're not so different from you all up north. We know we can't stay here forever. We're going to have to leave eventually too. There aren't enough of us in this little camp to sustain a healthy, viable community. We need to grow. The only way to do that is to find our other communities. Before the end—"

"Diindiisii—" Biiyen stood and took a few steps towards Linda, a worried look on his face.

The elder waved him off before rushing back into her speech. "Before the end, Melissa and I knew some other Anishinaabek who were doing the same thing we were, a bit farther south. Their plan was to lay up on the islands on one of the big lakes just south. If they made it through, the same as us, the same as you, they might—" She coughed and for a few seconds couldn't seem to catch her breath.

Biiyen shot his brother a glance, and Shkaabewis ran to the copper pot, filled a cup with water, and walked it over to Linda, who took it without drinking.

"They might be there now, for all we know," Linda wheezed. Her coughing continued, and she eventually relented and sipped from the cup. "So we are slowly planning to go there too."

Nangohns, who had been transfixed by the old woman's words, looked at her father. Evan was bent forward, his eyes levelled at the fire. He looked up only when he realized Linda was staring right at him, waiting for his attention.

"And this is what I've wanted to tell you since you got here. I know you want to go down to your old homeland on the north shore. But first, I want you to think about something. I want you to think about the future." The elder's wide eyes bore into Evan. "When you go back up north to get everyone," she said. "Think about bringing them here. There is big strength in big numbers."

The proposition triggered a flood of homesickness and yearning in Nangohns, and tears brimmed in her eyes. She barely noticed Melissa return to the fire with a copper pot and a stack of mugs. She offered tea to everyone, and as she poured it into each cup, a strong aroma of sumac and dandelions drifted around the circle.

Seemingly fully recovered from her coughing fit, Linda sipped her tea and smacked her lips. "That's a lot, eh?" she said. "A lot to take in, for sure. But I want youse all to know you can stay here as long as you need to. Even if it's over the winter. But I know you got that binoojiins, that little baby, to get back to. Ever lucky you, mishoomis!"

Nangohns looked again at her father, whose face had lost almost all expression but now thawed into a smile that she knew was genuine but must have been masking something like the niggling homesickness she was feeling. She would speak to him before they slept and finally find words for everything. She would tell him that she wanted to return home, but not until they had seen the north shore. Whether or not they found Linda's Anishinaabek in those islands, they would soon start their journey home and be reunited with their family, hopefully with a plan to return to Saswin.

Linda looked from Evan to Nangohns and put out her arms, beckoning for the girl to come closer. She took Nangohns's hands and looked down at her stomach. "Those babies are the reason we're still here. If we wanted to give up after everything that happened to us, we woulda stopped having babies. But this world needs them, and that's what we all know deep down."

Nangohns thanked her in the old language and pulled her hands back, a bit more abruptly than she had meant to. Linda maintained her gaze, and her smile turned into a knowing look before she sat back in her chair and took another sip of tea.

The heat from the flames caressed their faces and bare shins, chasing away the chill of the evening. The wood popped and crackled as it combusted, and the children's voices nearby faded as their day of play and celebration drew to a close. The twilight darkened as the sun escaped the horizon to the west. Melissa poured more tea.

"Nangohns, my girl," Linda commanded, "tell me more about your shimis, that little niece of yours. What's her name?"

Nangohns felt a rush of blood to her face. She looked down at her callused palms, imagining the soft baby in her arms. "Waawaaskone," she said.

SIXTEEN

THEY REMAINED IN THE settlement for five more days. Evan told himself they needed the time to regain their strength and resupply for the next leg of the journey, but they were also getting to know their new allies, who were quickly becoming kin. In the evenings, the five walkers sat around their own fire next to their cabin and debated what to do next. Biiyen and his scouts had flagged what they thought would be the safest and fastest route south to the east-west highway intersection that would lead them to the north shore of the big water. They pointed out the old logging roads that paralleled the highway, which, if passable, would keep them in the bush and off the major thoroughfares, but using them would add time to the trip. According to the map, they were less than two hundred kilometres from their destination. If the trails were navigable, getting there would take them five days, six at the most.

The world that had opened up for them at Saswin raised questions about their mission. Even Linda admitted that they didn't currently have room for the entire community from Shki-dnakiiwin, and Evan and Tyler doubted it was possible to bring everyone down before the snows. The sojourn with this community had cemented their resolve to return home with news of the world to the south, and hope for their future. But the spectre of new dangers haunted them too.

They departed after a sunrise ceremony on the sixth day, their packs full of provisions and clean clothes. Biiyen, Shkaabewis, and their fellow scouts had taught Cal and Nangohns several paths into the settlement from the main road, to use if they couldn't retrace the trail left by Kevin and Izzy. Final goodbyes were short, and Evan promised their well-wishers that they would return.

The land around them was new to all of their eyes. They paralleled the main road, cutting their way through the bush, wary of walking out in the open. By the end of their first day back on the move, they had passed several ravaged homes and could occasionally make out the remains of vehicles scattered at intervals along the side of the highway. For Nangohns, these ramshackle images had now become synonymous with Zhaawnong.

The next day, the overgrowth made the bush trails impossible to traverse, and they had no choice but to walk along the highway. Around midday, a green road sign appeared on the southern horizon, the first they had seen since leaving Gibson. It didn't reflect in the sunlight. Nangohns squinted, but the lettering was still indiscernible as the group moved closer. Beyond the sign she could see several structures laid out in straight lines on either side of the road. The walkers picked up their pace, eager to pass through the remnants of the town as quickly as possible.

The now familiar shape of a gas station appeared up ahead, and in the distance they saw the white spire of a church. Evan slowed his steps as they passed a rectangular board that once marked the entrance to the village. It had been defaced with a strange marking: a long, thick, black diagonal line that stretched from the bottom left of the sign to the top right, intersected horizontally by a shorter straight line.

The group fanned out, with Evan and Tyler making the most direct approach.

Tyler's face scrunched. "What the hell does that mean?" he asked Evan.

"Maybe a warning," replied Evan. "It looks . . . fresh." He thought back to the broken, torched, and fallen signs and billboards in Gibson, which had been weathered by wind, rain, and snow, apparently untouched by humans for years.

Biiyen had assured them that the lands along their route weren't contaminated, but the fact that someone had apparently been here recently made the sparse hair on Evan's arms stand on end.

The gas station on the west side of the road had been ransacked just as much as the ones they'd come across in the city. All four pumps lay on the cracked asphalt. The convenience store and coffee shop behind them looked to be emptied of all goods and supplies.

They pressed on through the small town. Nangohns observed the abandoned structures, scanning for anything different from the destruction that had surrounded them in Gibson. To her, the town looked like a solitary city street, picked up and plunked down in the middle of the bush. It was a strange strip of buildings, slowly being swallowed up by the abundant forest around it, and she wondered why the houses and other buildings were built so close together.

"How many people lived here before, Noos?" she asked Evan, to distract herself from the repetitive beat of their nervous feet on the crumbling pavement.

"Maybe around three hundred," he replied. "This was just a pit stop on the way up to the big city."

"Pit stop?"

Evan laughed. "Just a place to stop and gas up, and maybe take a piss and grab food. People used to drive for hours without stopping."

Nangohns looked around for cars. Not seeing any, she imagined being confined in a speeding vehicle for that long.

As they neared the church on the east side, a newly recognizable sight stopped them in their tracks.

"Shit," Cal said. "See that?" He pointed to the left.

Smeared along the outside wall, beside the vacant front doorway to the church, was the same marking as on the town sign, but much larger. It spanned roughly two metres wide and about a metre high at eye level. It was a sideways cross, tilted up at an angle. They stopped on the road in front of the tall white structure and peered through the gaping entrance. They could see that the interior of the church was bare as well.

Evan inspected the symbol. The lines were thick and appeared hand-painted. A few dark drips streaked beneath it, where the material used to paint it—mud or some other concoction—had splattered and dried. Manufactured paint would shine in the daylight, even from this far away, Evan thought.

"I guess the last ones through here had some kind of point to make," Tyler muttered.

"Let's keep moving," said Evan.

They walked down the main street, but grew warier as more buildings clustered together along the simple strip. More of the slanted cross symbols showed up on the sides of buildings and on the front walls of former stores and homes.

Finally, the road opened back up ahead of them, and Evan told Tyler they should try off-road trails again. As they turned back for a final look at the vacant highway town, the sharp crack of a rifle rang out from somewhere nearby. All five froze and frantically scanned their surroundings. A gun fired again, and Nangohns saw the bullet ricochet off the grey asphalt just a few metres behind them. Another shot came from somewhere on the west side of the road.

"Run!" cried Evan.

Cal, the fastest, darted off the road onto a nearby driveway, and the others followed, sprinting around the dilapidated remains of a house, through the backyard, and into the forest.

Another two gunshots echoed through the air.

The panic in Nangohns's chest silenced everything but the blasts. Her vision narrowed to the bush in front of them. She managed to glance back quickly to check on Evan and the rest.

They darted through the narrow trees. Nangohns kept pace with Cal as he bounced over the rocks and branches scattered about the forest floor. In the thick terrain, they fell into a line, with Evan bringing up the rear, checking to see if anyone was on their tail.

In front, Cal dodged and ducked tree branches, and stuttered his steps down hills and along rockier terrain, and Nangohns did her best to keep up, looking over her shoulder every few steps to make sure the others were following. She felt an adrenaline surge unlike anything she had experienced before, and her throat burned as she pulled air into her lungs.

At the back, Evan, panting heavily, started to lag, causing the line of runners to space out, but he could still make out Tyler running ahead of him. His pack slammed against his soaked back with every step, and he felt it weighing him down.

Nangohns couldn't tell how far they'd run or how much time had passed since they'd heard the first shot. When she turned her head, she could see Amber in her shaky peripheral vision, and she could only hope that the other two were following.

"Hold up! Hold up!" Tyler shouted.

The three younger ones stopped and turned to see Evan struggling to his feet at the bottom of a long ravine and Tyler running back to him. Nangohns bolted back down to check on her father. She reached Tyler's side, gasping. Evan struggled to stand and dust himself off. He had shed the backpack and was covered with scrapes on his palms and elbows from breaking his fall on the rocks.

Cal and Amber came down the hill as well, their foreheads shining with sweat.

"Come on, sit down," commanded Tyler, as Nangohns inspected Evan's injuries. "You gotta recover from that."

Nangohns grabbed Evan's backpack and brought it over for her father to sit on. He rested his elbows on his knees and took long, measured, deep breaths through his nose. Nangohns placed her palm tenderly on his shoulder and then stroked the top of his tied-back hair.

"Let's get him up that hill," said Tyler. "Then we'll all take a breather."

Nangohns and Tyler each took an arm and walked Evan slowly through the birch trees that lined the slope. His feet shuffled through the leaves and twigs until they reached the peak. They lowered him slowly to the ground, and Cal handed him an open water bottle.

"We shouldn't stay long," Evan said after catching his breath and drinking. "Whoever that was might still be following us."

"I wasn't just dreaming that, then," said Cal. "Someone was shooting at us, right?"

Nangohns confirmed that she had seen the second shot bounce off the road.

"We better get going," Evan said again, and tried to stand, but Nangohns gently nudged him back down.

"Where to?" asked Amber.

They resolved to keep going east, since that was the direction they had to go anyway.

The sun had begun its descent in the west behind them. They carried on through the woods, Cal continuing to lead the way. No one spoke for a long while.

The compass Biiyen had given them allowed them to stay oriented east even with no sun in the sky, and Evan insisted that they keep moving even as the darkening landscape became treacherous around them. Fatigued and struggling in the dark, Cal and Amber pleaded with him to stop and rest, but he refused.

"We gotta stop at some point, though, Ev," pointed out Tyler. "We don't wanna gas ourselves out too soon after that good break we had."

"We will," relented Evan. "Let's just get as far as we can first." He made his way forward to take over the lead, stepping around Cal as the canopy above them dimmed.

The others fell in line behind him, intently watching the feet of the person in front of them. The stars emerged above, and the moon slowly climbed over the horizon. The only speaking came from Evan in the front, warning of fallen branches, large rocks, and other hazards. Eventually, exhaustion set in, and he began looking for a sheltered stretch of even ground. He saw the outline of a rock outcrop on the plateau atop another hill. He walked to it and dropped his pack against the natural bunker, and the others followed. Tyler took his new lighter, which Biiyen had given him, out of his pocket and flicked it alight so the others could retrieve their blankets and warmer clothing for a brief sleep. They agreed they wouldn't light a fire.

Evan insisted on staying up to keep watch. He sat at the base of a thick tree and eased his back against the trunk. An eerie stillness came over the forest, and he kept his eyes trained on the gaps between the trees all around them for as long as he could.

When Tyler snapped awake a short while later, he found Evan slumped forward, asleep where he sat. Tyler lowered his friend to a prone position and covered him with his wool blanket. As he did, he felt something cold and metal, and realized it was one of the handguns. He checked the safety and tucked it into the top of Evan's pack. He sat down and kept his eyes to the west, awaiting a brightening sky behind him.

The spaces between leaves and the outlines of branches and rocks on the ground began to reveal themselves as the faint blue light of dawn crept into the forest. Nangohns stirred atop her blanket, and it bunched and twisted underneath her. She opened her eyes to see Cal and Amber still sleeping a few steps away. She rolled over, and Tyler greeted her with a sarcastic whisper of "Rise and shine!" She noticed her father balled up in the fetal position on the ground beside him.

"How long you been up?" she asked Tyler.

"Not too long," he said. "Let's let these guys have a bit more rest, though. I think that run took a lot out of your dad."

Nangohns looked over at her slumbering father. His hair had come loose in the night, and black strands ran across his face. His sparse, wiry facial hair became more visible as the light increased, but something about his vulnerability at rest made him look innocent and childlike.

Tyler watched her examine Evan. He saw her eyes soften in the pre-dawn glow. "He's been through a lot," he said, as if reading her mind.

Nangohns felt her throat tighten, and swallowed before responding. "Yeah, he really has," she said. "I hope he's having a good dream."

"He's getting some rest, anyway. That's the most important thing. I think what happened back there was pretty hard for him. He hasn't been shot at since . . . you know." Tyler paused, realizing he had never discussed Evan's injury with Nangohns before.

"I didn't think of that," Nangohns said. She kept her gaze on Evan and away from Tyler to conceal the tears forming in her eyes.

"He's a tough guy, your dad, where it counts."

Nangohns watched Evan shift in his blanket, and realized they'd all be awake soon.

They were still rattled by the gunfire by the time they broke camp. Progress through the bush was slow, but returning to the level ground of the road no longer felt like an option. The terrain they were covering was new yet familiar, and the rocky shield beneath their feet made walking fairly easy as they circumnavigated smaller lakes and swamps.

By the time the sun had started to sink behind them, they had arrived on the shore of a much bigger lake. The south shore, to their right, wrapped around a cove and out to a point, while the bulk of the lake, to the north, stretched far into the distance. The treeline on the north shore shrank into a green strip behind the whitecapped waves kicked up by the strengthening wind.

Cal noticed a dock jutting out from the shore on the other side of the point, and pointed out the partially sunken and broken raft to the others. The thick leaves of the trees that crowded the shore concealed what lay beyond it. He moved higher into the forest to seek an easier way through, and the others followed. As they neared the area uphill from the dock, a tall, broad brown structure appeared in a clearing ahead.

Evan pushed low branches away as he walked forward to get a closer look at the two-storey log cabin. He stopped at the edge of the trees, and the others stood beside him. A long staircase led from the ground up to a wooden deck that surrounded three sides of the house. Massive bay windows—miraculously unshattered—peaked just below the pitched roof and reflected the churning lake. The long curtains were drawn, so they couldn't see what was inside. To the left, a path led down to the dock, which appeared to be the only way in. Tall pine and spruce trees sheltered the residence, and a thick coating of dead brown needles covered the roof and deck.

"Looks like a cottage," said Evan.

"Pretty big cottage," noted Cal.

"Probably wasn't cheap to build. I don't see no roads around to truck in those logs," added Tyler.

"Doesn't look like anyone's been here in a while. Let's go check it out," Evan said.

They made their way up the stairs to the deck. The pine needles swished underfoot. The five of them spread out on the deck, looking out at the lake and into the bush around the structure.

"Totally off the grid," Tyler noted. "No hydro lines or anything coming in here."

"Must be a generator somewhere. I dunno why you'd go through all this effort just to have to haul gas in every time," said Evan.

"How did they get out here, anyways?" asked Amber.

"Probably a float plane. Unless there's a marina nearby. But there'd be more cottages on the lake if that was the case."

Cal walked over to the side door. "Shall we?" he asked the group.

"Give'r," said Evan.

Cal kicked open the door. The waning daylight exposed a luxurious, lodge-like interior. Shiny leather furniture sat in the centre of the main floor. A large flat-screen television hung on one wall. A massive stone fireplace was the centrepiece of the other. Colourful artwork hung everywhere, and towards the back there was a large kitchen with marble countertops and a wide island with tall chairs ranged around it. Wooden doors opened to bedrooms, and a dark wooden staircase led up to a massive loft. A thick layer of dust coated everything.

They scattered through the cottage for a closer look. Amber went upstairs to assess the sleeping arrangements there. Tyler and Evan went to the basement to scope out supplies, while Cal rummaged through the cupboards and drawers of the kitchen. Walking through the living room, Nangohns examined the framed colour photographs adorning the walls around the fireplace. Most were of the same family, two parents and three children. There was a photo taken at a lavish wedding, the groom looking dapper in a black suit and with short black hair, the bride's blond hair elaborately styled. There were baby pictures, and then shots of two blond children together. They were eventually joined by a third in subsequent photos. The collection of photos expanded into their teen years, and by the time the kids reached young adulthood, the father was bald but the mother's vibrant blond sheen remained.

On the adjacent wall hung older, black-and-white photos of what Nangohns assumed were other family members, and pictures of people who were likely extended family. The more recent images were crisp, taken in exotic locations against landscapes that Nangohns had never even imagined—sunny beaches, snow-capped mountains, and shiny dining rooms. The backgrounds and poses were all strange to her, and she wondered what these people would have been like if things hadn't come crashing down.

"They're probably all dead now," Cal muttered behind her.

She started, and turned towards him. "Geez, you scared me," she said. "You think so?"

"Probably. Do they look like they could hack it in the bush?" Cal tilted his head.

"Nope," agreed Nangohns.

"Then they're probably dead. Especially if they got stuck in the city."

"How do you know all the cities ended up like that?"

"Most of the ones down south are bigger. More people means more chaos."

"I guess so," she said, unconvinced. She turned back to the array of photographs.

They regrouped in the darkening main room. They were still well supplied from their stopover at Saswin, and there was little room in their packs, but some of the tools Evan and Tyler had found in the basement might come in handy. They had even found a generator and a solar panel rig, but those were as good as useless. Still, Evan and Tyler tried to determine where they were on the map, in case they ever found themselves back this way in the future.

Night fell, and there seemed to be a tacit agreement that they would spend the night indoors.

"Big step up from last night's accommodations," said Tyler, taking one last look out the huge bay windows before pulling the curtains closed.

Nangohns hadn't realized how much the exertion of the day and night had taken out of her, and was grateful when Cal volunteered to stay up a while and keep watch from one of the windows in the loft. Amber and Nangohns propped the front door that Cal had kicked in back into place before preparing a smudge. They scattered once again through the house to stake out places to sleep, Cal and Amber in the loft and Nangohns in one of the bedrooms off the main floor. Evan and Tyler would crash on the couches in the living room.

The five ate together, inside without a fire, and went to sleep early.

SEVENTEEN

WHITE LIGHT SEEPED THROUGH the narrow cracks in the curtains and around the edges into the large room where Evan and Tyler slept. The trace of early daylight cast a blurred streak across the matte-black TV high on the wall, which was nearly as wide as the brown leather loveseat across from it. Amber and Cal were still asleep in the loft, and Nangohns had yet to emerge from the bedroom on the main level.

Evan stirred, sat up on the leather couch, and rubbed his eyes. His back was soaked in sweat. Tyler snored quietly on the couch across from him. The stale, warming air told him that sunrise had already come and gone. He stood and stretched his limbs and back. He inhaled deeply through his nostrils and let out a slow exhale, his eyes adjusting to the dimness. He stepped around the thick wooden coffee table and passed Tyler's sleeping head on his way to the front windows. The hardwood creaked beneath his bare feet. The curtain felt soft and heavy as he ran his hand across the thick fabric and pulled at the edge slightly to peer outside.

A group of men were gathered on the ground beyond the deck, long rifles pointing in his direction. He saw a quick flash and, with a heart-stopping *bang*, the windowpane beside him exploded and crashed to the floor. Darting back from the window, Evan saw Tyler bolting up, the whites of his eyes blazing in the darkness. The gun cracked again and another window shattered. Thick shards of glass bounced across the wooden floor.

The sound of the gunshot rang in Evan's ears, drowning out his rapid breathing. He croaked at Tyler to get down, and they ducked behind the couch. After a few breaths, Nangohns came crawling towards them.

"Get back in there!" Evan commanded in a harsh whisper, and she scurried back into the bedroom where she had slept.

Evan heard stirring upstairs and glanced up to see Cal leaning over the loft railing. Evan waved him away, and Cal pulled a stunned Amber into the confines of one of the upstairs bedrooms.

"I missed ya on purpose," called a voice from outside, muffled by the curtains. "But if I have to come in there, I guarantee I ain't gonna miss. Come on out, now."

Lying on their stomachs, Evan and Tyler locked eyes. Evan felt his heart beating into the thick rug on the floor.

"Ya hear me? We know you're in there. We're giving ya a chance to talk."

Evan saw Tyler's hands trembling in front of him. He nodded frantically at his friend to reassure him and prompt him up to his feet.

"Don't make me count down like no fuckin' bitch-ass schoolteacher." The man outside sounded more agitated. "Five, four . . ."

"Okay, okay!" Evan shouted from the floor. "I'm coming out."

"What's this 'I' horseshit? We know there's more than one of ya."

Evan jumped to his feet and hurried to the side door. He turned the handle and pulled it open. He halted before walking out into the daylight.

"Hands up, if ya want," the man said with a chuckle. "There's five guns trained on that door. You try some shit, you'll be taking some heat real quick. You best just make a nice easy stroll outside here."

Evan held his breath and raised his hands. He stepped over the threshold and into the daylight. Wind blew in cloud cover that spanned the sky, filtering the sunlight into an ominous light-grey hue. Evan walked along the side of the log cabin towards the front deck, and heard Tyler making his way out. Through the clear Plexiglas railing, he saw their heads and shoulders, and their guns drawn on him. He stepped carefully to the edge of the deck. Four men stood in a staggered formation, outfitted in assorted shades of camouflage and black tactical gear. Each wore a baseball cap over short, shaggy hair, and their faces were mostly concealed by thick beards. The auburn beard on a burly man in the back caught Evan's eye. The water lapped gently at the shore behind them.

"You're probably wondering, Where's that fifth piece, then?" said the one in the front, taller and more wiry than the others. "Well, don't you worry about that. He's out back with his sight on the back door, in case you injuns try any funny business."

The man grinned, exposing missing front teeth and blackened rot around the ones that remained. His greasy beard hung to his chest and shook up and down when he spoke. The beak of his cap sat low on his forehead, concealing the hollows of his eyes.

Tyler came up slowly behind Evan, holding his hands high in the air.

"So don't try any funny business," the man repeated. "That's two of ya. Where's the rest? Come on out, y'all."

Evan heard feet bound down the stairs from the loft and then slow as they approached the door going outside. He looked over his left shoulder to see Cal emerge with his pale palms spread outwards. The braids in his hair were loose. He had pulled his lips tight and creased his brow to conceal his fear.

"Step up to the railing, boy," demanded the leader. "Alright, the three of y'all stay put. Line up nice, now."

The black assault rifles held steady on the three of them. Evan scanned the group below as inconspicuously as he could, careful not to move his eyes too abruptly. Their fatigues were faded but largely intact. The pockets in their cargo pants and shirts looked packed. They each wore black utility belts with ammo clips and other combat gear.

"Okay, that's the men. Where are them young ladies?"

The three on the deck didn't speak or flinch. Evan's jaw clenched.

"Oh, come on, don't try any kinda hero shit. We seen them with ya. We can smell them too, eh, boys?"

Evan felt a burning in his stomach. A few seconds later, he heard a door hinge creak as Nangohns and Amber emerged. The leader's eyes followed Nangohns, whose face bore no expression as she came around the side of the cottage.

The man lowered his rifle. "Ah, there's a fine young Pocahontas," he cackled.

Amber walked a few steps behind Nangohns, sniffling and clearing her throat to mute fearful whimpering.

"And another one! Been a while since we seen any little redskin girls this y—"

"How can we help you today, gentlemen?" Evan asked in a steady voice.

"Oh, he speaks! Hear that, boys?" the leader swivelled his head around to the others. "How about that. Are you the chief or something?"

"Who are you?" Evan asked, almost without thinking.

"Who am I? Just another man of the people looking to secure our existence for future generations and all that."

"What do you want from us?"

"Well, we seen you walking the road, and we just wanted to get to know y'all."

"You were the ones that shot at us?"

"We was just trying to get your attention. We didn't mean no harm."

The others seemed keen to let Evan do all the talking. Their guns were still packed away inside.

"Why did you follow us here?"

"You know what?" the man said, anger rising in his voice. He jerked the rifle up to put them in his sights. The five on the deck jolted. "See this?" he aimed it at each of them. "This means *I* ask the fuckin' questions. Got it?"

Evan replanted his feet on the deck boards to steel his legs, still jittery from the gunshots moments earlier. He nodded at the man.

"So tell me," the leader said, "where y'all coming from?"

"Up north."

"Where up north?"

"North of Gibson."

"That's a long way to walk." The command in the man's voice faltered slightly. Evan wondered if he was calculating the distance. "Now you can't tell me you came all that way with just them clothes on your backs," he went on in his lilting drawl. "Where's all your gear?"

"Inside," replied Evan. He looked beyond the leader to the burly man in the back. The beak of his cap was raised enough to expose his wide blue eyes. The black muzzle of his rifle dipped slightly, and his eyes darted to the side as a short blond man, who had been posted behind the cottage, walked to the front to join the rest.

"You two go in and get their shit," the leader commanded the man who had just arrived and a younger-looking one with a sparse black beard.

Inside, the men would find their unpacked backpacks lined up on the floor, and the supplies they'd found in the drawers and cupboards all laid out on the kitchen counter. And they would find their guns.

"So where y'all headed, then?" the man with the long beard continued his interrogation.

"We're going to the north shore of the Great Lakes," said Evan, keeping his eyes fixed on the leader now.

Behind her father, Nangohns scanned the three remaining on the ground while she listened to the heavy footsteps behind her on the main floor inside. The man beside the leader looked like him, with a similar medium build, though with less grey in his beard. Their fatigues made them otherwise indistinguishable.

"What north shore?"

"They used to call it Lake Huron."

"What the fuck you plan on doing there?"

"We wanna see what's there. Haven't been down this way in a long time."

"Holy shit, you ain't been around since shit hit the fan?"

Evan shook his head.

"Wow, this is some real quest for fire shit, then!" The leader let out a high-pitched giggle and looked at the one on his left, who laughed along with him. The red-bearded one in the back only smirked. The leader steadied his rifle again and fixed his eyes on Evan.

The boots of the two who had gone inside clunked along the deck boards as they came up behind the walkers. A stench of body odour trailed them. Evan noticed the small camouflage backpacks under their rifles as they tossed the confiscated packs off the deck onto the ground below.

"Bring 'em on down. Let's see what they got here," the man with the long beard instructed his fellows on the deck.

They raised their rifles and trained them on Evan and Cal, who stood closest to the stairs. The taller one motioned for them to move, and they made their way down at gunpoint. The men on the ground pulled the backpacks away from the deck to make space for the search. Evan noticed the redhead, still in the back, following them closely with his eyes, rifle ever drawn. From closer up, Evan was struck by how gaunt several of the men looked. The faces of the leader and a couple of the others had an unhealthy pallor to them, despite their exposure to the sun.

"Hands on your heads now," said the leader in an even voice.

The first down the stairs, Cal raised his hands slowly and locked his fingers atop his scalp. Evan's mind raced, trying to think of a way out. The leader was about the same size as him, and the one beside him—who he assumed was his brother or cousin—was a bit shorter but wider. The one with the red beard was bulkier and would be harder to subdue if they got lucky and disarmed them. He was less worried about the younger men who had searched the house. The blond one seemed surer on his feet, but he appeared to rely on his gun for intimidation.

"You fuckin' deaf or what? I said hands on your fuckin' head!" shouted the weaselly frontman.

Standing in the middle of his crew, Evan saw them submitting to the command in his periphery. He placed his palms on top of his head and felt sweat soaking through his thick hair.

The lanky man with the thin black beard crouched to examine the backpacks. Evan watched his wiry fingers unbuckle plastic clasps and loosen drawstrings. The scabs and scratches on his knuckles led to long, black-tipped fingernails. His gaping mouth exposed a long overbite of yellow teeth, and his excited panting drove the stench of his foul breath into the line of hostages. Evan's nostrils twitched.

"Looks like y'all pack heavy," the man with the long beard said. "My nephew here's gonna take a look at what you got. We had a long night of walking, and I ain't had breakfast yet."

"Help yourself," said Evan, wondering if this was all about food.

The man identified as the leader's nephew—the youngest-looking of the ambushers—pulled food containers out of two of the packs and tossed them to the ground in front of the older men. They smacked their lips at the dried meat visible through the clear plastic. Then the man dug his hand a little deeper into the pack with most of the food and pulled out three loose carrots, dug out of the garden at Saswin just two days earlier. Evan watched the leader's eyes widen, and his throat tightened.

"Huh, looks garden-fresh," the leader said. "Where'd you get those?"

When Evan hesitated, Nangohns blurted out, "We found them."

The leader cocked his head to focus on her. "Well, well, well, the little squaw speaks! That sounds like some bullshit, but please, tell me more, sweetheart."

She looked at her father. Evan kept his eyes steady and reassuring. "They were in the ground, back a ways."

"That don't tell me much truth. I reckon the garden them carrots was pulled from ain't too far from here. Maybe that mouth of yours ain't too useful for talking. We'll find another use for it, though."

Evan clenched his teeth and tightened his fingers atop his scalp.

The leader tilted his head to either side to speak to his crew. "I dunno, boys. We could just shoot 'em and take their shit. Or we could spare them if they take us where they been. Either way, we'll keep them girls warm for a while yet."

The desperate flutter in his gut sent Evan's mind into a panic. He tried to remain still while scanning the faces of their captors for an opening. The leader bared his broken and sickly teeth. The short blond one supervised his young counterpart, who continued to rummage through the packs, scattering clothing about as he dug deeper into them. But when Evan met the eyes of the burly one in the back, the man raised his eyebrows once and lifted his chin like he was trying to communicate something.

"Wait!" Evan shouted, trying to buy time. "We got something you might be interested in."

As if on cue, the nephew of the leader pulled one of the black handguns out of a backpack. His palm wrapped around the grip, and he turned to show the older men.

"Now, where in the fuck did you get that?" asked the leader, agitated and curious.

The men on either side of him stared at the clean, shiny piece.

Suddenly, the one in the back screamed "Dbaziik!" and all of the men's hands went to their rifles. Evan frantically turtled, and Nangohns fell to her side as they heard the first gunshot. On her way to the ground, she watched a mist of blood burst from the exit wound in the leader's chest before he fell forward, dead. Evan looked up in time to see a spatter of red blood and pink brain matter explode out the side of the other older man's head just as he turned to look at the source of the gunfire.

The third shot was into the chest of the young one quickly enough to keep him from standing and unloading the handgun he'd discovered a moment earlier. He let out an anguished groan as he keeled forward and dropped the weapon to the ground, within Nangohns's reach.

The last man standing squared up with the red-bearded shooter and clawed for the rifle looped across his back.

The shooter's gun went quiet. "Fuck! Jammed up!" he shouted.

Tyler leapt up from the ground behind the man grabbing for his weapon and tackled him. They rolled in the direction of the water, towards the redhead. The blond man mounted Tyler's chest and heaved his gun up with two hands to plunge the butt into Tyler's face. Before he could drive it down, the shooter stepped forward and swung his dead gun like a baseball bat into the attacker's head, knocking him to the ground, unconscious.

Tyler rolled out of the way and scrambled to his knees. The rest of the northerners were all on their feet now, watching the finale of this chaotic standoff. Nangohns saw the big man's short, loose red curls bounce as he walked calmly up to his last victim. His camo hat had fallen off when he swung the rifle. He looked at the man's unconscious body for a moment, and then grunted as he drove his heel into his nose, cheeks, and jaw. The man's skull cracked open, blood spilling into the soft, grassy ground beneath.

When he was done killing the last of them, the man stepped back to his original position and turned to face the survivors. His chest heaved as he panted through the last of the adrenaline surge.

In the melee, Nangohns had grabbed the handgun that had fallen to the ground. She gripped it tightly with both hands and raised it, pointing the muzzle at him. "Drop it," she commanded.

He slowly lowered the jammed rifle to the ground and raised his arms. He clasped his fingers behind his head and cast his eyes to the ground. The sight of Nangohns holding the gun shocked Evan, but the steadiness in her hands soon soothed him.

"Anishinaabe ndaaw," the man said loudly into the ground. "Zhaabdiis ndizhnikaaz."

He was speaking to them in Anishinaabemowin.

The group shared confused glances. Nangohns's eyes darted from the man who had just identified himself as Zhaabdiis to the weapons lying idle on the ground.

Amber took a step forward and held out her palms in his direction. "Boozhoo, aapiish enjibaayin?" she said, greeting him and asking where he came from.

"Baawaating," he replied, calm but breathing deeply. "I'm sorry. That's all I can say in the language right now. It's been so long."

"You're Anishinaabe from Baawaating?"

"Yes. I know, I look like these guys. My mom was Nish. My dad was zhaagnaash. I look more like him."

Evan turned to Tyler, who looked stunned. He glanced at Cal, who was biting down on his bottom lip, and back to Nangohns, who kept the handgun aimed at Zhaabdiis.

"That fucker was just about to kill us all," said Cal.

"Please. This was my first and only chance." Zhaabdiis's voice trembled.

"What the fuck are you talking about?" snapped Cal.

"Cal, calm down," cut in Amber. "Pass me that water." She fixed her attention back on Zhaabdiis. "Sit down. Have a rest."

Nangohns suggested they search him before letting him get too comfortable, and Evan slowly patted him down and removed his utility belt and camouflage backpack, tossing both to where Nangohns stood, gun ready.

"He's clean," Evan concluded.

Zhaabdiis cautiously lowered himself to the grass, with his hands still behind his head. He sat cross-legged and stared at his boots.

Amber walked up and handed him a bottle. "Minikwen. Here, drink," she murmured to him. "Just sit here a while."

He looked at Nangohns, the gun still trained on him, and at her nod timidly removed his hands from his head and took the bottle. "Miigwech," he whispered, and sniffled.

"Gather up those guns," Nangohns said, still with both hands on hers.

Tyler nodded, and he and Cal moved out to the bodies to retrieve the rifles. When all five guns lay neatly in a row in the shade of the deck, Evan huddled with the others behind Nangohns. She kept her gun on Zhaabdiis, who remained still, sitting quietly on the ground.

"What now?" murmured Cal to the group.

"He saved our lives," Nangohns noted. "That gross guy in front was a breath away from shooting us."

"He surrendered," said Tyler. "We have to at least hear him out."

"I dunno if we can trust him." Cal glanced over at Zhaabdiis, leaning forward now, with his face in his hands. "Anyone can remember a few words and say they're from the rez."

"He threw down his gun," Nangohns stated, feeling the grip of the handgun in her palms.

"Let's just talk to him," said Amber. "That's a start."

The huddle broke and all five turned to face the man sitting on the ground, just a few metres up from the shore.

"Zhaabdiis," Amber called to him. "Is that what we call you? Aaniish eyaayin?" She took a step forward and tilted her head.

Zhaabdiis looked up. His red hair flowed in broad curls a few inches from his scalp. Light-brown freckles dotted his cheeks below his narrow blue eyes. His bearded face was full and round, planted on a thick neck atop a stocky build. His lips shook into a faint smile. "Not good," he replied.

"So, you're from Baawaating, then?" she asked.

"I grew up there. But in the city. Not on my mom's rez. We went there all the time, though. The rez on the east side."

"Prove it, then," Cal blurted before Amber could ask her next question.

"Never mind him," said Tyler. "I think we're all a little on edge right now."

"I don't blame you." Zhaabdiis's voice cracked. He took another sip of water from the bottle and handed it back to Amber. "We snuck up on you."

Nangohns looked from him to the dead bodies on the ground. The two shot in the torso lay in the middle, eyes closed and mouths agape. The two on the outside were unrecognizable, one skull destroyed by a bullet and the other crushed by a boot. "Let's go inside," she said to the group. "We should go in and sit down to talk."

"Before we do," said Evan, "he's going to tell us who else might be out there."

"Yes. They're out there. But nowhere near here," replied Zhaabdiis.

"Are they following you?" asked Evan.

"No, not as far as I know. We—they spread out. And then meet at a designated place and time."

"Is that place nearby?"

"No, sir. It's way back west and south. They sent us on a mission north. Our group had been out about fifteen days now. Some went before us. We'd been on that highway north for only a few days. And that's when we saw you."

"Who the fuck are 'they'?" Cal interrupted.

"Inside, now," ordered Evan. "And then we should leave. As soon as we can."

He took Zhaabdiis by the shoulders and got him on his feet, then led him up the steps into the cottage. Evan could feel the man trembling as he sucked in a light sob.

Trailing them up to the deck, Nangohns noticed a spatter of blood from the head of the last of his former partners climbing up Zhaabdiis's right leg.

Tyler, who had gone up ahead, threw open the curtains to let the light in, stepping around the long, thick shards of the shattered windowpanes. Evan led Zhaabdiis to the leather chair on the far side of the room, which was flanked by the long couches made in the same extravagant style. Nangohns hung back and slowly set the handgun and camouflage backpack on the kitchen counter.

The hard, shiny hide of the chair squeaked and crinkled as Zhaabdiis sat down. He placed his palms on his thighs and watched as the others arranged themselves around him. Evan sat closest to the newcomer. He unscrewed a water bottle and offered it to him.

"Miigwech," said Zhaabdiis again, but he waved the bottle away. He took a short breath in through his nose and exhaled out his mouth, staring straight ahead.

"Are you hungry?" asked Evan. "Your friends were pretty excited to see a carrot."

"Kaa, no, I'm not. Thanks, though," he replied. "I probably will be in a bit. My stomach feels like a cinder block right now."

"Just try to relax," Evan said.

He looked Evan in the eyes. "You can ask me anything. I swear on Mother Earth."

Evan asked who the men lying dead outside were and what they wanted out here.

"The colonel, the lieutenant, and the other privates. We— they—were looking for more settlements."

"Like an army colonel?" demanded Cal.

"No, not an actual army," Zhaabdiis replied, raising his voice slightly. "More like a militia. But a really big one."

Evan noticed Zhaabdiis's knee begin to bounce. He dug his dirty fingernails into the thick fabric of his pants.

"Okay, okay," Evan said. "Why were you following us?"

"Our commands were to find stuff and take it. The colonel thought you'd lead us to something. Or we'd go back where you came from. A camp or a town or something. The land out west, where they were based, went bad. Ain't been nothing to salvage for years. Nothing grows there anymore. People were dying off like flies from the sickness, so they've been spreading out, trying to find good land to resettle on."

"The colonel. Was that the one doing all the talking?" asked Evan.

"Yeah."

"The one you shot in the back?" asked Cal.

Zhaabdiis looked down at his hands, now dormant on his lap. "Yeah."

The meeting went quiet for a moment.

"If you shot him in the back," Cal went on, "why should we trust you?"

The red-headed man steadily squared his face with Cal's. His eyes hardened for a blink, and then cleared. His lips parted a crack, and he said, "There is no honour among men on this land anymore."

Nangohns felt a warm gust push through the shattered windows. She hoped the wind might clear away the clouds later in the day. She looked at Evan, hoping he would hurry the questioning along, but before he could speak, Zhaabdiis continued, explaining that he was the one who had shot at them at the crossroads.

"But I missed you on purpose. We saw you coming down the highway, so we holed up in one of the abandoned houses at the far edge of town. The colonel ordered me to keep watch and make first contact, if necessary. But 'first contact' is misleading—it's bullshit. It means if there's a group, shoot one first. They usually rush to help the one that's hit. Then we ambush them and have instant hostages."

Evan and Tyler exchanged an anxious glance.

"But you were the first Anishinaabek I'd seen on this mission. I aimed at the ground so you'd hear it, then I shot over your heads. You weren't in danger, I swear. But the colonel was pissed that I didn't hit you. We argued for a bit, then he said we had to follow you. We were coming up short on the mission. Hadn't seen anyone or found any place worth finding."

"And you say a group was sent up here ahead of you. That means they could be anywhere right now and even you wouldn't know it?" asked Evan.

Zhaabdiis looked at him with a pleading face. "Yes."

Evan addressed the whole group. "We can't stay here with those bodies out there. We gotta gather up our stuff and get ready to go." He turned his attention back to Zhaabdiis. "Did you lead them to us?"

"No, they knew how to track you. The colonel had been doing that since the beginning."

"Since the blackout?"

"That's how it started up here too, eh?"

"That's all we know."

Zhaabdiis took this in with interest. "Anyway, when he decided to follow you, I thought maybe I had found my chance to get away from them."

Nangohns stepped forward, to the slight surprise of the rest of her group. "We are new to this place," she declared. "We don't really know where we're going. We couldn't have helped your friends even if we wanted to."

Evan looked at her momentarily before turning back to Zhaabdiis.

"I've been lost for a long time," Zhaabdiis said. "I walked so far just to try to get back home. And when I finally made it there, everyone was gone. I think everyone's dead. I held out hope for a while, but that light is almost out. There's not much left in my homeland anymore." He straightened himself in the chair, and the whole group jolted. Zhaabdiis raised his hands reassuringly. "I need to be with good people. I can't go on with people like them." He turned as if to look out the shattered window, but his eyes stopped at Evan. "I am humbly asking to join you. For however long you'll have me."

Evan silently surveyed the others.

Cal leaned forward on his knees and looked intently into Zhaabdiis's blue eyes. "So, from what I know, Zhaabdiis is the

Nish version of John. I guess that's your real name, eh?" he asked.

"Yeah, legally. But my nookomis always called me Zhaab-diis."

"It's a good name," said Evan. "Doesn't mean anything, does it?"

"No, but it sounds cool," the man replied, his body relaxing slightly.

"Yeah, it does," confirmed Evan. "Well, Zhaabdiis, you saved our lives. We got more to talk about, once we've put some distance between us and this place. We can't let you be armed."

Zhaabdiis's brow creased, and his head tilted like he was going to protest, but after a quick breath, he seemed resigned. He nodded at Evan.

"Don't take offence if we keep a pretty close eye on you for the time being," added Tyler. "Or take offence. But that's how this goes, for now."

"Okay," Evan said. "Let's get our shit together and get outta here."

The overcast sky had brightened and cracked, hinting that the sun would soon push through. As they returned to where their packs lay strewn among the dead, Evan's eyes fell on the collapsed face of the last man Zhaabdiis had killed. The body lay prostrate with an undisturbed torso and a flattened head. He walked closer. The man's face was entirely unrecognizable. The top of his forehead and his blond scalp were intact, but from his brow down to his chin, all that remained was a bloody, fleshy tangle of muscle, skin, bone, and hair. Cal and Zhaabdiis followed Evan as he walked past the array of bodies. Cal stopped at the feet of the blond corpse and opened his mouth to comment, but the shock of the gore left the words in his throat and his jaw dropped.

"We had a history," Zhaabdiis said, his face expressionless.

They looted the camouflage bags, which were slightly smaller than theirs but packed much more tightly. When they were finished, they debated what to do with the rifles arrayed under the deck.

Zhaabdiis sighed and placed his hands on his hips. "Well," he said, looking from gun to gun, "I'll let you in on a little secret. Only three of them actually work. Mine, the colonel's, and this one right here." He gestured to one of the rifles. "And this one is pretty unreliable. It jams a lot. Just like mine, apparently," he added.

"So the other ones are just for show?" Cal asked.

"Yeah, pretty much. The guy who tried to brain Tyler with the butt of his gun? His was totally useless."

"But you stomped him out anyway?" asked Cal.

"Yeah," replied Zhaabdiis evenly.

Cal snorted a laugh. But the shock of the killings hadn't worn off for Evan and Tyler.

"They were running out of ammo," Zhaabdiis continued. "There's nowhere to make it anymore, as far as we know. These rounds we have now are from the stockpiles of the before times. So everyone spares what they can. No wasted shots, as they always say."

"You shot quite a few at us back on the road, though," noted Tyler.

"Yeah, and the colonel was pissed about that. But those were warning shots."

"So what are we thinking, then?" asked Cal.

Tyler turned to Zhaabdiis. "How many people have these guns killed?" he asked.

"A lot."

Tyler frowned. "Well, I think we should ask ourselves if we want to bring that spirit with us," he said.

"You guys can decide if you want to take those guns," Evan said, "but we have to remember why we're doing this. Why we're walking this far. It's because we wanna survive. We wanna build a future. That spirit is most important."

"There isn't much ammo left anyways," Zhaabdiis noted. "I'll take the one I had."

"Maybe," Evan said, his voice hardening. "But not for now you won't."

"I'll take the good one, then," said Cal. "Even just for show."

EIGHTEEN

THEY WOULD GO EAST for two more days—through the bush to avoid the main highways—and then south for one last day-long trek to the north shore. Before they departed the opulent cottage, Zhaabdiis had told them of another group like his that had embarked eastward from the old border crossing at the river ten days ago. He estimated that they would be farther east than their destination by the time they arrived, but he couldn't be sure.

"They call themselves the Disciples," he said as they walked, loud enough so everyone in front of and behind him could hear. "They started as a militia down in Michigan a few years before the end."

"Are they, like, religious whackos too?" Tyler inquired.

"They worship the gun," replied Zhaabdiis. That, he explained, was why their symbol was a cross on its side. "To make it look like a rifle."

They were unorganized at first, before the blackout, Zhaabdiis told them. Typical militia types, all about the right to bear arms. But after a while they grew. They got popular online, and more chapters started popping up in other parts of the United States. They only let white people join, and they got more and more extreme.

The Disciples and similar groups sounded familiar to Evan and Tyler, but it had been so long, and they had been relatively insulated from that sort of thing up on the rez.

As Zhaabdiis told it, when the power went out and shit went down, the Disciples had a plan, taking over the towns they were in, ruling by the gun. They created a network with other like-minded militias and consolidated their resources— guns and ammo, water, canned goods, gasoline and vehicles— mostly in what had been southern Michigan. Because a lot of them were cops or ex-military, they had access to arms, and they'd had a head start building up stores of food and survival gear like water purifiers and fertilizer. They took over tanker stations, so they had plenty of fuel for vehicles and the generators that still worked.

"After a while," said Zhaabdiis, "any car or truck running on any road was guaranteed to be one of theirs, because no one else could gas up. They had a system to siphon and pump all that manually too, with no power. They spread out. Expanded across the midwest. And now they're trying to see what they can claim up here."

Cal interrupted from behind him. "You keep saying 'they,' but you were one of the Disciples, or whatever they're called."

Zhaabdiis hesitated. "I ain't proud of it. It was how I stayed alive."

"How long have you been with them?"

"The last few years."

"Did you kill any brown people?" asked Cal. The group came to a halt, and Nangohns turned to see Cal glaring at

Zhaabdiis and then at the rest of the group. "Sounds like they're into some white power shit."

Zhaabdiis stepped out of formation to address them all. "No. I swear to you. It's been a long time since I've seen anyone who's not white, not until we found youse—"

"Heads up," Nangohns said. "Looks like a swamp up ahead. We should go around if we want to keep our feet dry." She pointed to the higher ground to the right and started off in that direction.

"Keep an eye out for a spot to make camp," said Evan. "Looks like we're getting close to suppertime." He squared his shoulders in front of Cal and Zhaabdiis, looking at them both sternly. "It's been a long day. We need to keep moving."

They rounded the swamp in silence. Nangohns weighed the details of the newcomer's story. She had heard about the kind of men Zhaabdiis had lived among, but the evil of the south had never seemed this real. She wondered what she would do if they encountered the Disciples again, remembering the hard steel of the handgun in her palms that morning.

They were nearly around the murky wetlands when she heard a familiar flutter of sound from the bog on their left. It stopped her in her tracks. A massive brown moose with thick, wide antlers was wading into the swampy water up to its torso, dipping its snout into the moist vegetation. It looked up as it chewed, briefly regarding the humans walking by before returning to its food.

Nangohns momentarily considered reaching for her bow, then let out a weary sigh. "Meh, woulda been a pain in the ass hauling that thing outta there," she muttered.

"Been a while since I ate moose," said Zhaabdiis. "Deer is pretty much all I've had lately. They're all over the place down south."

"How do you hunt them? With those things?" She pointed at the unloaded assault rifle on Cal's shoulder.

"Yeah, they're what we had on us most of the time."

"Looks like those would make a mess of a deer," replied Nangohns.

"Depends where you shoot it, I guess," said Zhaabdiis, his voice unsure.

Nangohns intuited that he didn't do much of the hunting. "Seems like a waste to me," she said, and he shrugged.

She led them past the moose and through the trees beyond the swamp until they arrived at a flat clearing surrounded by pines, where they would stay for the night.

Dusk arrived. The fire burned steadily, smoky enough to keep the evening mosquitoes at bay. Zhaabdiis asked Evan and Tyler about their home, both before and after the collapse. They explained their move into the bush after the first deadly winters. They told him how the present expedition had come about, and what they'd experienced so far: their exploration of the dead city and their friend's accident and death. They stopped short of telling him about Linda and the community at Saswin, still wary of their new companion.

Then it was his turn to tell them his story. After a brief stint in the Canadian army, Zhaabdiis had become a long-haul truck driver and was trucking through the American southwest when the power went out. That November, he told them, he was hauling a load of California strawberries.

"I'd been driving a rig for a few years. That time of year is a busy one down that way, because that's where Canada used to get a lot of its produce."

The names of faraway places and details of bygone routines intrigued Nangohns. Up until now, she'd imagined Zhaawnong as a not-too-distant land of past luxuries and lost foreign customs, but as Zhaabdiis spoke, she realized it was much bigger and more complicated.

"I hit the desert in northern Nevada, and the sky opened right up. As soon as the sun was gone—bam! These awesome green lights dancing across the sky. It was the weirdest thing. We called that waawaate, right?"

Amber nodded.

He drove under those lights until two in the morning, when he pulled into a big mall parking lot—he couldn't remember where exactly—to get some rest. When he woke up, his cellphone had no service, and a dozen or so people were standing around one of the mall entrances. "It looked like they couldn't get in," he told them. "I didn't think too much of it right away, but I remember looking out at the street and all the traffic lights were out."

It was soon clear that the power was out all over town. He drove on to the next town, hoping to find something to eat, but all the lights were out there too. "I didn't even bother stopping. People were out on the main street, just waiting outside stores. Lines of cars were waiting at gas stations. I had maybe a third of a tank left, which I figured would get me through Utah and maybe into Wyoming. I just hoped that the power outage was a desert thing, and that when I got to land that wasn't as dry and harsh, everything would be all good."

The group listened intently, silently. Nangohns resisted the urge to ask questions about every detail. She wished someone could point out these strange-sounding places on a map. She knew what a desert was, in theory, but couldn't imagine what it would feel like to drive through one.

In Wyoming, Zhaabdiis told them, his fuel was running out, so he stopped at a truck stop. The power was out there too, but he lined up at the pump anyway and got out to see what people knew. No one had any cell service. The CBs in the trucks were working, but the people on the other end of those radios were just as clueless as everyone else. The truck stop itself had a generator, and he was able to get breakfast and wait to see if the power would come back on.

By the time supper rolled around, he told them, there were probably about thirty people in the truck stop diner. The manager told the cooks to make as much food as they could before it went bad, and the mood was pretty decent that first night.

"Me and a couple of the truckers stuck around the next day. The manager of the truck stop had sent his people home, and a bunch of drivers rolled out, decided they'd risk it and see how far their fuel would take them. At one point, a few guys broke into the truck stop to take whatever they could get. Even the TVs and stuff. Once the dust settled, the rest of us went back in just to hang out. Some of us were holding out hope that things would go back to normal. But it seemed like some people saw it as their chance to smash shit. It was scary to see how fast some of them turned."

After a breath, the pace of Zhaabdiis's speech picked up. He told them how, the next day, he woke up to someone banging on his cab window, asking him what was in the truck. "I wouldn't tell him, and he got all worked up, but eventually he left me alone," he recollected. "People rolled in and out all day. Some were out of gas. It was their last stop. There were families with little kids. A couple bikers. A few dudes tried to crack open the tanks to find a way to siphon gas, but they couldn't figure it out. The workers from the truck stop were long gone. I waited around inside most of that day. I didn't want to be alone. But then this one guy came into the busted-up diner, making all kinds of demands—he was obviously starting to lose it—and shoved one of the truckers, shouting for food. That's when the first shots went off. One of the other dudes, who was there by himself, shot that guy. And then all the guns came out. The guy who was shot just bled out on the floor. Most of the people there went and hid in their cars at that point. Especially the ones with kids. I waited out the rest of the day in my cab."

Zhaabdiis thought he had enough diesel to go a few hundred kilometres, so he took off that night. "Just fired up and rolled out," he said. He saw some of the men in the cars watching him leave—a couple got out and ran after him. He could see them in his mirrors, grabbing on to the rig, but they gave up as he picked up speed. "They disappeared, and all I could see was the road ahead of me in the headlights. It was the last time I saw people for a while."

Zhaabdiis took a left off the main interstate and headed north. He had no real plan, he said; he just wanted to get as far away from the traffic artery as possible. He drove along a narrow two-way route that wound through sprawling hillsides, and as the fuel gauge dwindled down to empty, he turned onto the first dirt road he saw. He couldn't tell where it led; he just drove until he couldn't go any farther. The road wasn't built for a big rig like his. Not wanting to get stuck—he figured he'd need to drive out of there eventually—he stopped when the bush started to squeeze in around him.

"I sat in the cab almost that whole next day, thinking about what I was gonna do."

As the days went on, though, the more paranoid he became. He had a trailer of unripe strawberries, and a personal stash of chips and nuts and jerky that he was trying to save for when he eventually walked back to the road to see if he could flag anyone down.

The northerners let Zhaabdiis speak. Nangohns noticed the relief in his eyes and the relaxation in his shoulders as his story went on.

After about a week, he told them, he was sick of eating berries and could feel the cold setting in. He decided to pack up what he could and start walking. "It only took a couple days to get really rough, though. My food was gone, and those hills and mountains down there—I wasn't prepared for that kind of land."

Finally, after several cold nights, he got lucky: he found a cabin in the bush, built next to a lake in a secluded valley. It had a wood stove and insulation, and was even stocked with some supplies for the winter. He shacked up there hoping to rest for a few days, all the while expecting to see a truck come down the little driveway anytime. But none came, and days turned into months. "Whoever had supplied that place didn't make it," Zhaabdiis speculated.

"So that was your first winter," responded Tyler.

"I just about went crazy from being all alone. I figured if the owner of the cabin showed up, it would mean things were back to normal and I could get a ride back to the real world, but nobody ever did turn up, and when spring came, I started walking."

He eventually found a group of two dozen people in the grasslands to the north. They had claimed a farming compound and were growing enough food to sustain themselves, far away from the cities and towns. They let him stay in exchange for manual labour. He ended up staying there for three years. He still had his gun, unlike the rest of the people on the commune, and he had to chase off desperate survivors a dozen or so times while he was there.

What he learned while living there wasn't so different from what they had heard from Linda and the others: fragmented stories about the chaos that followed the blackout, and the easy spread of sickness in those first few months. The flu took out a lot of people everywhere, followed by a mystery illness that came to be known as "the Dog" because of the barking cough of the afflicted, which signalled a drawn-out, agonizing suffocation to come. Sickness eventually claimed some of the commune dwellers, said Zhaabdiis, and they started to succumb to their own inner turmoil. Some of them broke away, and that's when he decided to move on.

"You left on your own?" asked Cal.

Zhaabdiis nodded. "There was no trust there anymore. Everyone was paranoid. I didn't really sleep in the last couple weeks before I left."

Nangohns watched the brief exchange. Cal was clearly still suspicious, but said nothing more and let the newcomer continue his story.

The next part of his journey took him into the prairies of Lakota territory, in what used to be called South Dakota. He found another community, who after some initial trepidation and awkwardness, took him in, and he stayed for more than six years. "I probably coulda stayed there for good," Zhaabdiis said. "They were real good to me. They even offered to adopt me. But they knew I wanted to get back home eventually, even after all those years."

He left at the beginning of spring the following year, as soon as the snow melted, although he was warned about flooding along the rivers to the east. He planned to go through Minnesota and Wisconsin, and then up through the northern part of Michigan to the land that they used to call Baawaating.

He raised his eyes to see the faces around the fire looking back at him. "I slept in abandoned houses and under trees," he continued. "Fished in whatever lakes I could find. I shot and trapped rabbits and squirrels when I could. I was alone the first couple weeks, but when I started seeing signs of activity—coals from recent fires, and seagulls picking away at things here and there—I knew the Great Lakes must be nearby. Dogs ran on and around the roads. I saw deer in the fields."

Near a town in what he thought was Wisconsin, he told them, he saw a symbol painted on a sign on the side of the road. The cross on its side, like a rifle. Soon he was seeing it everywhere. At that point, he kept his gun at the ready. He came upon the Disciples as they were rooting through an abandoned house. Seeing their numbers, he called out to them, and after a tense interrogation, they took him at gunpoint for several kilometres to a small, ramshackle settlement, which was, to Zhaabdiis's surprise, abundantly populated.

"I got the impression newcomers weren't that out of place there, as long as they looked white," he said. "It was mostly men in their thirties and forties. There were only a few women out and about, and I didn't see any kids. But I would see more women and children later. Everyone's clothing was pretty ragged. I probably looked the worse for wear too, but they were pretty much in dirty rags."

Zhaabdiis was marched into a large house on the far side of town and sat down in front of their leader—a man they called the general. In his fifties, he looked a lot cleaner than the rest of them: clean-shaven, with short hair, a square jaw, and wide blue eyes. He was wearing what looked like full-camo combat gear, with medals pinned on his chest. Another interrogation ensued.

"I talked about how I'd been in the military and knew how to use weapons. That part was true," he explained. But on the march into the town, he had formulated a back story based on the life of one of the men he had met at the commune. He told the general he had grown up in Colorado, served briefly in the army and had been getting by doing odd jobs when the lights went out. And that he'd spent months off on his own, scavenging eastward, eventually winding up in that spot in Wisconsin.

After a long series of questions, the general said he had one more. "He asked how white I was."

"And what did you say?" asked Cal.

Zhaabdiis looked into the fire, then to the ground, and then back up to the eyes gazing back at him. "I didn't hesitate," he replied. "I said, 'One hundred fuckin' per cent.' I knew by then what those guys were about, and I knew I was passing for white."

The onlookers had been expecting this and waited in silence for him to continue.

"Like I said, I'm not proud of it, but I wanted to keep living, so when I saw the opportunity, I took it."

The general, apparently satisfied with Zhaabdiis's account of himself, set about telling him the rules. He was to cut his hair and keep it short at all times. After some basic training, he would be issued a rifle and was to keep it with him twenty-four seven. He would be assigned a group leader, whom Zhaabdiis would report to and obey or be shot.

"He told me all about the Disciples, how they came to be. He talked about their 'missions' abroad, exploring the land and expanding to new settlements," Zhaabdiis said. "Right away, I thought that would be my chance to get back home. Go with them on one of those missions close to home, and then just stay."

Zhaabdiis paused for a drink of water. Nangohns noticed a vein bulging in his forehead. Here he was, accounting for himself once again, she thought. But he'd lied to the general, out of desperation, he claimed. A sinking feeling came over her as she realized that, like Cal, she didn't trust him, and probably wouldn't for a long time.

"Before I left that room, he—the general—told me their overall objective. The point of all those missions." He swallowed once more. "He told me they wanted to recapture the original heroic spirit of the white man and reclaim the land for themselves."

Zhaabdiis looked up, searching for sympathy in his listeners' faces. They looked back, and Nangohns noticed that even Cal's accusatory glare had settled into a stern but neutral expression. They waited for him to continue.

"And yeah, that scared the shit out of me. I was outnumbered."

So he played along, he admitted, and was assigned the rank of private. He told them his name was O'Brien—a name pulled at random from his memory that he hoped would be convincing given his red hair. They fed him and assigned him a bunk in the same house as the general's office. "I accepted the hospitality," he said. "I didn't really realize what I was getting into."

He went to countless drills and training sessions over the following days. It was all very cult-like, and as time went on, he felt their way of life tighten its grip on him.

"If it didn't feel right, why didn't you just leave?" Cal asked.

"After that first day, I don't know," Zhaabdiis answered. "Then the days turned into weeks, and it just didn't seem possible. I felt like I was being watched the whole time. Guns everywhere. I started getting used to it. I started going on missions. I kept telling myself my chance would come sooner or later. My chance to go back home."

In the months and eventually years that followed, he visited all the other outposts along the shore of Lake Michigan. He started getting a better idea of the scope of their network, which seemed unstoppable. "But it was faltering at the same time," Zhaabdiis qualified. For all their guns, the Disciples didn't have a way to make more bullets. They had a lot of ammo stockpiled, but Zhaabdiis knew they worried that it wasn't going to last. And they couldn't maintain the guns all that well, so the broken ones started piling up.

But they did know how to survive. They hunted deer, grew big gardens in the towns they controlled. There was still no power or functioning heavy machinery anywhere, but they had laundries where clothes and gear could be washed and maintained, and field hospitals where recruits with medical experience treated the sick, sometimes at gunpoint, and stock-piled what supplies they could scavenge.

Nangohns was struck by what she was hearing. If it was true, the Disciples had accomplished what they were trying to do, in their own way. They wanted to connect with their kind and build their ancestors' vision of what the world should be. Their world had no room for *her* people, though, she realized, and her mind moved on to what she would have to do if confronted with these men again.

Zhaabdiis was visibly tiring, and seemed unsure of how his story was being received. He straightened his back and took a breath. "After a year of going on those missions, I realized we never went that far north."

"They were only interested in expanding south and west?" asked Evan, clearly wanting him to keep going, still hungry for details about the Disciples' current whereabouts.

"Looked that way to me," replied Zhaabdiis. "It was only last summer when I managed to convince them to go on a mission up to the border—what was the border, I guess. But even those big cities on either side of the river were all but empty, and all but burned to the ground. That's what made me think everyone back home must be dead or gone. I kinda gave up then. Figured I had no choice but to just stay on with them."

His story ended abruptly there. The fire popped and shot glowing embers upward.

"Miigwech, niijii," said Tyler, taking the lead and glancing at the others. "How are you feeling?"

Zhaabdiis opened his eyes wider and exhaled heavily. "Oh, good, I guess," he said. "Chi-miigwech, thanks for letting me share. There's obviously more there. But I think I'm done for now, if that's okay with youse."

"Sure," said Tyler, ignoring emerging sounds of protest from a few of the others. "It's been a long day."

The still night amplified the steady hiss from the campfire. Everyone was starting to stir and get up to prepare for sleep when Cal broke the silence. "Hey, Zhaabdiis, did you learn any Lakota songs when you were out there?"

"Yeah, I did, actually." His eyes lit up. "They still had some big drums out there. We—uh, they had powwows all the time."

"We don't have a big drum anymore. But we brought some shakers with us. You want to teach us one of those songs sometime?"

"Nahaaw," Zhaabdiis proclaimed.

"We'll have time to sing," said Evan, "but for now, let's all get some rest."

NINETEEN

THE NEXT DAY, AFTER a long morning of walking, they stopped on the rocky shore of a small reservoir to eat. In the easier moments, Cal and Amber, and to a lesser extent Nangohns, peppered Zhaabdiis with questions about his life as a vagabond in the aftermath of the collapse.

"You sure got a lot of stories," Evan remarked as he pulled his boots back onto his feet before they set back out.

"Saw a lot of shit, I guess," Zhaabdiis replied matter-of-factly.

"Yeah, I've been listening. It'd be pretty easy for you to bullshit us bush Indians, though."

Zhaabdiis froze almost imperceptibly before relaxing and looking at Evan, stone-faced. "That's the thing about stories about the end of the world, I guess," he said.

Evan raised an eyebrow. Zhaabdiis kept steady eye contact with him.

"You don't know what's true and what ain't," he continued. "You just got to worry about yourself. At first, anyway. But then, if you wanna see the future, if you wanna survive, you gotta find others. If you think you care about the future and your life ends alone, what was it worth?"

The other four tied their shoes silently, listening.

"You have to walk with a purpose, that's what my nooko-mis always told me," Zhaabdiis went on. "You need a destination and a reason for getting there. Otherwise, you'll get lost. Forever. I know you know what I mean, if you've been walking for as long as you say you have."

Evan's cheeks warmed in a brief flash of defensive ire, with his doubt about Zhaabdiis thrown back at him. He drew in a breath. "I do know what you mean," he replied coolly. "And we're getting close to where we're trying to go."

As they finished gearing up, Nangohns caught Zhaabdiis eyeing her bow and quiver on the ground beside her pack.

"Get anything with that lately?" he asked.

"Yep," she replied. "Some rabbits. A deer back a ways."

"A deer? Really?"

"No one's as good with the bow as her," Cal cut in.

"It's a cleaner kill," Nangohns added. "Plus, if you miss with an arrow, the animal might not hear your shot and may stay put. Can't say the same for hunting with a gun."

Zhaabdiis glanced down at the rifles on the ground and back to her. She raised her eyebrows.

"Think you could show me how to take a few shots with that bow?" he asked.

"Maybe once we get somewhere we can target practise. With those shaky hands of yours, we'd lose some arrows for sure out here in the bush," she teased him.

"Cool," he smiled and turned to hoist his pack onto his back.

Tyler led them back through the trees, with Evan keeping watch at the rear.

In the afternoon they spotted a clearing in the forest ahead and soon emerged onto an overgrown dirt road. They hesitated at first, wanting to avoid major routes, but the knee-high weeds and shrubs punching through the surface along the way made it seem remote enough, and they decided to follow the road as it meandered southeast, sheltered by tall deciduous trees. Although the overgrowth was thick, the even ground gave their muscles and joints some relief.

The buzz of crickets and the chirps and calls of various birds echoed all around them. The sun pummelled through the green awning, concentrating radiant heat in slivers and swaths of yellow beams. The weeds on the road dragged against the bare shins of everyone but Zhaabdiis, who still wore full-length military-style fatigues from the waist down, but was now sleeveless up top, like the rest of them.

The road carved through the bush in a more or less straight shot, occasionally wrapping around large rocks or dodging ponds and swamps that now crept across the route. They followed it for the rest of the afternoon, until it stopped at a rusted, tangled fence overtaken by saplings and brush. Tyler guided them over the crumbled barricade, and they passed slowly through thick scrub that grew up through and over a wide concrete platform, cracked and worn from twelve years of temperature extremes. The staging area, which would once have been busy with trucks and shipping containers, led to a wide, deep quarry. Approaching the edge, they looked down into a dark pool at the bottom.

"May as well stay on the south side," Evan said, and he set about leading the six of them around the quarry, staying several metres from the edge to avoid pitfalls. It had caved in here and there, years of snowmelt and rainfall pushing brown and grey dirt and gravel from the wall to the bottom of the quarry.

Evan's eyes followed a small landslide of rocks and natural debris to the water pooled at the bottom. On the edge of the pond, a white crane stood in shallow water. Its yellow beak swerved from side to side as it flashed its red feathered crown like a beacon. Evan stared at the tall bird, which didn't seem to notice the walkers several metres up on the ridge. Its long, thin legs propped it up out of the water, putting the majestic plume of white feathers that covered its wings and entire body on display. He was mesmerized by this crane, a species he hadn't seen before.

"Hey, Evan, eyes ahead!" Zhaabdiis blurted out from behind.

Evan turned his head forward and noticed a gap in the grassy floor just steps in front of him where the ground had given way. "Shit, thanks," he said, and veered away from the edge.

They soon found themselves trudging through the bush once again, and as dusk fell, they looked for a suitable spot to set up camp. They navigated the craggy terrain and kept watch for even ground with enough firewood around. Sunset had darkened the leaves above by the time they settled in place for the night.

Nangohns had been sleeping soundly for several hours when she was jolted awake by a voice coming from her right, just steps away from where the six walkers circled the fire.

"Gshkozik." It sounded like a man. "Gdoo-nsastaanaawaa na Nishnaabemang?"

Her eyes opened wide and her heart pounded. The campsite was still shrouded in shadows in the pre-dawn light.

"Do you understand me or what? Wake up," the man repeated in English.

Nangohns heard the others rustling around her. She raised her head in her father's direction. He was looking at her, making sure she was safe.

Evan turned in the direction of the voice and said, "We hear you," his voice croaking awake.

Nangohns sat upright, a bit frantic, trying to get a better look at whoever had woken them up. In the thinning darkness, she could make out a tall figure with long hair. Behind him stood another man, slightly shorter and wider.

"Where are you coming from?" the taller man asked.

"We came from up north. Been walking all summer," Evan replied. He tried to slow his breathing.

"What about that one?" The man raised a hand in Zhaabdiis's direction on the far side of the extinguished fire. "He come down with you too?"

"No, we just met him," Evan confirmed.

Everyone was sitting upright now, their hands flat on their knees or the ground to deter any sudden movement. They were waiting for the man to speak again, but he didn't respond at first. He seemed to be scrutinizing the campsite, thought Nangohns. She focused on the two visitors. They had similar facial features to folks back home: narrow, piercing eyes and long noses. These two could be brothers, she thought. They stood at attention, and yet now they didn't appear threatening to her.

The one in front spoke again. "You should stay off the roads," he said, "even if they seem safe."

"You saw us back there?" asked Tyler in disbelief.

"We heard you coming even before that. Crashing through the bush like a moose."

"And you followed us all the way here?"

"Not exactly. We had some other stuff to check out. But it was pretty easy to pick up your trail again."

"Who are you?" asked Evan.

"I think you owe us your introduction first. You're the visitors in our territory."

Evan stood, and the others got to their feet as well. He cleared his throat and introduced himself by name and home community. The others did the same. Zhaabdiis mentioned his clan as well. The others from the north often omitted that detail, because not all of them were sure of their clans in their traditional system.

"You really have come a long way, then," the taller man said. "We figured as much. You looked like this was all new to you. Where are youse going?"

"We're told our original home is called Wiigwaaswaati-goong." Evan kept speaking for the group. "The place where the birch trees grow. None of us have ever been there before."

The one in front looked back at his companion, and they shared a silent glance. Evan perceived their recognition as a good sign.

"You know it?" Evan asked.

They only nodded, their faces betraying nothing.

"We've also heard the big island near there might be safe for us. If we can, we want to get there."

"Who told you about the big island?" The taller man's tone sharpened.

Evan hesitated, then said, "Some Anishinaabek we met along the way. But we also know of it from the old stories. We know it's a special place for our people."

The two men conferred silently again. When the tight-lipped one gave his companion a curt nod, the tall man looked back to the group. "My name is Anakwad," he said. "And this is my brother, Giizhik." He gestured back at the silent one. With the morning light, the two men had come into sharper focus. Anakwad wore black nylon cross-training pants and a blue light-fleece sweater; Giizhik was dressed in a similar way, in grey pants and a faded green shirt that looked to Evan like gear from an outdoor outfitter. Their clothing was patched and stitched in spots, and they both wore weathered brown moccasins. Long black hair draped their faces, which were tanned and slightly creased in the forehead and around the eyes. Evan estimated they were roughly the same age as him.

Continuing in Anishinaabemowin, Anakwad identified the island as their home. Making out these words, Nangohns felt an excited chill run up her arms.

"You're a couple days out," Anakwad continued, switching back to English. "It's not far. You won't make it, though, if you keep this shit up."

Evan asked him what he meant.

"You should stay off the roads," Anakwad repeated. "Only the weak and desperate keep to the roads. And they're the most dangerous."

"Did you see something? Somebody?" asked Tyler.

"No, but we've heard of some movement again," Anakwad explained. "It's been a long time since we've had any wanderers out here."

Another ripple of anticipation ran through Nangohns. She thought of the men they had encountered just a few days ago and steadied her head, knowing a glance in Zhaabdiis's direction might give him away. But she suspected they already knew.

"Youse guys seem to be in pretty decent shape," Anakwad went on. "Youse made it this far. Looks like you know how to live out here." He glanced in Zhaabdiis's direction. "It's the ones that only knew how to live in camps and cities and who walk on roads that we worry about. Some come running from trouble, some come looking for it. That's why we're out here."

"You came to check it out?" asked Evan.

Anakwad explained that they came to the mainland every once in a while to look for medicines that didn't grow on the island. "We have eyes out on the mainland all the time. Our friends told us about some stragglers that passed through this way a while back."

"How many of them?" Cal asked, stepping forward abruptly. "What did they look like?"

The two visitors simultaneously took a fluid step back, seemingly back on guard.

"They counted four altogether," replied Anakwad, as he redistributed his weight on his back leg in response to Cal's sudden movement. "All zhaagnaashak. Didn't get a good look at them, though, I'm told."

The lifeless bodies of the Disciples sprawled in front of the cottage flashed through Evan's mind, the horror still fresh. He turned to look at Cal, now at his side, and nodded. Cal's eyes widened and he bit his bottom lip.

Evan looked back to the brothers and cleared his throat. "We saw some of them too," he said.

His proclamation seemed to hang in the cool morning air, triggering fear in his group and intrigue in the strangers.

Anakwad raised an eyebrow. "Where did you see them?" he asked.

"In the bush, a ways back to the west."

"Where are they now?"

Evan looked down at the twigs and rocks at his feet. "They're dead," he uttered.

Anakwad's jaw tightened as his head swivelled slowly in his brother's direction. Their brown eyes met under down-turned brows, but they said nothing.

To Evan, the silence was excruciating. His mouth smacked as he opened it again to speak. "When are you going back home?" he inquired, a slight tremor running through his voice.

"We can't take you with us," said Anakwad, intuiting Evan's next question. "We have more business out here, and we don't know how long we'll be. Plus, if we're a bigger group, we're a bigger target." He glanced deliberately at Zhaabdiis again. "We've been watching you, and we think we know good people when we see them. But you'll have to make your own way. We can tell you how to get there. It will be up to our people there if they want to let you in."

Amber approached and stood beside Evan. She extended her closed left fist to the men. "Boozhoo," she said. "We offer this semaa as guests in your territory. We don't have much, but we would be honoured if you accepted our offering. We thank you for receiving us here."

Giizhik walked to her and held his left palm upward and smiled. She placed a small pouch of tobacco in his hand. He wrapped his thick fingers around it and bounced his fist up and down. He extended it upward and said "Miigwech."

"Looks like this is your territory too," Anakwad spoke again, smiling for the first time. "We'll welcome you home properly when it's safe to do so."

Evan had retrieved the tattered road map, but Giizhik softly waved it away. "You're on the right track," he said, indicating east with the side of his hand. "Eventually you're going to get to a river. Large, with lots of rapids. Just follow it south for a ways until it bends hard to the west. Don't follow it that way. Look for a forest of birch trees to the east, and from there move south. The river is calm and shallow there, so you can cross safely. Keep looking for those trees as you go south. They will lead you to where you need to go: the place of the birch trees, just like our ancestors called it. It's not just a clever name." He too broke his hitherto stony expression, giving them a gentle smirk and a wink.

"But," Anakwad warned, "there's a couple of settlements between here and that river. We know them all, and everyone is peaceful. We have an agreement, have had for a while now. Just be mindful of them. And if you do come across them, don't stay for too long."

Evan's mind was swirling with questions, but before he could ask, Anakwad continued, reassuringly, "There's no one settled here that you need to worry about. They aren't Anishinaabek. There might be a few among them, but not many. We get along with them well enough, but we all try to keep our distance."

The two brothers readied to go.

"Youse all just lean south," repeated Anakwad. "But be careful, and be quiet. You'll end up at the road before you know it."

"You should go," said Giizhik. "Hopefully we'll see you on the other side."

"Nahaaw," Anakwad nodded. "Baamaapii."

The two brothers walked away, in the direction the walkers had come from the day before. They both looked back and nodded one last time before disappearing over the hill and into the bush.

The six that remained in the small clearing were speechless for a moment. The quiet of the morning had become a swirl of wonder and confusion, and Nangohns could feel herself processing the strange exchange.

"Did . . . did that actually just happen?" Cal asked aloud.

"I felt his hand," Amber said. "Felt pretty real."

"How long do you think they were following us?" wondered Nangohns.

"Probably longer than they admitted," said Evan. "But there's no point worrying about it. If they wanted to stop us from getting to where we're going, they could have. But they're right. We should get moving."

As they mobilized, Nangohns's mind buzzed. For the first time, the homeland their elders had told them about, and the island foreseen—or remembered—in so many dreams and visions felt absolutely real. The chill of the morning air as they broke camp foreshadowed the impending fall. The leaves on the trees were still a vibrant green, but summer's descent had surely begun. When they finally made it to the north shore, they'd have to set out for home almost immediately if they were to get back before the weather turned. If they made it back and through the winter, she thought, it could be the last northern winter for her and her family.

They entered the basin of Lake Huron, a rugged terrain carved by ancient waterways that still nourished the land. They climbed up and down rocky crevasses all morning, circling lakes and stepping through streams. By midday, the summer heat returned, and they shed the outer layers from the night before. They watched majestic birds of prey soar and circle high above, and they stopped at midday to offer semaa for the eagles that comforted them on this last part of their journey.

"Take this all in," Evan reminded them as they paused to eat on a sandy beach on the edge of a still lake. "We are lucky to be here. It's a beautiful place. And we're almost home."

That afternoon, Nangohns led them farther east, back into the thick bush that closed in around them. The perpetual layer of dead leaves crunched below their feet. Nangohns remembered what the brothers had said about them lumbering like moose through the forest, and she made a point to move as silently as she could. After a while she sensed that the others were following suit, or trying to. She became increasingly aware of the sweat beading on her brow and dripping from her armpits and down her back. Her legs ached. When she occasionally glanced back at Evan, he looked markedly weary but determined as they pressed on.

The afternoon had just begun to wane when they heard the rapids through the trees ahead. They were getting close to the river that they would follow until it bent west, when they would look to the east for the birch tree forest. They walked straight through the thinning brush and down an embankment to arrive at the swiftly moving water. The din of the rapids expanded into a roar as they approached. They stood high on a natural causeway, a safe distance from the churning river that pounded over and through large, treacherous rocks. The booming rush of the white water awed them. Even standing away from the maelstrom, they had to shout to communicate. There was no way they could cross the bone-crushing rapids to the eastern side, so they pressed on south.

Downriver, the channel widened and the rapids calmed slightly, but the current itself didn't relent, swirling along the surface in a soothing, spiralling pattern that disguised a potentially deadly current below. The river remained impassable.

The clear water gave Nangohns a look at the sand and rocks on the bottom, and she thought of the lake back home that she had fished in since childhood. In her mind, she saw her mother, her brother, and his young family all waiting on the shoreline for them. Longing welled into her throat.

Shouts from the others up ahead on the causeway pulled her from her reverie. She heard Cal's voice and wished he'd keep it down, thinking once again about the brothers' warning. Then she saw what the commotion was about. A hundred metres downstream, a strange structure protruded from the lush branches that covered the shoreline. The others went silent as they assembled and slowly made their way farther along the ridge for a better view. In front of them, a large wheel-like structure, turning with the flow of the water, came into view where the river bent. The green overgrowth concealed anything else around it.

"Looks like a water turbine," said Zhaabdiis.

"What's that?" Nangohns asked. She had never seen anything like it, and was struck that something so unfamiliar even had a name.

"You can rig those to generate power. Somebody set that up to power something."

"Must be one of the settlements those two told us about," said Evan.

As the water wheel churned downstream, they examined the bush behind it for any sign of life.

"We must not have gone far enough south," Cal said. "What should we do?"

The rapids remained impassable, and Evan urged them to continue following the river, even at the risk of encountering whoever lived here.

"What about these?" asked Cal, pulling at the strap around his chest that held the assault rifle on his back.

"I don't think we should be packing those on the way in, no matter who's there," said Tyler. "It could be asking for trouble."

"But what if they're packing too?" asked Zhaabdiis.

Nangohns felt the uncertainty that had taken hold of the entire group.

"We're wasting time," Evan declared. They would have to continue as they were. Ditching the weapons wasn't an option; they didn't know when they might be back through here. If the brothers were right and they didn't have to worry about the people who had settled here, they would just have to make it clear that they were passing through.

They decided to move farther into the bush to avoid detection, but to their surprise, the densely wooded ground became clearer with each step. Occasionally, they saw the flat surfaces of tree stumps and other signs that the forest had been worked with tools and cleared away.

They were once again feeling exposed. Nangohns suggested that a river as big and old as the one they were following usually had higher ground nearby and they should try to find it. They traversed the lip of the slight river valley and soon reached a ridge, where the canopy opened to offer more light. Nangohns scrambled up the ridge ahead of the rest and stopped at the summit. The others caught up and gathered around her. From the higher elevation, Nangohns pointed out the river to the east and the outline of several cabins and other buildings spread out on the west side of the waterway.

"I count about seven buildings from here," Tyler said, scanning the shingled roofs. The rest of the settlement was obscured by thick green leaves in their sightline.

"Check that out over there." Evan pointed to the west of the cabins. "Looks like a wind turbine. With that water wheel too, they must have some power here."

Nangohns followed her father's finger to a tall white structure that towered over the trees. The slow-turning blades mesmerized her; back at the old reserve, the cell and radio towers that stood taller than the trees didn't move like this. She caught herself staring, and squeezed her eyes and shook her head to snap herself out of it.

"We need a better look," Nangohns said. She walked up to a rock outcropping a few more steps away from the river. She hoisted herself up onto the grey stone, leaving enough room on the jagged platform for Tyler and Zhaabdiis. "Stay low," she advised. "We're a bit out in the open up here."

Tyler squatted and turned to the three on lower ground. "Pass up those binocs," he said.

Cal dropped his backpack and opened it to pull out the binoculars he'd raided from the pack of one of the dead Disciples. He handed them to Tyler, who slowly stood to take a look.

He raised the green camouflage field glasses to his eyes and adjusted the focus wheel in the middle with his fingers. He exhaled and steadied his hands, like he was sighting an animal through the scope of a rifle.

"I see some kids," Tyler said. "There's six of them there. They're kicking a ball around."

"Keep still," Nangohns said. "What else do you see?"

"There's an older guy watching them. White hair. Maybe in his sixties. Looks like a younger guy there too, maybe your age, Nang."

"How do they look?" Evan asked quietly from below.

"They look . . . okay," replied Tyler. "No guns or camo. They look healthy, I'd say. I can't tell for sure, but looks like they're all zhaagnaashak."

"Sounds pretty harmless," noted Evan. He looked at Nangohns crouched on the rock for affirmation. She tightened her lips and shook her head.

"There's a couple more people coming into the clearing," Tyler continued. "Looks like an older lady in a wheelchair. Oh . . ." He froze, his mouth slightly agape. "There's another guy coming in from the right. Camo hat and shorts—"

Zhaabdiis bolted upright. "Gimme those," he said, grabbing the binoculars out of Tyler's hands. Nangohns saw his fingers tremble as he brought the lenses to his eyes. He rotated his head until he found his target. "We gotta get the fuck outta here," he said. His head pivoted nervously towards the others. "Now."

Amber gasped and they all snapped to attention.

"He's one of them," rasped Zhaabdiis in a loud whisper. "A Disciple. I know him—and he knows me." Without looking, he handed Tyler the binoculars and hopped down from the rock. He approached Evan, eyes determined. "If he sees us, there'll be trouble," he warned.

"Are you sure?" asked Evan, keeping his voice low and firm.

"I'm sure as shit. He's a younger recruit. I remember him from one of the boot camps last fall. I think his name's Holden."

"Looks like he's by himself," said Tyler. "He stands out among the rest of them. I don't see any guns."

Zhaabdiis shook his head, now clearly panic-stricken. "It doesn't matter. They know how to take over places like this. He's scouting ahead, but more will follow. We gotta fuckin' go!"

"Okay," Evan said. "Let's go."

Nangohns and Tyler leapt down from the outcropping. The group strode quickly along the ridge, following it away from the river. They descended into the shallow valley, and soon they were all running. They vaulted over rocks and branches, and hustled into the unknown expanse of forest. They stopped only when they felt they had put enough distance between them and the settlement, and when the fire in their lungs and throats was too intense to ignore.

TWENTY

BYPASSING THE SETTLEMENT AND its impressive turbines
had thrown them dangerously off route, and after a precipi-
tous rush west, away from signs of human life, Tyler used
Biiyen's compass to set a course southeast and back towards
the river. By dusk, the rush of the rapids beckoned them
back, and they were once again treading carefully along the
bank as the gloaming closed in around them. Finally, when
they couldn't go on any longer, they found enough space on
the ground to sleep.

They took turns keeping watch, but no one had a comfortable sleep that night. Their meat was dwindling, and the
vegetables Linda had sent them off with were nearly gone.
They would need to harvest more soon.

The next morning, they set out again in single file along
the riverbank. Nangohns noticed Amber take her place behind
Zhaabdiis, and detected an air of anxious anticipation. They
all had questions, but exhaustion and fear of being found had
kept them mostly silent since beating their retreat the day
before. But that morning, after another extended jaunt in
silence, Nangohns saw Amber tug on Zhaabdiis's pack. Her
ears perked up.

Without breaking stride, Zhaabdiis turned his head to listen.

"You're sure you've seen that guy before?" Amber asked.

"One hundred per cent," Zhaabdiis repeated without hesitation.

"Tyler's not sure he saw us," Amber continued. "Do you think he'd try to follow us if he did?" She kept her voice low, almost inaudible, but Nangohns made out every word.

"It depends," replied Zhaabdiis. "He was probably with another group that split up. The ones who know how to handle themselves in the bush do that. If he's trying to track us down, he'll probably try to find his associates first."

"Another group?" A hint of incredulity had entered Amber's voice, and she spoke louder now. No longer satisfied with a private word, she wanted them all to hear. The procession came to an abrupt halt.

"What's going on?" said Cal.

Amber's gaze remained fixed on Zhaabdiis. "I thought you said only a small group of you came up here."

"Yeah, it was just us and the other crew who went east. He wasn't with them, though. So—"

"So you don't know what we might be walking into, here, or down south, or anywhere," deduced Cal, speaking sharply. His hostility towards Zhaabdiis had mellowed since their first few nights together, but it now seemed to be rekindled.

"Calm down," said Tyler. He turned to Zhaabdiis. "If he is who you think he is, what are the chances he wants anything from us? We're just wandering through. We're useless to him."

"Not totally useless," Zhaabdiis said. "Not if we lead him to something."

"No matter who's out there," Evan spoke up, "we carry on. We've already seen the good that lives on."

In front of him, Nangohns turned to offer a comforting smile.

"We've seen the evil too," he went on, walking up to Amber and placing his hands on her biceps. "We're not gonna get any guarantees out here. But I believe this is where we are meant to be. We know that the Anishinaabe way lives on down here, even after everything that's happened. For that reason alone, we have to believe in each other now." He looked up to the high ceiling of green leaves filtering the early-morning sunlight. "These trees give the breath of our ancestors back to us. This river returns the water that kept them alive. We have to carry that with us, follow the path."

He turned to Zhaabdiis. "I'm going to ask one more time. Is there anything you think we should know about your friends?" Zhaabdiis opened his mouth as if to protest, but Evan silenced him with wave of his hand. "Anything we need to know that you haven't told us yet. Like something you think we might not want to hear?"

Zhaabdiis's shoulders hunched, and he abruptly tightened his posture. Nangohns recognized the cringe of shame. He had been determined to earn their trust when he told them his rambling story. She believed most of it was true, but could taste his desperation, and it couldn't be ignored that he'd made his way the last few years by living a double life. Saying one thing but meaning another, lying to survive.

"By now you know we're not going to hurt you," Evan said to Zhaabdiis. "But we need to know that you're not going to hurt us, on purpose or by accident."

Zhaabdiis's indignation had faded away as Evan spoke. Raising his eyes from the ground back up to Evan's, he took several deep breaths before speaking. "I'm telling you the truth. If they sent more scouts up here, I didn't know about it—"

"But?" interjected Cal in a mocking tone.

"But the colonel and us had been marching north longer than expected. We were due to turn back around the time we found you guys. It's not unusual for missions to drag on, but it's possible they sent a few scouts after us."

"Okay," said Evan. "Nothing anyone can do about that. Anything else? Any reason any of them would have gone past the cottage and found their friends dead?"

Zhaabdiis tightened his lips and shook his head determinedly.

"For sure?" Evan probed.

"One hun—"

"Do me a favour," interrupted Evan. "Stop saying that. There's no hundred per cent anything out here."

Zhaabdiis nodded. "Look. Holden, the guy I saw, he's a scout sent from the border camp. The second group wouldn't have had time to double back from their eastern mission by now, but it's possible they've been having luck scavenging around here and are preparing to send men in. What we did—"

"What you did, you mean," corrected Nangohns.

Zhaabdiis shuddered, as if twinging from pain. "What I did." He took a breath. "I'm pretty sure they don't know about their dead friends, is what I'm saying. On my life," he said, his voice gravelly. "And if they find out, and we run into them, I'll take responsibility. But they'll kill us all."

"Well," said Evan, "I guess that's about what I figured." He addressed the rest of the group. "We're pretty much in the same boat we were in when they found us. Only now we're within striking distance of what we came to find. If they're sending more guys up here, they're a problem that isn't going away soon. But maybe, if those brothers were speaking true, we don't have to face them on our own."

"Hell yeah," said Tyler. His face remained serious, observed Nangohns, but his eyes were full of love for her father, his best friend. "And hey, chin up," Tyler said to Zhaabdiis. "We haven't gotten each other killed yet." He gave him a playful punch in the arm.

Zhaabdiis jolted and tensed up at the unexpected contact, his eyes wide, but when Tyler started cackling mischievously, Nangohns saw the pressure that had been building up in Zhaabdiis since Amber's first question dissipate. He was, in some way, one of them. At least for now. And that was alright.

Satisfied that the air was cleared, Tyler pulled Biiyen's compass from his pocket and said that south was across the river.

"So now we've gone too far?" asked Cal, sounding more worried than angry.

"We musta hit the bend in the dark last night," Tyler said. "That was supposed to be our cue to bank east."

"There's no avoiding it now," said Evan. "We're gonna have to cross the river."

"And keep an eye out for birch trees," said Nangohns with a subtle grin.

They walked down the bank to the edge of the river. The distance across was a good stone's throw. They could see the bottom of the river most of the way across, but there was a dark gap in the middle. The water was still running fast as they took off their packs to hold above their heads as they forded the river.

The chilly grip of the waterway wrapped around Nangohns's ankle as she stepped in. She steadied her foot on the rocky bottom and carefully lowered the other into the flow. Evan had treaded forward to lead the others. He had just about reached the darker water in the middle when Nangohns heard a loud splash and looked over to see Tyler staggering, nearly losing his balance as a submerged branch popped up from beneath the surface, dislodged, she figured, by his steps. The long, glistening, awkward branch was immediately seized by the current, which sent it hurtling downriver. She whistled to Tyler, and when he nodded that he was alright, they pressed on and were soon crawling up the other side of the bank.

Nangohns caught a flurry of movement in the corner of her eye as she stepped up to dry ground. Startled, she looked downstream to see a small, wiry brown marten dart along the rocks and come to a stop a few metres away. It stood looking at her with its soft, foxlike expression, exposing the yellow fur on its throat. "Boozhoo waabizhishi," Nangohns whispered through a smile, and followed the rest away from the river.

Their shoes slopped one foot in front of the other over a wide span of bush. The trees spread and the ground lowered the farther southeast they went. Soon enough they found themselves passing clusters of thin white birch trees, growing tightly together in pockets—their cue to straighten southward. To Nangohns, they were hopeful beacons in the green woods, marking the way every few dozen steps.

Buoyed by this sign, the walkers followed the trees until the morning passed and the sun beamed at its noon peak. Through the forest up ahead, the sky opened up, which usually meant water, but the shade remained thick. Still at a considerable distance, they couldn't tell if what they were seeing was, in fact, the vast shoreline of the mighty lake. Nangohns looked up through the gaps in the leaves for birds, but none dashed across the fleeting blue patches of visible sky.

"Shit," Cal said. "If that's not big water up ahead, it's the road." He planted his feet, and the others came up beside him.

Nangohns's heart sank. She suspected Cal was right: what they were seeing was the highway that once carried cars and trucks clear across the country.

"I'll go up first and take a look," said Tyler. He walked towards the open air and stopped at the bottom of a gravel incline. His torso twisted as he turned back, gesturing for the others to stay a safe distance behind him while he looked around. They stood together in the safe shade of the trees on the other side of the ditch.

Tyler's feet slipped on tiny stones as he climbed up cautiously, staying low, parallel with the rough slope. He peeked out above the pavement, looking in both directions. After a few breaths, he turned back to them and extended a palm outwards, telling them to stay put.

Nangohns's throat constricted with thirst as she watched Tyler turn back to the road. He leaned forward and placed his hands on the gravel shoulder to extend his torso upward while keeping his legs below the surface. He didn't want to give himself away. He again looked in both directions, then scanned the treelines on the other side. He then turned back and descended the embankment to rejoin the others.

"It's a long stretch," he said. His pupils were constricted at the centre of his dark-brown irises by the bright morning sunlight. "To the west, the road goes straight and then eventually up a hill. There's big rock cuts on either side that way. The other way, to the east, it gradually goes around a long bend. Can't see nothing around that corner."

"What about straight ahead?" asked Evan.

"I couldn't really tell. There's just trees."

"But we know the lake is that way," said Cal, pointing across the road. "That's south. The lake is south. We should make a run for it."

"That ain't happening," said Evan. "A few seconds is all they need to spot us. They followed us for more than a day, remember."

Cal lowered his eyes and nodded.

"Let's go that way." Evan pointed east. "We can stay low, down here in the ditch. We might find a culvert to crawl through."

They walked silently in the shade of the trees that towered over the ditch, making their way as quietly as they could over the brush. As they approached the curve in the road above, Evan listened for a stream, but nothing babbled nearby. He noticed a slough caressing the side of the ditch up ahead and slowed. The ground softened, turning to thick mud the closer he got. The other five tempered their pace behind him until he stopped. He scanned the surface of the water in the ditch and saw the upper lip of a rusted culvert about halfway across. He faced the others and said, "It's all clogged up."

They stood in a tight bunch, uncomfortably close to the sparse gravel of the embankment up to the deteriorating asphalt.

"What about the river?" proposed Amber. "It leads to the lake somewhere down there. If we go west, we'll find a bridge to go under. Easy cover."

"We crossed hours ago," said Evan. "And it goes a ways west before it runs back south. We might overshoot where we're trying to go by a long way."

"Walking along this ditch can't be much better than walking right on the road," said Nangohns. The others turned to listen. "The brothers said to stay off the road. We just need to cross it. We want to put it as far behind us as we can."

"We could wait until dark," suggested Tyler. "May not make any difference, but we'd be harder to shoot at, at least."

Nangohns, Cal, and Amber turned to Evan, apparently supportive of this plan.

Evan squinted up at the sun. "Let's head back into the bush and double back to where we first came out. We'll lay low until dark, scout around as best we can, and make a run for it. We'll want to walk all night and get as far from this damn highway as we can." He looked deliberately at the rifles looped around the arms of Tyler, Zhaabdiis, and Cal, ensuring the rest of the group followed his eyes, then gently tapped the handgun tucked into the back of his shorts. "Stay sharp," he advised in a low command.

Nangohns reached across her chest to feel the cool synthetic material of her sturdy bow. The trusty grip reassured her, even amongst these louder and deadlier firearms. She craned back her head to take in the azure dome above her. She closed her eyes and breathed in the humidity and decay of the ditch, then exhaled and took the lead, heading back to the treeline before turning west, back to the cluster of birches that first marked their arrival at the road.

They settled in behind the trees and passed around their last bit of food. Once they were clear of the highway, Nangohns thought, she'd have to go looking for something substantial, perhaps a deer. There was something terrible about sitting in place when there was so much to do. Amber and Cal were lying a few metres from where the rest of them had hunkered down. Maybe they needed this downtime more than they realized, but sitting still with her thoughts was becoming untenable. Getting away from the perilous highway, dodging Disciple patrols, finding food, making the trek back home, and all the other uncertainties in between: she couldn't calm the churning thoughts that flashed through her head, unsought.

It was nearly dark by now, and visibility in the clearing beyond the trees had diminished considerably. Tyler and Zhaabdiis had managed to fall asleep, and Evan, who sat upright against a large tree trunk, seemed to be nodding off himself. They had discussed doing some scouting before crossing the road, and Nangohns knew she'd be the stealthiest one for the job. To her, there was comfort in twilight. Leaving the group dozing, she silently bounded off, bow in hand. She paused at the edge of the trees and observed silently for several minutes, looking east and west, before darting through the ditch to where the steep escarpment began. She found a patch of high grass where most of the gravel had washed away and stayed low enough to the ground that, if she hadn't been seen sprinting through the ditch, she was likely invisible from where she crouched. After watching the eastern and western approaches for another few minutes, seeing and hearing nothing, she scrambled up the escarpment, knowing she was once again exposed.

Flat to the ground, with her palms in the dirt by her sides, she allowed her head to break the plane of the road's surface. She twisted it slowly to the east, to look to the bend in the road that passed through the rock cut, and then to the stretch that led west. Like the other big highway up north that led into Gibson, the pavement wasn't as cracked and overgrown as the smaller routes through the region, but the annual freeze and thaw had left some gaping potholes and wide cracks in either direction. She saw no movement on or near the road.

The sudden gnashing of gravel startled her. She retreated as fluidly as she could into the grass and slowly slid out of sight into the ditch. She listened, swallowing her last bit of saliva. She pushed herself to her feet and carefully rose to a half squat to look back out at the road. The pounding of her heart echoed in her chest like the honour beats of the drum at the peak of grand entry at a powwow. Some fifty paces down the road to the west, she made out the silhouette of a large deer's abundant antlers against the pink remnants of sunlight. It stood still, the breadth of its rack clear in the dusk. She knew it heard her and was looking in her direction. A sharp snort came from its snout, and then another. The beast turned to face the north side of the road and lurched forward. Its hooves clumped along the pavement, then upset the gravel again on the other side. Once out of sight, the deer was absorbed into the dark bush without a sound.

Preparing to approach the road once more, Nangohns crouched into a starting position. In the opposite direction of the deer, about the same distance away, she saw something move and realized it was Evan and Tyler, their heads swivelling left and right, scanning the ditch. She felt a sharp pang of guilt for leaving without a word. It took everything not to call out to them. They shouldn't be out in the open like that, she thought. But it was her fault.

She was just about to make a run for it when the bang of a firearm rang out. She splayed herself flat in the high grass. The shot had come just as she readied to sprint back to the trees, but she couldn't tell if it had been directed at her or at Evan and Tyler. She saw her father duck, but he was still visible, crouched low at the treeline. If they didn't start running soon, she was going to have to. Another shot sliced the air, closer to her this time. She had to move. Her bow in hand, she rolled onto her stomach and exploded into a sprint, back to where she had seen her father. Her legs burned, and she could hardly feel herself breathe. The boom of the last shot was all she heard, and she kept her eyes fixed on the clump of birches straight ahead, beacons in the early evening. Suddenly, a third shot rang out. She thought she felt something zip past her ear, then saw the bullet hit the tree trunk she was running towards. She instinctively put her arms over her head and tried to lower herself even more as she ran.

The shot had been at eye level, and when she glanced back towards the escarpment, she saw two men with shaggy beards training their rifles on her from the road. "Freeze!" one of them shouted. She knew they had her in their sights. She fell to her knees. "Don't you fuckin' move, now," she heard another voice shout. Nangohns tried to comply, but her chest was heaving and her hands were trembling. She heard the sound of dirt scraping and saw, out of the corner of her eye, a third man sliding into the ditch a little way down towards the bend in the highway. She saw him raise his rifle, and a devastating calm came over her. She was going to die.

The third man yelled into the woods just beyond her, and to her horror, Evan, Amber, and Zhaabdiis emerged from the shadow of the trees, holding rifles in outstretched hands to show that they weren't going to use them. The third man bellowed at them to drop everything.

"Hands where I can see 'em," the first voice hissed, right behind her this time.

She gasped and jerked around involuntarily; the start seemed to knock all the air from her lungs.

"Whoa, there," the man said quietly. "Do what they did. Drop that bow and anything else, alright?"

She could see him now. His low beaked cap concealed his eyes and accentuated his long blond beard. She couldn't see the second man, but she was sure there were at least three of them. She dropped her bow. She strained to listen over her pummelling heart and heard the third man—they were all nearly identical in size and shape—telling Evan, Amber, and Zhaabdiis to move into the opening beyond the trees.

The Disciple with his gun trained on her approached, kicking the bow away, never once letting his guard down. "Stand up, turn the fuck around, and walk," he said, keeping an ample distance between them.

When she saw her father and two friends kneeling with their hands on their heads, guilt and panic once again swelled in her chest.

"Two of 'em got away," the third man announced. "Took off into the bush."

The man with the blond beard spat on the ground. "They'll come back," he muttered. "They always do."

Another man approached from the west. He looked younger than the others, even in the fading light. Nangohns wondered if this was all of them. Anakwad and Giizhik had heard of a group of four.

"You three can go ahead and get down on your bellies," the blond one said in an even drawl. "Get them rifles," he commanded the young-looking one. The kid started jogging towards Evan and the others until the blond one barked, "Eh! You forget something?" He indicated the bow and arrow lying in the grass.

"Over there," the man ordered Nangohns, pointing with his gun to where the others lay flat. "Move." He took his hand from the barrel to tip his cap higher for a better look at her as they made their way to the other captives. The older man from the cottage, the one Zhaabdiis had called the colonel, had seemed to enjoy threatening them. This one seemed calm, almost disinterested. Nangohns figured he was the leader.

"This is a shit spot to hole up, but I guess you figured that out by now," he said. "Anything, private?"

The younger one was down on one knee, searching her friends' and father's pockets. He stood back up. "The big guy was hiding a Glock in his pants"—the blond one whistled as if impressed—"but otherwise, they're clean."

"As clean as injuns can be, I guess," the second one said. In the dim light, Nangohns could see that he was slightly stockier than her captor and had a patchy brown beard.

The men ordered them all onto their feet and lined them up on the flat ground between the trees and the road. The younger one bound their hands behind their backs with coarse synthetic rope, like the kind Nangohns used to patch her fishing net back home.

"Like I said, this is a shit spot to sit and wait," the leader said, "but we'll tolerate it in case your idiot friends come back to try to save you."

Nangohns hoped Cal and Tyler were still running. Part of her hoped they'd be smart enough to never look back. Her stomach fluttered.

The leader, whose gaze had hardly left Nangohns, walked up to get a better look at the others. It was nearly dark, but she saw the silhouette of his gun barrel lower for a moment before steadying on Zhaabdiis. "Well, fuck me sideways," he said. "O'Brien, what the fuck are you doing with these damn injuns?"

Zhaabdiis tensed. "Howdy, Sarge," he replied. His voice was firm. "Fancy seeing you all the way out here."

The man with the brown beard cracked Zhaabdiis over the head with the butt of his rifle. Zhaabdiis crumpled to one knee, letting out a pained groan. He tensed his abdomen and pushed himself back up to his feet.

"Answer the goddamn question, private," the sergeant said. "What in the name of firepower are you doing running with these fuckin' savages?"

Zhaabdiis swallowed. He took a deep breath through his nostrils, looked steadily at Evan, and exhaled. "These are my people."

"The fuck they are. Where's your troop?"

"There's something sketchy going on, boss," piped up the young one. "I think he's a goddamn turncoat."

"You shut the fuck up," said the leader. "This ain't your concern right now."

"I left them behind," Zhaabdiis said calmly.

"Where?"

"A ways up north. Like Holden here"—Zhaabdiis nodded at the youthful one—"I went out solo for a bit."

The sergeant raised an eyebrow and spat. "I think that's some bullshit," he said.

Zhaabdiis stared straight into his eyes but didn't move. After years of drifting, he'd mastered an inscrutable gaze.

"Well," said the sergeant, after what seemed like a full minute of leering, "I am curious and all, but I ain't wasting no more time on a motherfuckin' traitor."

A deafening bang exploded from his rifle, and the force of the shot knocked Zhaabdiis onto his back. He lay motionless on the ground as blood from the hole in his chest soaked his white T-shirt. Amber stifled a scream. Evan gasped.

"Now, you all tell it to me straight, or else I'm gonna do you all in like this dirty fuckin' turncoat," the sergeant said. "So, where y'all headed? Where were you taking O'Brien?"

Evan looked up from Zhaabdiis's body. "This is as far as we were going," he said. "I swear."

"That right?" The sergeant looked at Nangohns.

"He's telling the truth," she said.

"Well, what's down here?"

"We don't know. We came this far to see."

"They're keeping secrets, boss," said Holden, stepping to the sergeant's side.

Evan stared at the young man. "We saw you at that camp," he said. "Did you tell the people there that you're a Disciple?"

"It don't matter now." Holden smirked. "The buzzards are probably picking at 'em right about now."

Evan winced and looked at the ground.

"The fuck is he talking about?" the brown-bearded man asked.

"A settlement less than a day's walk from here. They had some off-the-grid hippy shit rigged up. More shit than we could ever carry back, so I cleared 'em out. That's our place now. Just waiting for us."

The sergeant nodded, and Nangohns could tell it was the first he was hearing of this. She thought of the people who'd lived in the houses they'd seen from the ridge. The children gleefully kicking around a ball. *If we hadn't run away, would they still be alive?* she wondered.

"We were just there." The words escaped Evan's mouth. "How did you—"

"We don't sleep," said Holden. "When you sleep, we move."

Amber whimpered and bowed her head, unable to cover her face with her hands tied behind her. Nangohns could see her friend's shoulders shaking.

Evan turned back to address the sergeant. "I'm telling you the truth. We heard there was good fishing down here on the big water," he said. "Our home is gone. We needed somewhere to start over."

Holden scoffed. "You were going fishing with all them guns?"

"You're lying to me," the sergeant said.

"Why would I lie?" said Evan through clenched teeth.

"Enough of your fuckin' questions." The sergeant raised his voice. "I think you're meeting someone here. Someone's been following us the last few days. Following us following you. We wanna know who. We might let you live a little longer just to find out."

Evan hesitated. Nangohns looked at her father. She wanted him to say something, anything, to prolong their lives. But what? In the brief hush, she heard the faint crumple of a leaf in the bush behind her. When their captors didn't respond, her heart rate slowed.

"Sergeant, what the fuck are we doing here?" The man with the brown beard broke the silence. "If those guys who escaped have any firepower at all, they could get the drop on us." He turned to indicate the high rocks on the far side of the highway. "I say we shoot 'em or else haul them up to higher gr—"

A faint hiss whispered through the air, and an arrow landed in the man's chest with a thud. He looked down at the shaft protruding from his solar plexus. As a line of blood escaped his lips and ran down his beard, another arrow struck Holden in the belly, and he crumpled to the ground, wheezing for air.

The sergeant's eyes widened, and he spun in the direction the arrows had come from, raised his rifle, and fired into the trees in two controlled bursts. "What the fuck?" he muttered. He stepped back and was retraining his gun on the three captives when a third arrow whipped through the air into his right eye, felling him where he stood.

Two lean silhouettes slid fluidly out from the trees behind them. Their chests and feet were bare, and they wore only dark shorts and thin bundles around their shoulders. Their black hair was tied back tight to their scalps. They moved in unison, like twins, melding with the land below and around them.

Evan dove to the ground, pulling at the cords tying his arms.

Nangohns recognized the brothers and cried out, "Gii-zhe-giiwewak!"

Rolling in the dirt, Evan struggled and flopped to free himself, but Amber's soft voice stopped him. "I got you," she said. While Evan had tried to reason with the Disciples, Amber had been loosening the cords binding her hands. Nangohns had thought she was just trembling with fear. But after the first Disciple went down, she had crawled over to him and, her hands free, removed a large knife from his boot. Now she placed a hand on Evan's shoulder until he stopped writhing, then carefully cut the nylon ropes around his wrists.

Suddenly, more arrows flew over their heads towards the escarpment. In the dark, Nangohns saw, to her horror, three more Disciples running toward them from the road. A few shouts went up, and a flurry of gunfire washed over them. Hands freed, Evan ran to where the sergeant lay twitching and removed a pistol from his holster. He fired towards the men above. Even in the dark, Nangohns could see blood spray out the back of one of the men's heads.

"Get to the trees," Evan yelled. Amber, who had flung two of the rifles over her shoulder, ran towards Nangohns to untie her. Walking backwards, the sergeant's pistol at eye level, Evan fired two more shots in the direction of the advancing Disciples. The whoosh of two more arrows rushed past him. One of the two remaining Disciples had made it to the bottom of the slope only to take an arrow in the groin. As he doubled over with a piercing shriek, his gun went off in his hand, firing at random.

Evan felt a hot blow to his gut and crumpled forward in crippling pain. He saw the man lumbering towards him, the arrow sticking out of his groin, and struggled to lift his pistol.

"Naadmooshin!" Nangohns screamed, as Amber struggled to cut her free of the nylon bindings.

The Disciple, gasping and holding his wound with one
hand, had straightened himself to fire again when two arrows
struck him in the face and shoulder, knocking him flat on his
back. He shuddered for a few seconds, then went still.

Giizhik and Anakwad moved smoothly into the clearing,
bows drawn and trained at the last Disciple, who, seeing his
friends lying dead in the ditch or writhing in their death throes,
spitting blood and grunting, was scaling the escarpment back
up to the highway.

Nangohns, her hands now free, ran to her father.

"Evan!" Tyler's voice cried out. He and Cal ran into the
clearing.

Amber, who had a rifle aimed in the direction of the fleeing
Disciple, dropped it when she saw Cal and ran into his arms,
weeping.

Tyler joined Nangohns at Evan's side. "Hold on, bud.
We're gonna fix you up," he said, but his voice trembled in
unmistakable panic.

"I can't believe," Evan said through pained breaths, "it
happened again."

Tyler let out a stunned laugh and grabbed his friend's
hand. Evan gripped back, and Nangohns was relieved to see
that he still had some strength in him. She whispered to him
in the old language, offering thanks and prayers. "Bizaanyaan,"
she whispered. "Be still."

Giizhik and Anakwad were suddenly there next to them,
crouching beside Evan. Giizhik inspected where the bullet had
entered Evan's gut. Blood had soaked the bottom half of his
shirt. Nangohns followed Giizhik's eyes to the wound. Giizhik
looked up at his brother and nodded.

278

"To the water," Anakwad said calmly. "Our boats are there. Let's get him up and move."

He waved to Tyler, and as the two tallest of the group, they wrapped Evan's arms around their shoulders and lifted. They moved quickly up to and over the road, and then down a hill on the other side, with Cal, Amber, Nangohns, and Giizhik following. The rugged slope gave way to a sandy beach, and the trees opened to reveal, in the bright moonlight, the softly rippling water of a lake that seemed to go on forever to either side. They'd been much closer to the big lake than they'd realized.

Two rowboats sat on the sand. Anakwad and Tyler carefully placed Evan in the one on the left, sitting him upright. He was lucid, but clearly in pain, holding his belly, occasionally pulling his hand off the wound to look at his bloody palm.

"Gegwa, don't," said Anakwad, and he produced a thin blanket, which Evan clasped over his wound.

Nangohns, who was carrying his pack along with her own, dropped both into the bottom of the boat and climbed in to sit across from him. Cal, Amber, and Tyler threw theirs and an extra into the other boat. They'd left Zhaabdiis's body behind, Nangohns realized. Anakwad stepped in and grabbed the oars of the first boat. Giizhik shoved them out into the water and splashed over to the second boat. Amber and Tyler jumped in as Giizhik and Cal launched the heavier of the boats from the sand and guided it out into the open lake.

"Giizhik! Dbaziin!" Anakwad shouted at his brother from the water.

Holden was stumbling down the hill, gripping the broken-off shaft in his gut with one hand and firing a handgun erratically with the other. Cal ducked, still guiding the boat into deeper water. Nangohns reached for her bow from the ribs of the boat, but Anakwad leaned forward and put his hand over it, shaking his head and nodding towards the receding shore. The bullets strayed far from the crew in the other boat, and a moment later Nangohns heard the gun click empty. Holden lunged forward and screamed, cursing the fleeing party.

Giizhik took one last look at the figure on the shore before climbing over the gunwale and taking his place at the oars. Cal, the last one in the water, gave the aluminum boat a final push forward and clambered in. With heavy pulls on the oars, they slid into the open water.

Holden collapsed on the beach and struggled to get back to his feet. As the small flotilla escaped, they watched his silhouette go still, and shrink into the distance.

TWENTY-ONE

THEY ROWED LATE INTO the night until they cleared a point and entered a wide cove. Behind a long sandy beach stood a tall backdrop of homes and former shops that reminded Nangohns of the buildings they'd seen in the highway town where they'd first encountered gunfire. Crumbling docks, barely afloat, bobbed in front of an abandoned marina, where a paved boat launch ran into the water. Anakwad steered his boat that way. "Biinaak daabaan!" he shouted as they neared the shore. Two figures emerged before darting back into one of the buildings. Nangohns saw dim orange light flicker in the windows, the same colour as a small fire that burned down the shore in the cove. Nangohns heard a few more shouts, but couldn't make out the words. The two figures emerged again with a long wagon.

Nangohns held Evan's hand. He slumped forward in pain. Her eyes darted from him to the landing and the people there. "It's okay, Noos," she said calmly.

The aluminum rowboat slid up onto the beach, the sand grinding softly on the keel. Anakwad hopped into the water with a splash and waved Nangohns in as well. He grabbed Evan under the armpits, and she lifted his feet. They carried him over to the cart that waited on the boat launch. Evan groaned with each step. They placed him gently in the wagon, and he let out a deep breath as he lay back. When he was settled, the two figures—a young woman and a young man—tugged on ropes to pull the wagon slowly up the incline. To Nangohns, even in the dim light, neither the woman nor the man looked Anishinaabe.

She looked at Anakwad, and he motioned her on with his chin. She turned her head to her fellow travellers, who were unloading the boats.

"Go on," Tyler said. "We'll catch up with you."

She felt a pang of sadness and fear about splitting up the group in a strange place. She looked down at her father's blood on her hands, and immediately thought of her mother. She followed the wagon up onto the even pavement, tinged a dark blue by the moonlight.

The pair pulling her father turned left down a short, broken road, past old storefronts to a stand-alone house with peeling white paint on the outside. They carefully manoeuvred the carriage up a ramp. At the front door, they crouched to talk to Evan.

"Can you walk?" asked the woman, adjusting her headband over her high, tightly curled dark hair, which formed a halo around her head.

Evan shook his head no.

The young man, who had sandy-blond hair, nodded at his counterpart. "Okay, we'll get you up and in there," he said.

Nangohns noticed she was clenching her fists and teeth as she watched.

The door opened and an older woman with long white hair ushered them in. "Biindigek," she said. The helpers hoisted Evan up, with his arms around their shoulders, and stepped inside with him. They carried him through the foyer and past a large wooden staircase into an adjoining room, where they set him down on a bed, cradling his head as they eased it onto a pillow. Nangohns knelt on the floor beside him and smoothed back the hair on his scalp. It felt hot and damp with sweat.

The woman who had let them in walked into the room and placed an unfolded metal chair beside the bed. She wore long blue shorts and a sleeveless white top. "Boozhoo," she said with a hint of serious cheer. She looked Evan up and down, then introduced herself. "Noodin ndizhnikaaz. Migizi ndodem. Aaniish ezhnikaaziyin?"

"Evan," he croaked.

"Aaniish na?"

"Nwiisgines." He clenched his eyes and pulled his lips in tightly. "It hurts."

"Oonh, gwiisgines." She turned to Nangohns and asked, "Giin dash?"

"Nzegis," she replied, admitting her fear and worry.

The woman, who had introduced herself as Noodin, switched to English. "So what happened?"

"He got shot."

"By who?"

"Some guys with beards who attacked us on the highway."

"What did they shoot him with?"

"I think it was a handgun, but I wasn't right there."

"Right in the belly, eh. Hmmm. Okay, Evan, I'm gonna lift up your shirt and take a look." She peeled the soaked tank top from his torso. He gasped as the dried blood yanked at the wound. She leaned in to inspect the hole. "Not a whole lot of blood, all things considered," she said. "But that's not to say there's not a lot of damage. I'm gonna touch your forehead now." She placed her palm on his sweaty brow and frowned slightly. "Okay, Evan, we'll try to get you fixed up here. And you, daanis, what's your name? I'm sorry I forgot to ask."

"Nangohns."

"Ah, that's a beautiful name. My nooshenh, my grand-daughter, is named Nangohns. You'll see her toddling around here somewhere. Anyway, Nangohns, let's let your dad rest a bit before we start treating him. Darren and Kayla here will get him cleaned up and give him some medicine to start. Come outside with me."

Noodin got up from the creaky chair and walked out of the room. She went around the staircase, through the foyer, and out a back sliding door that led to a wide deck with a view of the water. Nangohns followed her slowly, taking in as much of this strange house as she could. Candles and lamps had been lit, and Nangohns could see that the walls were bare and everything including the sparse furniture was made of wood. When she stepped through the glass door, she could see out to where the boats they'd rowed in were beached, but no one was there.

The elder woman placed her hands on the weathered deck railing. Nangohns took her place beside her, feeling the wobble of the old structure. Noodin kept her eyes on the water as she spoke. "Just so you know," she said, "I was a doctor before the end. I had a clinic here. So I'm not some random whacko who looks at gunshots for fun." She smiled kindly, her white teeth beaming in the moonlight, but it did little to ease Nangohns's fears. "I know you're worried about your dad, and I wish I could say it's all gonna be okay, but I don't know that for sure. I don't know what that bullet did to his organs. We're good at treating most things nowadays, but bullets are still an X factor. This is the first one we've seen in a long time."

"What's an X factor?" Nangohns asked.

"That just means it's unpredictable. It's gonna take time before we know how best to help him."

Nangohns looked back out to the water, and then to the buildings lined up on the street, moonlit from above. "Where are we?"

"Oh, this place used to be called Sunrise Harbour. We just call it Oodenaang now. Our town. There are other old communities here on this island, though, that still have their Anishinaabe names."

"Are we safe here?" Nangohns asked, looking out over the water.

Noodin moved in closer and wrapped her arm around Nangohns's shoulders, turning her towards her. She looked her in the eyes. "Yes, you are, my girl. I promise."

Nangohns began to weep, and Noodin held her tightly, stroking the top of her hair even though the younger woman was nearly a head taller. They stood for a moment in silence.

Noodin let go and moved back, gripping Nangohns's elbows sympathetically. "Let's go inside," she said. "We'll have some tea and get you something to eat."

A kettle was already boiling on the wood-fired cookstove in the kitchen. Noodin invited Nangohns to sit at the wooden table. She prepared tea and brought a pot and cups to the table. She went back to the counter to scoop something out of a large bowl into two smaller ones, then brought Nangohns a serving of wild rice and blueberries. "Just picked those blueberries yesterday," she said. "They've been growing pretty well in the patch just on the other shore there. I'll take you over there later."

The wild rice was chewy and was complemented by sweet bursts from the berries. The food reminded Nangohns of home.

The blond boy named Darren came out of the room where Evan lay and summoned them both over. He explained that they'd cleaned the entry wound and applied a salve, but the bullet remained lodged somewhere in his abdomen. They'd been able to sit him up and give him some tea of hemlock bark and other medicines. Evan had fallen asleep right afterward. Darren invited them in to check on him.

Noodin walked in first and felt his forehead once again. "He's still pretty hot," she said.

Nangohns stepped around her for a look. Evan lay on his back, with his head tilted away from them, resting high on the pillow. A blue sheet and wool blanket covered him up to his neck. The creases in his forehead and his downturned brow marked a painful sleep. Nangohns extended a trembling hand and rested her palm against his sweaty scalp to feel his warmth and the life left in him.

"We'll let him rest, my girl," said the doctor.

Nangohns thanked them all, and they left the room. They returned to the back deck, where Giizhik had brought Cal, Amber, and Tyler.

"How's he doing?" Tyler asked.

"He's in pain," Nangohns said. "But I think he's in good hands here."

Noodin introduced herself, and so did the others. She explained Evan's situation. "A person can live with a bullet in their belly," she said. "But only if it hasn't done a lot of damage."

She offered them some tea. Anakwad arrived with an older man in tow. He was shorter and stockier than the two younger men, with much more grey flowing in his black hair. Anakwad introduced him as Ogimaa.

"That's just my nickname," the jovial man assured them. "I'm not really the chief. People call me that for fun because I came up with the idea to move to this place. We don't really have chiefs and councils or anything like that. Peter is the name I was born with. Call me Pete if you want."

He approached Nangohns and held out his arms for a hug. She embraced him easily, and he broke away and smiled. She watched him go around the circle to welcome their group to the community. His warmth seemed counter to his thick, defined arms and barrel chest. The crow's feet at the corners of his eyes conveyed an eventful and emotive life.

"I heard you came pretty far to get here," he said. "I want you to know there is lots of room for you here. Stay for as long as you need to. And we'll talk about getting your relatives down here too."

Ogimaa told them how they came to settle in this town. The island had been home to a few permanent towns and reserves since the mid-nineteenth century, he said. The original idea was to make the entire island Anishinaabe territory as the region eventually known as southern Ontario was being settled by Europeans. But when the government learned of the resources on the island, they walked back that initial promise and created towns on the shorelines where Anishinaabe inhabitants had fished since well before the arrival of settlers. Authorities would not allow the new reserves to touch the water.

Nangohns recognized this account of the time they called Jibwaa from stories she'd heard before, in her village.

Ogimaa jumped ahead to the time of the blackout. Most of the people who had lived in the nearby towns took off back south, he explained. Some who stuck around "couldn't hack it"; some died. Some came to the reserves—even up from the cities—desperate and needing help. Some of those people were still there now. "After a while," said Ogimaa, "we hand-cranked the swing bridge to the mainland open so no one could walk across anymore. Too many people kept showing up. A lot of trouble. Some still tried to boat and swim over. That's when we decided to fully move into this town, to set up a kind of outpost, about a year and a half after the lights went out. No one's tried to come to the island for a long time, though. You're the first new people we've had here in at least a few winters."

"How many people live on this island?" Tyler asked.

"I dunno exactly. It's a big island. People are spread across seven or eight communities. A good five hundred or so, anyway. But we got lots of room. Lots of abandoned houses. Most of them are still standing good. A lot of them got wood stoves. Good furniture. Not many clothes left, though. Those all got raided early on. We took all the extras already. That's why I gotta cut the sleeves off these tiny-ass T-shirts all the time!" He flexed his arms irreverently and stuck out his tongue. "All that to say, we are ready to welcome you back, if this is the place you think you've been searching for. My heart tells me this is your home. I can't repeat that enough. We can make a plan tomorrow for how to get your people here. Maybe we'll send these two guys up with you to help." He gestured back at Anakwad and Giizhik. "Let's get you all settled in first, though. You need some rest."

"Come on in. I'll show you around," Anakwad said.

They walked back inside to the main foyer. The northerners' packs were stacked against a couch in the living room across from the stairs. Anakwad took them up to show them the rooms where they'd be sleeping. The beds were neatly made and appeared to have sat unused for a while.

A shrill wail from below bounced off the wooden walls. They froze, and the gaping whites of their eyes flashed at each other before they dashed downstairs. Tyler was the first into the room and saw Evan flailing in the bed, groaning in between shrieks of pain.

Nangohns pushed past Tyler to crouch by her father's side. "Noos, it's Nangohns. I'm here. What's wrong?"

She grabbed his hand, and he squeezed hard. His body stiffened as he sucked air through his nose. She tried to soothe him with affirmations, and in moments he relaxed slightly and his sweaty body settled into the bed. His breathing slowed, and he opened his eyes. His head turned in her direction, and she smiled. Her eyes were wet, and her bottom lip trembled.

"Boozhoo, n'daanis," he said.

"Hi, daddy," she said.

"Hi, my girl," he repeated. "How are you?"

"How am I?" She chuckled. "What about you?"

He smiled at her. His eyes were vacant, and he didn't notice the small crowd behind her. "Oh, my girl," he said. "I had the most amazing dream."

"Did you? Tell me about it."

"I dreamed I was high above the water. The sun was shining so bright. There wasn't a cloud in the sky. The blue water stretched as far as I could see. And then I was falling. I looked down, and the ground was coming up real fast below me. It was a beautiful rocky island. I was falling, but I wasn't scared. I watched the land get bigger and bigger. I saw the waves rolling into the rocks. I saw the green moss. I saw the blueberry bushes growing in between the rocks. And when I hit the ground, I bounced right back up. I was jumping. And then I realized I could jump from island to island. So I jumped all the way up and down this long shoreline. The islands and the mainland looked so beautiful. So many trees, so many beaches, and big, strong rocks. And bushes that feed everything. I jumped so high I could see the land on the other side of the lake. The lake was so huge and blue. Just the most beautiful water you could ever imagine. So full of life. So full of history. And every time I came down to jump again, there were Anishinaabek there. They waved at me, and smiled, and cheered me on. I jumped and jumped and—"

Evan fell into a coughing fit. His body heaved forward, curling his torso upright. Droplets of blood splattered from his mouth onto the blankets in front of him. He collapsed back into the bed, his body heaving. "Nbi," he said. "Water."

Noodin rushed in with a bottle and tipped it into his mouth. Water spilled over his face and neck, and he choked on the rush of liquid into his throat. He raised to his elbows on the bed and caught his breath, his chest surging. His face contorted and he groaned in pain before falling back to the pillow.

Nangohns gently placed her palm on his forehead. "Nbaan, Noos," she said, softly encouraging him to sleep.

She looked back at Noodin, who gestured them all out of the room with a tilt of her head over her shoulder. They quietly stepped out one at a time to let Evan sleep.

Evan woke in pain and thirst twice more in the night. Nangohns lay on the floor beside his bed, trying to calm herself enough to sleep while nurturing her father when he needed it. By dawn he was sleeping soundly, and she arose when she heard the footsteps of the others upstairs. The young helpers, Kayla and Darren, arrived shortly after, with baskets of duck eggs, potatoes, and apples for breakfast.

After they ate, Noodin came to check on Evan and assigned a rotation of watchers to stay in the room and monitor his condition. Darren took the first shift, and Ogimaa returned to take Nangohns, Cal, Amber, and Tyler on a tour through the town. They met about a dozen other community members while walking along the short streets, but Ogimaa was careful not to overwhelm the newcomers, given their ordeal and the condition of their leader.

After the tour of some of the buildings, gardens, and gathering spaces, they returned to the house for lunch. Evan remained in a deep slumber. Giizhik and Anakwad brought over fresh fish, fried in a pan, and stayed for the afternoon to discuss the journey back north and the eventual exodus of the people of Shki-dnakiiwin to the south. Ogimaa and Noodin joined the planning session as well. They sat in a circle on the deck deep into the afternoon. Tyler, Cal, and Amber shared specifics of their home community, like who lived there and the roles some would play on the trek. Anakwad and Ogimaa worked out logistics, like routes and supplies. Nangohns and Noodin dipped in and out of the conversation to check on Evan.

The sun moved to the west, and the supper hour approached. Nangohns and the doctor went together once more to assess Evan before preparing food. Their footsteps on the wooden floor stirred him. Nangohns stood silently at the foot of the bed, while Noodin remained by the door. Suddenly, he shrieked and bolted up to his elbows, his eyes blazing wide in the faint light of the room. Both women jumped, and Nangohns rushed to her father's side.

"Noos, I'm here," she said just above a whisper. "What's wrong?"

His head fell back to the pillow and thrashed from side to side with his eyes squeezed shut. He calmed, and opened them again to look at his daughter. His heavy panting scared her. "Water," he said, and Noodin moved to give him some.

"No, take me to the water."

Nangohns looked gravely at Noodin. She tucked in her lips, and early sympathy softened her eyes. She only nodded, and reached down to squeeze the young woman's hand. Nangohns squeezed back, and choked back a sob in her throat. Evan lost consciousness again.

The commotion had drawn the others on the deck back inside. Tyler tapped Nangohns on the shoulder and motioned her out of the room. Evan was sleeping deeply, so they wrapped him in the coverings on the bed, and six of them carried him out to the same wagon that had rolled him in. Nangohns followed, unable to break her gaze from his pale, worn face. They placed him gently in the flat bed of the cart. Tyler insisted on pulling him alone.

Ogimaa directed their procession past the beach where they'd landed and through the town. On the far side of the main road, a footpath originally carved for tourists wove high onto a rocky ridge to a lookout over the shore. The sun lowered slowly to the horizon in the west and brought a lively hue back to Evan's skin as the cart bounced along the cracks and bumps of the trail.

They stopped at the lookout. Evan's breathing became erratic, and his body tensed up.

"I want to bring him closer," said Nangohns. "I want him to be near the water."

Tyler, Anakwad, Cal, and Giizhik leaned down to wrap their arms underneath Evan's shivering body. His lips were dry and his face was drained. They lifted him from the wagon and walked carefully down the massive rock that sloped to the water, stepping around blueberry bushes and evergreen shrubs. Nangohns walked ahead to pick a spot. She stopped at a smoother plateau where the lime-coloured lichen softened the hard edges of the ancient stone of the island. She looked back at them and nodded. They descended the pitch carefully and set Evan down on the rock. They untangled the sheet and left the wool blanket beneath him.

Nangohns stepped away to allow them their final moments with Evan. A man who silently led. A man who had humbly carried a dying community on his back into a new era. A man who would help his people return to their true homeland and be among their relatives, the descendants of their common ancestors.

Giizhik and Anakwad each gave brief, thankful farewells and left. Cal placed his hands on Evan's chest and head, and spoke to him for a long while. Amber stood behind him with her hand on his shoulder. He stood and wiped his eyes, and walked back to hug Nangohns. She thanked him, and he walked back up to the lookout. Amber crouched, closed her eyes, and whispered a long prayer, before joining Cal and the others up the slope.

Tyler sat cross-legged in front of Evan, looking out to the water and then at his friend. Nangohns couldn't hear him speaking, and she didn't want to eavesdrop. But then he began to mumble. And then laugh. After talking some more, he cried. He repeated this cycle over and over until he was ready to leave his friend, who was still breathing but wouldn't open his eyes again.

Tyler stood and wiped his eyes. He returned to Nangohns and embraced her. "It has been the honour of my life to know him," he said. "I am in your family's debt forever. I love you all."

"I love you too, Tyler. We'll start over in his name and spirit."

They hugged once more, and he went up to join the others.

Nangohns breathed in the moist air. She let out her breath in both relief and despair, then walked down to sit with her father in his final moments. She lowered herself to the rock and felt the layer of soft lichen on the outside of her calves as she sat, lifting Evan's head and shoulders and resting them on her lap. His body eased and tensed in fits. His face had lost most of its colour, and his eyelids were stretched dreadfully thin. Air came in spurts from his open mouth. She looked at his yellow teeth against his pasty lips, and yearned for one last communication from him. She cradled his head in her arms, stroking his sweaty scalp and savouring the last of his warmth.

From behind her, she heard the group that had welcomed them here begin a travelling song. They'd brought no drums, so hands tapped the beat on the loose wooden railing of the lookout. Evening was nearing. A few others had emerged and, hearing the travelling song, had come to pay their respects. Cal led the song, and Noodin, Ogimaa, Anakwad, Giizhik, Darren, and Kayla sang along in simple harmony. Tyler stood on the rock in front of them, dancing and singing, his eyes shut tight.

Nangohns looked back down at her father and smiled. A faint hum came from his throat, nearly in harmony with the song. It was his final message from the physical world.

Nangohns's eyes flooded with tears. "Miigwech, Noos," she said. "Pane ga-zaagi'in."

The song ended, and the sun began its crawl down to the vast water in the west. The light shifted from yellow to orange as Evan Whitesky stopped breathing. His body stiffened in his daughter's arms, but she held him close nonetheless. She looked back to see Tyler all alone on the rock, watching them with his elbows resting on his knees. She turned down her lips, and he knew. He buried his face in his hands, and she looked back to the vessel that had been her father.

The sun touched the western horizon. Nangohns looked around at the blueberry bushes and the strong, ancient rocks. The humble waves rolling in from the big lake caressed the hard shore, welcoming her home.

EPILOGUE

WAAWAASKONE CROUCHED IN FRONT of the bush and reached for the ripe blueberries among the tiny green leaves. The hem of her rainbow-coloured ribbon skirt brushed the rocky ground and bunched as she lowered. She stroked the plump blue cluster of berries with her fingertips. She brought it out from under the bush's leaves and into the morning sunlight for a better look.

"Waabdenoon na?" Nicole asked from a few steps up the slope. Her grey hair waved in the warm summer wind.

"Mii go gnabach," the girl replied to her grandmother. She tucked loose strands of long black hair that had fallen from her braid behind her ear, squinting in the bright summer radiance.

The blue water behind her rippled under a steady breeze, soaking up the vast, cloudless sky above. Nicole watched her granddaughter gather the berries with intention and care. The girl's dull-white T-shirt stood out among the grey rocks and green bushes of the shore and the wide lake so immense that the shore on the other side was imperceptible. The massive, life-giving body of water still impressed Nicole, eleven winters after they'd walked to this place to settle forever. She had never lived on water like this.

Nicole had brought Waawaaskone to the bushes on the edge of the water to pick the berries the girl would offer to her family and community at the feast that would finish her year-long coming-of-age ceremony. She came to this spot often to revel in the magnificence of the lake, to harvest berries on her own, and to remember Evan. She regularly offered semaa here, in the place where he'd taken his final breaths.

"Nookomis," Waawaaskone said, "Gii-ntaa-miin'ke na nmishoomis?"

Nicole laughed at the image the girl conjured of Evan crouching down and picking blueberries, and tried to remember if he was particularly skilled at it.

"Gaawii nmakwend-ziin," she replied. "Gii-ntaa-miijnan sa wii go miinan!"

The girl chuckled, thinking about the grandfather she never knew enjoying eating blueberries rather than picking them. The only image she had of him was as a young man in an old printed family photo Nicole had salvaged from their old home before they left. In the faded image, her father, Maiingan, and her aunt, Nangohns, were only five and three years old, respectively. It was the last picture the four of them had posed for before the lights went out.

Waawaaskone had no memory of that place. She wasn't even a year old when they'd walked through the old reserve on their exodus to the island on the big lake. That day, Nicole had stopped to grieve in front of their old house on the rez for a long while, knowing she would never see Evan again.

The months after Evan, Nangohns, Tyler, J.C., Amber, and Cal left had been agonizing for her and most of the community. There had been no way of knowing where they were, or if they were alive. The ones left behind carried on as best they could, summoning patience and hope, making preparations in the event that they would soon head south themselves.

When the fall came, at the end of the month some people called Waabaagbagaa-giizis, or the Moon of the Turning Leaves, four of the walkers returned home with two strangers. Evan and J.C. had been replaced by two brothers, Anakwad and Giizhik. Nicole could remember the relief and heart-break she had felt all at once. Her daughter had made it back, but her partner in life had not. Her grief hadn't relented until she had finally arrived, the next summer, at the spot where he had died.

The mass departure was carefully calculated and surpris-ingly swift, but executed in careful stages. Tyler and his partner, Nick, went immediately back south with Anakwad and Giizhik. Their goal was to arrive at the island before snow-fall. Along the way, they cleared a trail with machetes and marked the route with whatever expendable colourful materi-als they could use to tie around tree trunks and branches.

After what felt like an endless winter, the entire commu-nity left at the end of the flooding season, travelling in groups, allowing the older and physically challenged ones more time to traverse under the guidance and protection of the young. They rested at Linda's camp for many days on their way through, and many of the elders and children stayed behind while a core group of adults—including the veteran walkers—went ahead to assess the safety of the road. Once they made it to the island, the two brothers came back with Nick and Tyler to help the remaining northerners who would migrate to the big island for good. Some had decided to stay behind at Saswin and settle there instead.

They met no human threats in the ghost towns or hiding in the ditches of the crumbling roads, for which Nicole gave thanks. She, Maiingan, Pichi, and the toddler Waawaaskone had gone with the first group. There was no question that they would make the Anishinaabe island their new home, with others from all walks of life. They needed to see where Evan had ended his journey. Where this land and their people had been renewed.

Waawaaskone returned her attention to the blueberry bush. She tenderly plucked the ripe fruits from the stems and dropped them into her birchbark basket. Nicole caught a glimpse of her haul, berries nearly cresting the rim. The girl, also noticing the nearly full basket, gently placed it on the rock. Standing to stretch her legs, she turned to face the water. Moving down along the slope to stand beside her granddaughter, Nicole put her arm around the girl's slender shoulders and pulled her in. They gazed out to the undulating lake.

"Nookomis," Waawaaskone said, preparing another question for her grandmother, "mii na go maampii pane da-yaaying?"

Nicole breathed in, smelling the moisture of the summer air and the vegetation that thrived on the rocks around them. Just twelve winters old, the girl knew her people's history of wandering, pushed north and south by tragedy and necessity. She squeezed Waawaaskone's thin shoulder tight and kissed the top of her braid. Small waves smacked lightly against the rocky shore in front of them.

"Enh, nooshenh," Nicole replied, "mii go maampii pane da-yaaying."

She repeated it once more, almost to herself, in the language her granddaughter didn't understand, as if to remind the ghosts of history who had tried to destroy them but failed.

"We'll always be here."

ACKNOWLEDGEMENTS

Writing a novel is not an individual endeavour. There are several people I want to acknowledge and thank now that this one has been published.

First and foremost, the generous and supportive readers of *Moon of the Crusted Snow* who wanted a sequel made this book happen. I am forever grateful to you all for kindly and enthusiastically encouraging me to re-enter this world and walk with these characters again.

My stellar agent, Denise Bukowski, picked up on that enthusiasm, and emphatically suggested I develop a story idea for a sequel. She has been one of my greatest advocates in this industry, and she was confident she'd find a home for it.

Denise invited Rick Meier and Anne Collins of Penguin Random House Canada to meet with me in the fall of 2019 to discuss the possibility. It turned out to be one of the most important meetings of my career.

Rick and I then embarked on the journey of making that story idea into a book. He was there from the beginning: a keen ear when it was all just thoughts in my head, and an expert editorial eye when those thoughts became words on the page. His careful guidance and brilliant suggestions as editor helped push this story beyond my own imagination, for which I'll always be thankful.

It's an honour and a pleasure to have this story published under the Random House Canada imprint. Sue Kuruvilla and her team have made me feel at home, and that support is invaluable. Big thanks as well to copy editor Sue Sumeraj for fine-tuning the final version.

I'm also very grateful to Mireya Chiriboga and the team at William Morrow/HarperCollins for publishing the U.S. edition of this novel. It's exciting to have this story available throughout Turtle Island.

Meeting readers in communities everywhere is my favourite part of being an author, and I'm very thankful that my publicist Sharon Klein has ensured that this book will reach as many people as possible.

The Canada Council for the Arts and the Ontario Arts Council provided essential financial support in developing and writing this novel, as they have with all of my books. Both agencies have been crucial in my advancement as an author.

Writing about Anishinaabek requires a strong cultural foundation, and for that I'm fortunate to be able to turn to my dad, John, for the stories and teachings of our people.

Anishinaabe culture and language go hand in hand, and although I'm not a fluent speaker of Anishinaabemowin, I did my best to include our language in this story. To ensure I wrote everything properly, I consulted the astute Dr. Mary Ann Corbiere, who with great care and enthusiasm helped fine tune my grammar and phrasing.

The primary reviewer of all my ideas and writing is my wife, Sarah. She nurtured me and this story from its inception, and it wouldn't have taken shape without her love and analysis.

Big thanks to Sarah Gartshore, Waawaate Fobister, and

Lenny Carpenter for reviewing earlier drafts of this story and offering crucial feedback. You all helped make this story better.

It's important to stay busy with other creative endeavours while writing a novel, so I want to thank Naben Ruthnum, David Bertrand, Jennifer David, Cherie Dimaline, and Kevin Hardcastle for inviting me to participate in other exciting writing and storytelling projects over the past few years.

I was also able to fully immerse myself in fiction during the writing of this novel because of jury opportunities. My gratitude to the Writers' Trust of Canada and the Scotiabank Giller Prize for inviting me to serve on their juries in 2020 and 2022 respectively.

Every day I give thanks for the Indigenous authors who widened the circle for people like me. I especially want to acknowledge Richard Van Camp and Eden Robinson for their ongoing support and promotion of Indigenous storytellers.

My mom, Mona, has always been one of my biggest cheerleaders, along with my brothers. I'm very fortunate to have step parents, step siblings, aunts, uncles, cousins, and friends who have lifted me up my entire life.

On that note, chi-miigwech for the hometown support from Wasauksing, and nearby Parry Sound. Stories like this one are rooted in community and the land, thanks to life lessons I learned growing up on the rez.

Nmiigwechiwendam!

ABOUT THE AUTHOR

WAUBGESHIG RICE grew up in Wasauksing First Nation on the shores of Georgian Bay, in the southeast of Robinson-Huron Treaty territory. He's a writer, listener, speaker, language learner, and a martial artist, holding a brown belt in Brazilian Jiu-Jitsu. He is the author of the short story collection *Midnight Sweatlodge* (2011), and the novels *Legacy* (2014) and *Moon of the Crusted Snow* (2018). He appreciates loud music and the four seasons. He lives in N'Swakamok—also known as Sudbury, Ontario—with his wife and three sons.